THE RAINSBARGER BROTHERS

Based on a True Story

CHRIS SCANLAN

THE RAINSBARGER BROTHERS

Dedication

Dedicated to all Rainsbargers, near and far.
Let the truth be known.

Acknowledgements

A huge thank you to my wife for spending countless, exhausting nights editing this project. Thank you to my father, for listening to my incessant ramblings as I discovered something new about our family. And last but not least, thank you to my Uncle Dale for introducing me to this side of our family history!

-

INTRODUCTION

In the mid 1800's a man named William P. Hiserodt moved to Hardin County, Iowa from New York with his parents. Soon after, they died, and he worked as a farmer, as a blacksmith, and then joined the military. He was a Corporal in Company A of the 32nd Iowa Confederate Infantry. He was captured and wounded three times at Pleasant Hill. Hiserodt was later discharged on July 17th, 1865, due to a disability, after being held captive as a prisoner of war. After his time of service, he returned to Hardin County to open a saloon and hotel called the Western House. He became associated with notorious horse thieves, and eventually worked his way into counterfeiting silver half dollar coins.

In 1853, a family named Rainsbarger moved to Steamboat Rock, Iowa from Ohio. They lived with the Leverton family until around 1856, when they then built a log cabin down by the Iowa River and settled on a 160-acre plot of land a few miles Northeast of Steamboat Rock. The family had five sons: William, Finley, Nathan, Emmanuel, and Frank. The oldest, William, known as 'Old Bill', was a trusted member of the school board and respected farmer who owned nearly 120 acres of farmland. He was also known for harboring a flock of 70 wild geese that he had domesticated and used in local sport. Emmanuel, or Manse, was a local blacksmith who ran a program that allowed school kids to use his extra materials to make toys or snow sleds. He purchased the black smith shop from Henry Dinges in 1882. After their parents had passed away, Frank and Nate remained on the family farm by the Iowa River and were well-known within the community. Finley Rainsbarger was the only member of the family who had any reputable notoriety. As a young man, he was known as a 'sneak thief', and had once been removed from a gathering at William Boyles' home as he was caught stealing goods from William's guests.

The Rainsbargers were accused of many crimes in their time, but there was never any evidence to support the claims. Such accusations earned them the reputation of being a 'gang' rather than a simple band of brothers and were called the 'Jesse James gang of Hardin County'. The brothers lived in a time and place where the vigilante counterfeiters ruled that area.

Hiserodt, the ringleader of this crime gang, had nearly every person in the county in his back pocket. Hiserodt had lawyers, council members, mayors, attorneys, sheriffs, newspapers, judges, and other downright dirty lawless men all on his payroll. Hiserodt was a ruthless, yet sophisticated criminal, known by his vigilante criminals as 'Black Bill'.

It was during this time that Hiserodt employed a man named Enoch "Horsethief" Johnson. Enoch was known as a cattle thief, robber, and an all-around good-for-nothing lawless man. Finley Rainsbarger had been an associate of Johnson through the Boulder gang, which only added to the suspicion that the Rainsbargers were hardened criminals.

Enoch Johnson was married to a woman named Margaret, who was simply known as Maggie. Maggie was known to the higher-ranking members within the counterfeit gang, as two of the men were her uncles; John and Milton Biggs. She was a woman that can only be defined by her deceit and ruthless ambition, much like Black Bill.

William Hiserodt, Maggie Johnson, and a community full of thieves and liars wrought the destruction of the Rainsbarger family. These are the crimes of the gangs of Hardin County.

CHAPTER 1

FINLEY RAINSBARGER

I

February, 1866, in Steamboat Rock, Iowa...

The gavel slam echoed through the courtroom. A second thud followed immediately afterwards. Charlie Violes, the town's constable, had lost his day in court, and had pounded his fist down hard on the table after hearing the verdict. A thin man of medium height stood up a few feet to his right. He stared at Violes for a moment with a grin that said, *"I told ya so"*. The only noise in the courtroom was the sound of shuffling papers and feet as everyone stood up to exit the building. The thin man, still wearing his grin, shook hands with his defender, and headed toward the exit. Everything Fin Rainsbarger did agitated Charles and seeing him practically skip out of the courtroom was like adding an insult to an injury.

"That's it?! You're just going to let him walk free again?" Charles yelled as he banged his fist down a second time.

A man, well dressed, came and grabbed Violes by the elbow, and proceeded to escort him out of the room. "Not now, constable! Not here!" he said as he shoved Charles, who was much larger than he was, towards the front doors.

Stepping out onto the front steps of the courthouse, Finley Rainsbarger was already mounted on his horse, and speaking with his representative. Every so often, he would turn away from the man and spit in the dirt a clump of dirty brown tobacco. The sun was out, but it wasn't hot as a breeze stirred and made his hat move slightly with the wind. He had returned his side arm and dagger to their rightful places on either side of his belt.

Steamboat Rock, Iowa was still in its infancy, and its roadway was a crude track of dirt that had been trampled into dust by many horses, and buggies. Fin was resting his hand on his horse's saddle with its bridle in his hands in the roadway when Violes came plowing through the courthouse front doors.

He yanked his elbow away from the man's grasp, cursing as he did it. Even the way he walked sober looked like he had spent the night at the saloon. Violes was a heavy man and swayed between steps, pushing past smaller men as he went down them. "You chicken-livered son of a gun! Get over here, Rainsbarger! Screw the court's rule! You owe me, and I want what is mine! Pay up or I'll find another court willing to send you to the pen. I'd be delighted to take you myself!" he yelled as he shook his fist.

"Take it easy, Charles, you old mudsill. There's no need for empty threats. You're a veteran, and man of the law, ain't ya? Where's your honor?"

"There ain't no honor in this county other than what I find at the bottom of a bottle! Pay up, or I'll find a way to send you away," he demanded through gritted teeth, still swaying his way towards Finley.

"You get any closer, and I'll send you somewhere else," Fin replied with an upward inflection, showing his serious intent. His hand moved closer to the handle of his sidearm. Violes noticed the movement and stopped.

"You gonna shoot a public servant in front of a bunch of people?"

All eyes were on them now. All was silent except the occasional gust of wind that swept up the road's dust and hurled it at the brick building as it settled with the fallen leaves. Finley sucked in his tobacco juice and spit it on Charlie's worn out boots.

"Keep acting like you own the fires of hell, Charles. You just may end up there with them."

He tugged on his horse's bridle and rode off down the road at a gallop, leaving Charlie Violes behind. Violes moved into the roadway and yelled obscenities at Finley's back as he galloped further away. His voice was lost under the sound of the warm breeze.

II

The oil lanterns that lined the outside of the buildings on either end of the road were dimly lit as snow flurries began to fall. The Western House and local saloon was lit up the most out of any building on the block, which drew more patrons to it than usual. A dull roar of men giving cheers and playing cards could be heard. Sporadic laughter came from the hotel as someone told a good joke in *good* company and it could be heard from the street outside. Even with all of the noise from the inebriated patrons, one could talk at a normal tone over the laughter, and sound of poker chips being collected by the winner of that round. The hotel opened to the saloon with the rooms located upstairs. Finley sat at a table in the back of the room with his feet propped up on the table.

"I know you may come off as an outlaw to some, but please don't seem so lawless," said the man sitting next to him as he swiped Fin's feet off the table. "Besides, you may spill our drinks," he continued.

The man was Henry Johns, Finley's brother-in-law. He was a sophisticated gentleman from England who had swooned Finley's older sister, Martha. They lived near Abbott on a 1,200 acre plot of land, and owned three times that amount in other parts of Hardin County. This evening he was dressed in a suit and tie, standing out among the crowd that had infiltrated the saloon.

"You almost made me spill *my* drink! You best be careful Johns! I've already had a run in with a man today three times as ugly as you," he laughed.

"Three times as ugly?" Henry said, "That poor fellow's mother must have been a regular ole hedge-creeper." This time they both laughed so hard they almost missed seeing Charlie Violes enter the saloon. He swayed from side to side more than usual and already held a drink in his hand as he entered the building. Violes was accompanied by two other men who seemed twice as inebriated as he did. Moving past several tables, they crept their way over to a table in the opposite corner of Finley, and Henry Johns. Several patrons surrounded them and started a game of cards. More drinks arrived at their table, and they soon became the loudest crowd in the saloon.

Noticing Violes' arrival, Henry leaned closer to Fin and whispered, "I'm sure it's fine, gent, but if you'd prefer, we can head over to Wright's General Store across the way and get a bottle for the ride home. I'd say we nearly had our fill here, anyways. Wha'd you say?" Henry asked, hoping Finley would agree to his suggestion, knowing full well that John Wright didn't sell any alcohol.

"It may be entertaining to see Violes become more of a jollocks than he already is, but you may be right," he replied as he downed his last drink. Henry finished his drink as well, and then headed outside, relieved that Finley agreed to move on with him. Violes had been a thorn in Finley's side nearly all afternoon. He had followed him around from one place to another bellowing his childlike threats, which only made Finley more and more angry, not scared like Violes had hoped.

As they stepped outside, they both sighed as the wintery night air was much cooler than it had been earlier that day. Finley stumbled for a few paces as he stepped off the wooden porch onto the road.

"Who the hell put that there?" he asked.

Henry had a good laugh at his expense. "Perhaps we don't need anything for the ride home."

"No, no, now I definitely need a little liquid courage for the ride home, Henry. You know I'm afraid of the dark; besides, we need something to keep us warm," he joked. Of course, he wasn't afraid of the dark, but rather hoped he could have a bottle for the night to help him sleep. Finley believed a man slept better when he had some help and wasn't kept awake by his own dark thoughts. The bottle seemed to do the trick.

They had just reached Wright's front door as he was getting set to close for the evening when they heard it. Charlie Violes stood on the Western House Hotel's front porch with a bottle in his hand. He yelled again. "How many times am I gonna have to see you today, you dirty rat?" Violes yelled. "You're a liar and a cheat, Rainsbarger!"
"And you're drunk, Constable," Henry replied.

"I'm not talking to you, Johns! Rainsbarger! I'm gonna whip you better than that old man Rhodes did!"

At the mention of the memory, Finley recalled when he was nearly eighteen years old, he had said some less than kind things to two young ladies. Their father, Peachy Rhodes, didn't take too kindly to it and tried to put an end to his untamed manner. In 1860, Rhodes dragged Finley out behind his barn, tied him to the horse's hitching post, and whipped him until his boots were nearly filled with his own blood. In an attempt to retaliate, Finley had drawn his gun once he was let go. James Royal Jr. witnessed Fin's torment and had stopped him from fulfilling his revenge. Finley cringed as he recalled the feeling of being laid up for months afterwards. A year later, he burnt down that bastard's grain stacks. Since then, Fin kept a butcher knife in his right boot, and swore he'd kill Peachy Rhodes if he ever came near him again.

Finley pushed the memory aside. "It's been settled in court, Violes. You, more than anyone, understand how the justice system works. Now, I'm gonna go in and get me a drink, and be on my way home. You need to go on and get back to your game before you end up getting what you deserve." He turned and put his hand on the store's front door handle. It was cold from being beaten by the winter wind. In a single moment, he felt warm spit hit the back of his neck and heard the sound of heavy footsteps leave the wooden porch, a bottle hit the dirt, and then footsteps on the hard rocky road.

Finley turned around to see the drunk, heavy-set man shove his way past Henry Johns swiftly, with the speed, and power of lightning. Without hesitation, Fin brought his right knee up to his chest and grabbed steel. Charlie Violes swung at Finley's head with a fist that was almost the same size. Finley stepped backwards enough for Violes to nearly miss and stumble forward. Violes' fist grazed the side of Finley's head and flew through the air. Even though his punch didn't land true to its mark, it was enough to make Finley's head ring, and shove him into the store's front door, swinging it open.

Charlie realized his error too late, and instantly, time stopped. Still stumbling forward from his missed blow, he caught Finley's gaze, whose face showed no expression, and in another moment, time resumed. Fin stepped forward and stabbed Charles Violes in the heart. The impact of the blade made a thick moist noise as it buried deeper into warm flesh. Even warmer blood seeped out onto Finley's hand. Holding Violes up, he took out the knife with his right hand and buried it in his neck just under his left ear. Charlie died instantly and laid there in the dirt. Finley retracted his knife, cleaned it on Charles' shirt, and put it away.

A scream came from the saloon's front door as a young lady who had worked at the Western House had heard the yelling coming from Violes, and peered out the front door to witness what was happening. "Sheriff! Sheriff Thompson, hurry!" she cried.

And after that, the world around Fin Rainsbarger went silent. There was a commotion of men coming out of the saloon. He saw Henry Johns push past a few who were rushing towards Finley. He tried to explain to the sheriff that it was self defense. His pleas were lost to deaf ears. The men seized Finley and shoved him towards Sheriff Thompson, who was now very much drunk himself, and fumbling with the hand-cuffs in his pocket. Henry Johns was being shoved to the back of the crowd and his voice was lost over the shouting. Sheriff Thompson stepped towards him.

"Finley Rainsbarger, I hereby place you under arrest for the murder of Constable Charles Violes."

III

Finley was arrested by Sheriff Thompson and taken to the prison in Marshalltown. During the examination of the body, it was determined by surgeon Cusack and Dr. Underwood, that Finley stabbed Violes behind the left ear and in the heart. Finley was represented in court by Henry Huff and W.J. Moir.

Being that Charles Violes was the constable, Fin was sentenced to six years in prison. After only serving thirteen months, he was later pardoned by Governor Stone, as he determined that it was most likely self-defense. Henry Johns had also gathered all of the needed signatures for the petition for Fin's pardon.

When Finley was released from the prison he said, "I sent Charlie Violes to hell and the state sent me to the penitentiary. That makes it even. The one's as bad as the other."

This was the first recorded murder in Hardin County.

IV

From then on, Finley was feared within the community, and even more so when he associated with the Bolder Gang, and the notorious horse thief, and train robber, Jack Reed. Finley harbored the fugitive in his own home for some time while they ran a horse scam in the community. The gang consisted of Nate Thompson, Ed Cheney, Thomas Nott, Enoch Johnson, and the Biggs brothers, John and Milton.

Accepting the fact that Finley was now feared, he made a usual habit of petty crimes. In 1861, he had once driven his horse and wagon into a farmer's cornfield, loaded the wagon, and left as the farmer stood there and watched.

Another recorded account in 1882, states that Finley once stole two horses from Lyman Wisner's farm and set the crops on fire. Wisner shot Finley in the back and the bullet entered his lung. He was laid up for three months, and in order to avoid sentencing, he enlisted in the military. On his way to the enlistment office in Dubuque, he threw sand in his eyes to disqualify himself for service.

More notoriety was attached to the family name when another brother, Manse Rainsbarger, joined the Bunker Brother's gang in 1870. Shortly after, he was arrested for stealing horses near Vinton. The gang cleared his name, and he was released soon after.

V

Other crimes had become rampant in the area at the time. Many farmers had their cattle stolen or maimed. Goods left unwatched from barns were taken. Petty thievery of goods and small farm animals like sheep, lambs, and hogs occurred more often than not. The Rainsbarger brothers' names were often thrown into the short list of "who did it".

Gossip and Finley's one act, was enough to begin to spoil the Rainsbarger name in Hardin County. This led to many accusations, however, none of these accusations had any validity against the brothers and were only speculation. The Rainsbargers were known as "no Sunday school boys". Their cabin and farmland spread far throughout the area, and many referred to it as 'Rainsbarger country', believing it to be the headquarters for their crimes. Only family, close friends, and those who knew the truth came near. The people often accused them of having secret meetings to plan to steal cattle, or threatening a witness into leaving, or even making them disappear altogether. After becoming somewhat of a notorious family, disappearances were often blamed on the brothers and the community nicknamed the forest surrounding the farmland, 'Rainsbarger Cemetery'.

They lived like normal men, but were said to have mysterious associates, which only made folks even more nervous. It seemed a feud between the Rainsbarger family, and the quiet folks of Hardin County was beginning.

CHAPTER 2

BAD MONEY, BAD BLOOD

I

Steamboat Rock, Iowa, 1879, at the Western House Hotel and Saloon...

The buggy came to a jolting halt as Milton tugged the reins. The front wheel twisted and bent under the weight and then settled. The horse pulling the buggy was old and often skittish whenever it was harnessed. The horse was an old bay and it seemed to be less fearful when in the hands of Milton Biggs than when in the hands of his brother John. It tossed his head back and forth and let out a small snort.

It was a quiet night, and the only noises were the evening insects making their nightly music. As they listened, the two men waited for anyone unfamiliar to pass by their buggy a good distance before getting down from the high seat. John slid on his overcoat and blew out the lantern hitched to the buggy's side post. Side by side, they crossed the dirt road toward the hotel and saloon. Upon entering, Milton tapped a man on the shoulder who was seated at the bar. The man got up and followed the two brothers.

Near the eastern wall was the staircase to the rooms above. Near one room on the far side of the upstairs walkway, stood two confederate gunmen dressed in matching long dusters, and flat brimmed hats. Each carried a rifle on his back and a six shooter on the hip. They stood on opposite sides of the door, watching the saloon below.

The three men made their way through the crowded bar to the base of the staircase. Milton leaned over to Enoch Johnson, the man from the bar, as they approached the door guarded by the gunmen and whispered, "Now remember what we talked about, and try to act intelligent, will ya?"

Johnson gave Milton a small sideways glare and rolled his eyes. John slipped the armed guard on the left a note, he glanced at it, stepped aside, and opened the room door. Once they stepped inside, the door was promptly closed behind them. The room was furnished with a desk, two chairs facing it, a liquor cabinet, and a large bed. There was a door opposite the desk on the other side of the room that Enoch thought no doubt led to an adjoining room.

The trio was accompanied by two men who were already inside. One was seated at the desk sipping his drink and the other leaned against the liquor cabinet with his arms crossed. The man seated at the desk was of darker complexion and had a black beard, long mustache, and slicked back hair. He was dressed in a nice suit with a vest and carried a large knife on his side. The other man was dressed like the gunmen just outside the door, although he wasn't wearing his dark colored duster and was a heavy-set man. He wore a gray colored suit and carried a revolver instead of a knife. On his vest gleamed a sheriff's badge.

The three men greeted the man seated at the desk as they came in. The man had risen to greet them as well, and shaking Enoch's hand he said in a deep smooth voice, "Enoch Johnson, what a pleasure to finally meet you! I hear you're one of the most profitable horse thieves, knowledgeable in horse flesh, and the 'know how' to move merchandise. Just the man I think we need, or at least that's what John and Milton tell me."

"You flatter me, Mr. Hiserodt. I'm sure I'm nothing more than a humble thief," Enoch replied with a slight smile. His missing front tooth showed as he spoke, while the rest seemed to be slowly rotting from eating tobacco. Enoch wasn't quite sure yet why he was there, but he was happy to be; heck, he was always excited to be involved in anything that may make him a dollar.

"Well, gentlemen, this here is my associate. You may be familiar with him already," Hiserodt said as he pointed with his whole hand toward the man with the badge.

"Nice to see you two boys again," he said to the Biggs brothers, "And nice to meet ya, Mr. Johnson. The name's Wilcox, Sheriff Wilcox." While the men exchanged pleasantries, Hiserodt had poured them all drinks. He slid one over the desk towards Johnson and motioned for him to sit. Enoch sat down and gratefully accepted the drink.

"Mr. Johnson, I'll come out and say it, make it real plain and simple for you...we aren't dealing in stolen horses anymore. That's a young man's game and let's be honest, none of us are getting any closer to becoming a spring chicken. Most of us should have retired our worn-out bodies after the war, but time keeps pushing on. We need someone who can move our merchandise without raising any suspicions from any law enforcement personnel," he then nodded towards Wilcox, "Present party excluded." They all laughed at the remark. "The way Milton and John figure it, is that if a man like yourself can move horses across state lines and then back without getting caught, you may be able to with something *smaller*, and I'm in agreement."

Enoch was intrigued and smiled an ugly, stupid smile. He was a short man, unkept, and uneducated and it often showed. He looked to his left at Milton and then to his right at John, his wife's uncles, and saw their eagerness for him to join. He always thought Maggie's uncles liked him, but then again, Enoch Johnson wasn't exactly a smart man.

"Well, gosh, Mr. Hiserodt, I'm used to being the mule runner of sorts, and have been known to fool unsuspecting yellow belly beak runners, no offense, Mr. Wilcox. I'd be much obliged to join your operation. What kind of merchandise are we talking about if not horses? Sheep? Black Smith machinery? Liquor? Because we may have a supply problem if you leave me alone with the merch," Enoch joked.

They all laughed out of politeness at his awkwardness. "Don't be so daft, Enoch," Milton suggested, clapping Enoch on the shoulder, "Show him, Bill."

Hiserodt then reached into his vest pocket and tossed a silver object into the air at Enoch. It spun around and around in the air, sparkling in the lantern light. The object landed on the desk in front of Enoch. He slammed his hand down on it, pressing it into the desktop. Lifting his hand slowly, he saw what Hiserodt had thrown, and understood what he meant by moving something *smaller*.

II

At the home of Henry and Martha Johns, in Abbott, Iowa, 1880...

Henry Johns stood leaning in the entryway to his front door, arms crossed, looking out at the open prairie before him. The cool winter breeze blew brisk air all around and refreshed Henry's spirit. It was late afternoon, and the sky was now beginning to dim. As he contemplated the situation he now faced, he watched his two youngest children, a few yards out, playing with the family dog. Martha, his wife, approached from behind, handed him a hot cup of coffee, and hugged him. Standing on her toes, she placed her chin on his shoulder, as he was taller than her, and watched their children begin to play.

Henry sighed deeply and sipped his coffee, "Thank you for the cup."

"What is bothering you so much, dear?" she asked.

At first, he didn't know how to reply. He simply took another sip of his drink and breathed deep again. "We've lent out thousands of dollars in loans to those who needed it. We've given out over four dozen loans and have yet to be repaid even a portion of that. And when they do repay it," he paused and turned to look at her, "half of them are repaying us in counterfeit coins. Something has to be done, Martha. We can't keep losing everything we own, hand over fist."

As he finished, he looked back out to the two children playing. Martha placed her hand on his shoulder and rubbed it gently. For months her husband had been giving out loans to locals within the community, from Abbot to Gifford, and anywhere in between. The local banks weren't hard on funds but were rather hard on the patrons whom they thought wouldn't be able to pay back a loan. She knew that Henry was thinking about the children. This time of year was hard for the rest of her family as well, but she knew not to ask Henry to extend his pocket book out to them just yet. It might push him over.

"We have plenty, Henry, and the kids will have plenty when we're gone. All of this nonsense about money has kept you up more nights than not. Take what anyone is willing to give, forgive the rest of the debts, and move on, please," she pleaded as she rubbed his shoulder harder, "You know the good Lord loves a cheerful giver! Be happy about what you could do to help. But this counterfeit nonsense is eating you up."

Henry sighed again and downed the last of his coffee. He looked at Martha and then back at the children outside. A storm was starting to form past the tree line, and he could see lightning in the distance. "What about others who aren't as fortunate as us? The folks of Hardin County already suffer enough as it is. Wrong is wrong and right is right. It's that simple."

In her heart she knew her husband was right, and that Henry Johns wasn't a man to let go of truth and justice. "I just don't want to see you get hurt, Henry. What would we do without you? I fear your ferocity of searching out the truth may be the death of you," she replied, doing all she could to hide her tears.

"The truth is what sets a man free. It may just be what breaks the chains of the poor in Hardin County."

He kept staring at the approaching storm, and like the one on the horizon, she felt the one in Henry, and knew he wouldn't be eased of his burden until he exposed the counterfeiters. As the storm drew nearer, she pondered a question that had come up in her morning devotion. *What is truth?*

III

Standing on the opposite side of the street, Henry tied up his horse and buggy, and clenched the coin purse so hard, the palm of his hand almost had the coin stamp imprinted on it through the leather bag. As he stood there, he watched several patrons make their way in, and out of the Farmers Exchange Bank's double wooden doors. Some were rich, some were poor, very few lived in the middle.

Over the last few months, Henry had traveled to the surrounding cities and had even received an anonymous telegraph from a source in South Dakota. He had also procured rejected counterfeit money from Ackley and Grundy Center, Iowa. The counterfeit money he had traced always came back to Steamboat Rock. All Henry had to do was follow the receipts from the anonymous source, which led Henry Johns here, to the Exchange Bank.

He waited for horses and buggies on the dusty road to cease their constant passing by before he ran across the street to the front door. Catching the door as a patron came out, he quickly entered the bank. As the door closed behind him, a single bell chimed above the doorway.

"Hello, how can I help you today?" came a friendly voice from the front counter.

There stood a tall man with a long dark beard dressed in a nice gray coat. Henry recognized him instantly. It was Dan Turner, the first teller of the bank and town local who was currently running for Mayor.

"Hello, chap," Henry replied as he approached the counter, "Shouldn't you be out campaigning today?"

"It's a fine enough day to be out for sure, but duty calls," Turner said as he tapped the countertop. "How can I help?"

"Well, I need to speak with the bank's President, is he around?"

"Mr. Noyes isn't here today, but perhaps I can assist you. What's it in regards to?"

At that, Henry opened the bag of counterfeit coins and let them spill out onto the counter top. His hand shook with anger as he did it. They made a loud metal noise and some fell to the floor, making an even greater spectacle to those around him. The remaining customers stopped what they were doing and took notice. Henry stared at Dan Turner, waiting to see if he recognized the coins.

Henry thought he did.

"You can tell Mr. Noyes that he can keep these fake coins. I know there's counterfeit money being peddled in, and out of Steamboat, and the way I figure it, he has to be in the know," he said in a fury.

"Well wait just a minute—," Turner began but was interrupted by Henry.

"Shut it, chap, I'm not finished and I'm not stupid! Where do you think I got the coins? Johnson, you stupid son of a gun! Now he hasn't named names, but I've got my suspicions! This bank always accepts these rat-bag fakes and I want to know why! You tell Noyes I'm looking for him and he better be ready to talk!"

Henry Johns then threw the leather bag at Dan Turner's chest. It was empty and fell clumsily to the floor. Henry had already made it to the front door and stormed out before Turner even realized what he had just witnessed. He turned to the next customer, who was an older lady, and asked, "Did Henry Johns just threaten me?"

"To be fair, I think he threatened the bank's President, son," she replied.

Johns could hear the comment from the street corner just outside the bank door. He was mad, yet determined to stay calm, at least calmer than he had just been, when he heard a voice behind him.

"Excuse me, sir, I was just inside the bank and couldn't help but overhear you. I'd like to ask you some questions."

Turning around, Henry saw a man dressed in a nicer suit than the banker. He had a duster on even though it wasn't particularly cold out. Seeing the confusion in Henry's face, he opened his coat and flashed a silver badge. Stretching out his hand towards Henry he said, "I'm Mr. Norton; Detective Norton. Please...tell me what you know."

IV

Early fall, 1882, just outside J. Snyder's store...

"Pull the buggy around back, Frank," Enoch said as he lightly jabbed Frank Rainsbarger in the ribs and gestured towards the back of the building.

Frank had met Enoch Johnson only three times before today. The first time he had met Johnson was at his brother, Finley's home. He had gone to ask Finley if he was going to help with the thresher again that year and had stumbled upon the two men arguing in Finley's barn. They had just stolen a steer from William Haines' farm and couldn't decide what to do with it. There was a heated debate about reselling the steer or butchering it for meat and selling it back to the farmer in which they got it from.

The second time Frank met Enoch Johnson was at the home of Malhon Taylor. Frank had been meeting a young girl named Addie Williamson, who had been living at the Taylor's place. It just so happened that Johnson was bringing his daughter, Nettie, to stay at the Taylor's place. Nettie was a kind, soft spoken young girl who was always well dressed. After meeting Nettie Johnson, Frank never returned to visit Addie Williamson.

The third time was in late July. Frank had stayed at Enoch Johnson's home in Gifford for a week. He was there to speak to some folks about a loan, as he, much like many others in Hardin County, was having a rough year. It was during this time, that Frank fell in love with Nettie and began *keeping her company*. He often accompanied her to church and took her anywhere in town she wished to go. Frank loved to see her smile and hoped to marry Nettie one day. Every time he would ask Nettie her thoughts on marriage, her answer was always the same. She would politely smile and tell Frank good luck asking her father for her hand.

Enoch was a short stout man who always seemed to smell worse than an outhouse that had been baking in the sun. Nettie was the opposite in every way and most folks were amazed to find that she was his daughter. She had medium length, dark brown hair, hazel eyes, and soft white skin that had not been spoiled by the harshness of the world around her. Nettie was Enoch's first daughter, and his one true love. With the burning question of marriage on his mind, Frank found himself seated next to Enoch on this late-night errand.

Frank pulled the buggy around the back side of the store and brought it to a halt. There was a single wooden door and a torch mounted on the wall. Few people were out on the main road at the time and Enoch thought it was for the best.

"Well, old man, we're here," Frank said.

"Wait here a bit, Frank. I'll be back out in a little bit. I have a feller I need to speak with for a moment."

"Make it quick, it's cold out and I'd like to be home by morning. And Enoch...don't get into any trouble."

"Me not get into any trouble? I thought the Rainsbargers were the ruffians around here," Enoch replied jokingly. He then quickly jumped down from the buggy seat, and hurried into the single door in the building's rear brick wall.

As he waited, Frank sat and thought of Nettie, and wondered how he was going to ask Enoch for her hand. The wind blew quietly as he sat there in silence for some time, pondering life's hard questions. Would Johnson let him marry Nettie? Would she say yes? Could he provide for her in the ways he wanted to? Some time passed, and Frank started getting impatient, and after even longer, he nodded off. He wasn't sure what time it was when he was startled awake, but the sun had started to rise. The buggy he sat in was rocking from side to side like a boat in the water.

Sitting up, he looked over his shoulder through the wagon covering and saw Enoch standing with another man. They had loaded a wooden box into the back of Frank's wagon and covered it with a tarp. Whatever was in the box was heavy enough to shake the buggy and wake him up when they set it down. The two men shook hands and parted ways. The unknown man who had helped Enoch load the mysterious box was tall and dressed as a store clerk. As Enoch hoisted himself back into the buggy, the other fellow ran back to the back door and was met by a figure standing in the doorway.

The sun was rising opposite of Frank, so the man was only a silhouette. His face was unknown to Frank. The man blew past the silhouette and into the store. All Frank could see was when the man turned to close the door, he moved with a limp on the left side.

When Enoch sat back down in the buggy seat, a jingling noise, like coins, came from his pocket. Enoch pretended not to notice and gave a side glance to Frank to see if he had. If he did notice, he didn't mention it. Frank could tell that Enoch looked frustrated and decided he would only ask two questions and act like he didn't hear the money bag, which he knew Johnson had not had on him beforehand.

"Who was the gentleman in the door, and what's in the box, old man?" Frank asked. He tried to sound natural, but seeing the man run back to the building made him feel uneasy, like Johnson was hiding something. This was more than just a meeting. As he asked the question, he pulled the reins and started the buggy back towards home.

"Never mind what's in the box, boy, it's just something an old friend *owed* me," he replied, sounding queer about it.

"Fine then, don't tell me, Johnson."

There was a long silent pause between them. Enoch reached into his pocket and slowly squeezed the money bag so that it would stop jingling. He hoped that would be one less question that he may have to avoid. After a moment longer, Frank finally said, "I mean, I figure the man who helped load it, was Mr. Snyder, the store owner, but I reckon I couldn't tell who the other gentleman was."

"Why'd you need to know, Rainsbarger? He is a friend and I ain't telling you what's in the box. Now I assume you still have a question you wanted to ask me, now get on with it before I change my opinion about you," he said in a nervous way.

Enoch liked Frank, and knew what he wanted to ask, but he didn't want him involved in this, especially not for Nettie's sake. He had initially gone to meet with Mr. Snyder to talk about moving the product but wasn't aware he was actually moving it that night. Enoch was surprised to see Hiserodt there at all. He was even more surprised that Hiserodt talked him into taking the counterfeit goods at that moment.

Talked him into it wasn't exactly how Enoch would describe what had happened...

"I need you to take the money and ship it to Milton. He'll be waiting to receive the package in Dakota City, Nebraska. We aren't moving it through the Dakotas this time, Johnson."

"I can get the money to Milton, boss, but not now! How would I explain it to the man out there? He knows I don't own anything other than my house and the clothes I'm wearing now!"

"I don't care what you tell that rat, Rainsbarger, you just get it loaded! Take the box or soon you'll be in one, Johnson!"

V

On December 27th, 1882, Frank Rainsbarger married Enoch Johnson's daughter, Nettie. They eloped when she was seventeen years old after only six months of courtship. About three months into them seeing each other Nettie became pregnant.

During that time, Frank and Enoch Johnson had a bad disagreement, which led to Enoch telling Nettie not to marry Frank days before the wedding. He told her that Frank wasn't the right type of man for her. Nettie said that Frank was a good man and that she was still going to marry him.

Despite the disagreement, Frank was still fond of Enoch, and always called him 'the old man'.

CHAPTER 3

THE ARREST

I

August 16th, 1883...

Enoch Johnson's buggy's back wheels bounced two feet into the air as the two gray mares leading the wagon pummeled through the brush. They rode at a full gallop through the woods that was just east of the main roadway that led from Goldfield to Eagle Grove. With the Wright County Marshals shooting at him, he was forced off the roadway, and into the dense timber, parallel to it. Milton Biggs was in the back of the covered wagon with a rather large, thin box. He was lying down and using the box for as much cover as possible as he returned fire. Shards of the wagon's wood splintered as they went.

"Shoot them yellow belly bastards, Milton!" Enoch howled with laughter. The tall branches made several small tears in the wagon cover as he ran his two-horse team even harder. Timber shrapnel clouded Enoch's vision as he pushed onwards and closer to Eagle Grove.

Milton fired two more shots at the officers in pursuit. He missed both and snarled, "Can't you keep this blasted wagon a little steadier? I'm nearly out of iron and they're still hot on our tails!"

"I'll do what I can, but they came out of nowhere! Where's your buggy parked with the other coins?" Enoch shouted over the gunfire.

"If we lose 'em, you need to make a sharp left turn off Mainstreet, just past the mercantile. I stashed it behind the store near the bush," Milton bellowed as he fired his revolver again.

The two mares neighed their excitement at the fusillade and slid out of the ditch when Enoch pulled hard on their reigns. The buggy slammed against a nearby tree and found pace along the battered dirt road. "Whoa, whoa, easy girls, easy! Biggs, take my side arm, and pump someone full of fire iron already, will ya?" he yelled as he tossed back his revolver without looking. It hit Milton in the back and he yelled a curse at Johnson.

Milton then fired in rapid succession and managed to shoot two horses out from under their riders. About five other secret service men rode hard and wouldn't let up. "I don't think we're gonna lose these boys, Enoch! What's the plan? We're about to enter Mainstreet."

"I ain't got no plan, boy! I ain't the brains of this here operation! Hold on tight and keep firing! If we can lose them a bit, we may end up getting to the buggy and be able to sneak out through the timber."

The horses pounded the hardpan as the remaining deputies ceased fire upon entering the town of Eagle Grove. For a moment, the two counterfeiters thought they had driven into an area outside of their jurisdiction as one by one, the detectives broke away from the chase.

"By god, I think we got rid of those sons' ah b—," Enoch's were were silenced over the deafening noise of his buggy colliding with another. A four-horse team ran through a crossroad that intersected the main thoroughfare. The buggy slammed into the side of Enoch's wagon at full drive and in slow motion, shoved the counterfeiter's wagon onto its side. Milton hit the dirt hard inside the shredded wagon covering and grasped at the wagon's covering to stop his forward slide. The box between his legs slammed the ground next to him and shattered into five fragments, sending its contents in every direction. Enoch was thrown from the buggy seat upon impact and landed into a rather large pile of cattle manure near the road's curb.

When he landed, he watched the overturned wagon slide across the roadway and slam into a nearby building. Milton crawled his way out of the wagon cover and stumbled to his feet. "Damn, Johnson, what the hell did you hit?" he asked.

"I didn't hit nothing! Blasted buggy railed us on the approach to the crossroad," Enoch yelled back as he began to collect the counterfeit coins that had barreled out of the shattered box. Covered in horse manure, he began stuffing them into his hat and pockets.

"What are you doing? We need to get out of here, Enoch! These are only the fakes, we can reprint these! The real thousand is in my wagon! Now let's go before we lose everything and really have hell to pay with Black Bill," Milton said as he hit Enoch in the back with his sweat baked hat.

"Don't tell Mag, but I ain't never seen something so pretty in my whole damn life! I ain't leavin' a single coin," he laughed. As he crammed the silver coins and manure into his trouser pockets, he was stopped by the sound of a rifle being cocked, and several men shouting for him to put his hands up. Hoards of service men ran around the nearby corner near the mercantile with rifles at the ready. Milton cussed and put his hand behind his head.

With the overwhelming temptation to not part with his precious phony treasure, Enoch, still on his hands and knees, reached for one last coin. He screamed and cussed as well, as a heavy boot came down upon his hand. Looking up, he saw the barrel of a long rifle aimed at him. There in the glaring sun, was Secret Service detective, Alex Beach.

"Good afternoon, Johnson," Beach said with a sarcastic smile.

II

At the jailhouse in Fort Dodge, Iowa, August 17th, 1883...

Enoch Johnson sat in the cold empty room alone for what felt, at least to him, like forever. It was a small room made out of brick with two oil lanterns on either side of the walls opposite Enoch, and a barred window behind him. He sat at a small wooden table, no longer wearing the hand cuffs. He whistled in a melancholy manner while he waited and leaned back in his chair with his feet on the table. A small cup of water on the table was the only thing else in the room with him. Enoch began to wonder if the detectives had forgotten about him. He was just about to yell for someone when he heard movement on the other side of the door; the sound of several keys on a ring, then the twist of the door handle.

Two men dressed in suits entered the room and sat down on the other side of the table as Enoch. As they entered, Enoch removed his feet from the table and sat upright. One man was carrying several papers which he let drop onto the table. He was shorter than the other detective and had a long handlebar mustache.

"Good evening, Mr. Johnson, my name is Detective Norton, and this is Detective Steadman," said the man seated to the left.

"I'm sure you understand why you are here, and if for any reason it hasn't been made clear, let me clarify. You have been placed under arrest for the possession of, and intent to pass, five hundred dollars worth of counterfeit 1881 silver dollars," said Steadman.

Enoch snorted a small laugh. "You know, I could really use a drink," he said.

Norton slid the water cup closer to Enoch's side of the table, "You already have one, Mr. Johnson."

"I was thinking of something more stiff, perhaps something that burns as it goes down. Have any gin?" Enoch asked.

"This is not the time for any foolishness, Johnson. We already know that the money was sent out by you! We know the counterfeit coins go from Steamboat Rock to several different locations—!"

"South Dakota, Nebraska, Kansas, Missouri," Norton interjected.

"That's right," Steadman continued, "and then from there, they go back to Eldora to be distributed to different banks! We need the names of those banks, Johnson."

Enoch remained silent. He didn't know the names of the banks. Hiserodt didn't trust him with all of the information. He wondered how they had known where he would be in Goldfield in the first place.

He'd been careful, or at least he thought. "I don't know which banks," he said at last.

"Then give us the names of the men you work for! How many are there? This has been going on for the last five years and the time is up! Your attorney, Mr. John Duncombe, asked that we consider bail! We need a reason!"

"We know you know names, Enoch, now tell us! Our informant already aided us in picking up you and Milton Biggs," Norton yelled.

"Look, we know how it all went down! In June you express shipped a box from Cleves to a man named D. W. Ballard in Kansas. You expected he'd collect the box, hold onto it and then redistribute the money amongst the local banks! Only he never showed up to collect. The box sat there at the post master's office for weeks before he opened it."

"Who labels a box full of counterfeit money as Billiards balls?" Norton asked. "How stupid can you be?"

"That's not even the worst part, Enoch! All we had to do was follow the receipt. Which led us back to you and Milton Biggs," Steadman finished.

"You didn't even use a fake name, you poor stupid son of a gun," said Norton. "Now tell us the names and we may go easy on you! Hell, tell us the names and we *may not* have to go give your wife the shake down. Maybe she knows something? We need something before we transfer you to the Commissioner's office."

At the mention of Maggie, Enoch was furious! He stood up in an instant, threw the cup at detective Norton and took a swing at Steadman. Despite his rage, Enoch was too slow. None of the men noticed through the commotion of trying to get Enoch to remain seated, that someone else had entered the room.

"I ain't telling you nothing until I know Maggie is safe! What did Milton tell you?" he shouted.

Everyone stopped moving when they heard the door close. All three men turned to see who had entered the room. Norton, smiling, was the first to speak, "Let me introduce you to our insider on the case. He's been a real bloodhound in hunting down the counterfeiters. You're his first catch."

Enoch starred in unbelief. Not ten feet away from where he sat, stood Henry Johns.

III

September 1st, 1883...

The train pounded the tracks in an incessant beat that made Enoch's head split. The train's cabin was decorated with a reddish brown felt material that was outlined in gold. The elegant tapestry on the ceiling kept Enoch's eyes from focusing on anything and only added to his migraine. It had been at least an hour of constant noise from the train; kids screaming, other passengers arguing, and Detective Steadman humming. Enoch wanted a glass of warm gin, and he wanted it bad.

A few dim lights lined the inside of the cart and Enoch could see families with young kids trying to get comfortable to settle in for some sleep. With the lights on inside the cabin, there was nothing to be seen outside as the reflection blocked out any view. The train cart that he and Milton were placed into was only about half full. The three rows in front of them were left empty so as to not place normal citizens next to the criminals. Directly behind them sat the two detectives. Milton Biggs had the window seat with the window to his right, and directly behind him was Detective Beach. Enoch and Steadman were on the ends near the isle.

As the train chugged along, Milton just stared out the window, trying to get a glimpse of the passing scenery, fumbling with his handcuffs. Beach kicked the back of Milton's seat, "Will you knock that off?"

"They hurt my damn hands! Can't you make them any looser? Why do I have to be shackled to this animal, anyways? You smelt better with the cow shit on you, Johnson," he replied.

"Sure, sure...maybe I should just take them off," Beach replied sarcastically.

"Well it sure wouldn't hurt. Where the hell am I gonna go? Out the window?"

Enoch laughed a little at the idea of Milton going through the window until Steadman kicked his seat and told him to be quiet as well. For a long while after, the night was silent. Steadman hummed less, children fell asleep, and Enoch's migraine subsided. The two men were finally being transferred to the Sioux City prison to meet the U.S. Commissioner. Enoch wasn't sure what exactly that entailed or what prison life would be like. He imagined without any gin to calm his liver; it would be hell.

As time rolled on, Enoch thought of his wife, Maggie. He would miss her, but most of all, his heart broke for Nettie. How would he live without her? Panic struck his heart and he felt that he may need to do whatever possible to get back to her. Memories of her learning how to walk, or sing wouldn't be enough. She had so many more things in life to experience and he wanted to see them all. Criminal life wasn't easy for Enoch but it's what he knew how to do and how he was able to provide for her as a single father, at least until he married Maggie.

I've made a mistake! How could I ever leave her?

Contemplating his life's mistakes, Enoch lost touch with the noises around him, but only for a moment. All was silent. And then...

Chaos.

Enoch awoke to the sound of someone yelling for help. He tried to see clearly but wasn't able to. He looked over at Milton to see that in no way had he fallen asleep. He seemed alert like he had been waiting for some grand moment. At the cry for help, the two detectives jumped from their seats and began to look around. Women and children were startled from their sleep. Small children started to cry, and scared passengers began to argue again.

"Help! Help! Fire!" someone shouted from the train cart in front of them.

Enoch rubbed his eyes and still tried to see clearly. He then realized the cart was filling with smoke as young children began to cough behind him. The door at the head of their cart crashed open and a young girl stood in the doorway. "Please, somebody help us! There's a fire!" she yelled through sporadic coughs.

"Come on, chap! Let's go," Beach said, yanking at Steadman's shirt.

"We can't just leave these two here! They need to be watched. What if they try to jump?"

"They're going to jump out of a moving train that is possibly on fire? Think Detective, if there's actually a fire that can't be contained, the conductor will have to stop the train. Once we hear the brakes engage, we'll rush back. It's probably only one car away! They're in chains, aren't they? Now let's go!"

The two men rushed out the door and into the other cart. As soon as they were out of sight, Milton leaned down and put his right foot in the center of the handcuff's chains and started kicking as hard as he could. "Come on, Johnson! Try to get free!"

"And what then, Milton? Are you actually going to jump out the window? There's nowhere to go," he replied.

Women and children had begun, in a panic, to exit to the cart behind them, and soon the two men would be left alone. It was only a matter of time before the two detectives came back or the fire reached them.

"Trains don't just light on fire, you knit-wit! It's a distraction! And no, I ain't going out the window. We're *both* going out the window! Now get moving!"

Enoch froze.

How would they survive that? There was no way! They'd hit a tree, or a boulder and surely be done for. They may even break every bone. Enoch knew he couldn't handle the fallout of jumping from a train. Maybe the conductor would have to stop, he'd apply the breaks and then he could jump once it slowed down? Maybe. Only if the two men didn't return right away. Then he thought of Nettie, again.

In a furry, he began trying to break the chains like Milton. He kicked and kicked but to no avail. The force behind each kick only worked to slowly break his fragile wrists. The next thirty seconds were a blur to a worn out man like Enoch Johnson.

Milton screamed a deep agonizing scream and then turned to Enoch, "Mine are off! Let's go! I'll help you get yours off once we've landed." Milton then stood up, and leaning into Enoch, he then threw his right shoulder into the train window. He bounced back off it. It shattered in on his second attempt. Using his broken cuffs, he then cleared the remaining glass from the window frame. As soon as the window was cleared the train began to squeal.

"That's the brakes, Johnson! Let's move it!" screamed Milton. He then reached up to the open overhead storage compartment, lifted his legs and dove feet first out of the moving train. Enoch sat there unable to move as he watched smoke billow out the open window.

There's no way he survived.

Standing up, he tried grabbing the above compartment like Milton had just done, which proved more difficult with the cuffs still on.

For Nettie, he thought.

As he lifted his feet into the air, he heard a familiar noise. Peering over his shoulder he saw Detective Beach's six shooter barrel aimed at his head. The noise he had heard was Beach pulling back the hammer.

"If you try to jump, I shoot."

"You know, I didn't really think goin' out the window was the best idea, anyways," Enoch chuckled.

"Sit down and shut up, Johnson," Steadman added, shoving him back into his seat.

The cart was beginning to fill with smoke as the squealing came to a stop in tandem with the train. Enoch was jerked forward, and shouts could be heard from the remaining train cars. The overwhelming panic that he had felt before began to dissipate. Enoch thought that if the fire was actually close, the two detectives wouldn't be standing over him as calm as they were.

Upon the train settling on the tracks, Beach shouted, "Take this mangy mutt off the train but keep him away from the honest folks. I'm going after Biggs! He couldn't have gone far! Hopefully he impaled himself on a tree branch and we'll only need to be in charge of one rat."

Upon exiting the train, Detective Beach could see a few feet into the blackness of the night due to the engulfed cart near the head of the train. Even through the noise of panicked passengers, he thought he heard horse hooves riding the grassy hills into the dark.

This was planned.

IV

Several weeks later, at the Sioux City Prison...

The cool winter air crept into Enoch's brick cell like a thief. The morning light shining through the barred window had just begun to defrost the concrete floor. He was in a single person cell, and all that he had was a cot, bedding, and the clothes he wore. He was wrapped in his thin blanket, and lying down facing the wall when the deputy made the cell bars sing with his metal cup. He ran them back and forth and whistled while he did it.

"Wake up, Johnson, you have a visitor. She's coming down the hall now. Make yourself presentable," said the deputy.

She? Was it Maggie, or perhaps Nettie?

Enoch would have normally been excited by having a visitor, but he didn't want either woman to see him like this. His hair was matted, and even more dingy than usual, and he was still waking up. The cold had reached its way into his joints and they were stiff while he moved to sit upright. Licking his hands, he combed his matted hair as best as he could, and drew in his blanket tighter to hide the rest of his mess of a body. Then he saw her, Maggie, his wife, standing there watching him clean himself with his hands like a rat. He instantly stopped and smiled at her.

Maggie Johnson was a woman in her thirties. She was dressed in her best dress and her hair was done up tight in the back how Enoch liked it. A few stray hairs blew in the light breeze that was coming from the window. She normally had a warm and embracing look, but at the moment it was cold with her lips closed tight upon each other. She was a woman of fair beauty and she used it to her advantage.

"Hi, Mag, I've missed you! How are the girls?" Enoch began.

"Shut up, you gibfaced son of a—," she clasped a hand to her mouth.

She trembled as she stared at Enoch. Her lips drew in even tighter. The morning light from the window made her pale skin seem even more white. Seeing her, Enoch remembered why he had fallen in love with her but couldn't remember why *she* had taken to *him*.

Maggie opened her small purse, and took out several pieces of paper, and threw them at him. They reached the cell bars and fell to the floor, spreading out in every direction. "You got caught doing what you do *best,* and you have the nerve to send threats to your family, and employer! *How dare you!*"

Enoch didn't know what to say. He just stared at her and watched her anger unfold. Something in her demeanor told him she was no longer his and had possibly become someone else's.

She stepped closer to the iron bars until her face was in between them and she could feel the cold metal on her cheeks. Her eyes were watering as she said, "Black Bill sent me to tell you that if you talk you're gonna die with your boots on and when he's done...there won't be enough left of you to feed the crows."

"And what if I make bail, Mag? Run away with me!"

"I'd rather see you die," she said as she spit at him, "No one is coming to visit you, old man! You can either die in here peacefully, or you can die on the outside like a dog. Either way, you'll never be truly free." This time she spit directly in his face. "How dare you think I'd have any love left for you after you let Milton die! His body was found, broken and bleeding out!" she screamed.

She clenched the iron bars hard, which then made her white hands even more white. Spit hung from her lips as she stared at Enoch. He couldn't even bring himself to look at her now. He just stared at the floor and didn't dare wipe her spit off his face. He supposed it wouldn't help to tell her that jumping from the train was Milton's idea, and not his.

"I'd divorce you, Enoch, but if I can be honest with you...I'm hoping you'll at least have the decency to die in here and leave me the house. At least then I can say you *provided* something for your family. You'll never see the girls again, Enoch. Not Nettie, not Effie. Never!" She took a step backwards, "Goodbye, Mr. Johnson," she said nearly under her breath.

She then turned and began to walk away in a furry. Enoch jumped up and grabbed the bars in a panic. His heart raced and he no longer even felt the cold.

"Let me see them one more time, Maggie!!"

There was no reply.

Reaching the front door to the jail, all she could hear, was Enoch yell her name with immense desperation.

"MAGGIE!"

It echoed down the concrete hall as she left.

Enoch was the kind of man whom she would pity if she didn't hate him so much. He was the type to seem so pitiful you couldn't help but aid him and once you did, you resorted to hating him as he took from you everything he could get.

As she reached the bottom of the jailhouse steps, a horse and buggy pulled up in front of her, and she climbed inside as she wiped away her tears. Once she was seated, she turned to the man driving the buggy.

"Do you think he'll turn over any evidence? He'll have to be taken care of if he does," he said.

"I hope so, Mr. Hiserodt...I hope so."

V

At Mr. Sewell's Boarding house and infirmary for the Sioux City Prison, January 26th, 1884...

Detective Steadman grabbed a chair that was seated at the empty desk and dragged it over to Enoch Johnson's bedside. Enoch had become sick, and his health severely declined over the last few weeks. As a result, he was transferred to the minimum-security boarding house to be treated.

Steadman sat back, folded one leg over, flopped his newspaper down on the bedside table, and exhaled sharply. He looked around the room at the other sick inmates, wishing he wasn't there.

Only God knows what these folks were suffering from, he thought.

The room was long and lined with beds on either side. The window curtains were drawn back so that the sunlight could aluminate the room. There were only a handful of people in the same room and one or two of them had their own privacy screens drawn around their bed. Enoch was sitting on his own bed in his state-issued clothes with the blanket wrapped up to his waist.

Steadman folded his arms and breathed again. He looked anywhere but directly at Enoch and said, "Well, it looks like you're gonna die here, Johnson. Unless...you wanna make a deal."

Enoch had thought long and hard about this conversation, knowing it would come. How much time he had left, he wasn't sure, but he didn't want to spend it here or back in jail. If he gave up the counterfeiters, he may end up dead. There was no rejoining them now, even if he did get out. They feared he would turn over evidence to the federal agents and Enoch knew it. They had sent Maggie one time to come see him as none of them risked being caught. What options did he have? Stay here and possibly die due to an unknown condition, or leave and possibly die on some godforsaken lonely road, facedown in his own blood? If he played along with the state, maybe he could be protected until he left the country.

"What kind of deal?" he asked.

"The kind where you give us the names of the counterfeiters, and not just some, but *all* of them. You help us bury them, and we keep you out of jail. Sounds nice, right? You can be a free man again, at least for a while, but only if you agree to testify in an open court."

"What about protection? What's to say they won't just come grab me once I'm out. The docs think I have cirrhosis but they're not sure.

I can't defend myself in this condition," Enoch said as he lifted his arm and showed the detective his withered state.

"Protection may be difficult at first. This is Woodbury County and you'd be going back to Hardin County. Nobody wants to go there."

"No protection, then no deal, and what's the matter with Hardin County?"

Steadman shrugged, "You know the ruffians out there better than most. You tell me. I heard you know the Rainsbarger boys better than any. Isn't one of them your son-in-law?"

Enoch thought it was funny that Frank Rainsbarger or his brothers would be considered a reason not to go to Hardin County. Finley maybe, but not the rest. They seemed rough to the average folk, but they weren't any hardened criminals.

"I know they get blamed for most mishaps down that way, but being blamed, and being convicted, are two different things. Do them boys drink? Yep. Chew and smoke? Guilty also, but I ain't never seen them steal any cattle or burn any farms. Those stories are all hogwash...except when referring to Finley. Then they're all true," Enoch said while laughing.

"Maybe. Maybe not. All I really know about Hardin County is that y'all needed to start a horse and cattle association to stop thieves from stealing them. Petty thievery is pretty rampant in those parts. I know *that*, and the name Rainsbarger."

Enoch butted in, "And like most, you don't know the truth about 'em. The family was pioneers when the railroad came in and Steamboat Rock became a town. Either way, most people don't take kindly to the name. I think the bad reputation mostly came from Finley. Sorry to say, I played a hand in that. Of course, you know all about that and the Boulder Gang."

"All I'm getting at, is maybe it would be best if you stay with your daughter, and son-in-law if you get out."

Enoch thought it over. Most folks in Hardin County wanted to live a simple life and anyone that didn't fit their social norm was an outcast. The Rainsbarger brothers included. They lived behind miles of overgrown forest near the Iowa River, just outside of Steamboat Rock. Their seclusion from the daily folks only aided in the assumption that they were dangerous or up to no good. Maybe staying with Frank and Nettie would be best.

"I'll give you two names now, and if I ain't dead within a week's time after my release, I'll give you the names of the top men," he said at last.

Steadman stood up, grabbed his newspaper from the bedside table, and said, "I'll draw up the paperwork."

CHAPTER 4

TO KILL AN OLD HORSE

I

Enoch and Maggie Johnson's home in Gifford, Iowa, April 14th, 1884...

Nettie Rainsbarger was dressed in a long sleeve shirt and overalls underneath her raincoat when she had arrived at the Johnson's home. It had been raining for several days and hadn't let up. The rain made the air cooler in the evening, but also mostly humid in the afternoon, which made her undershirt stick to her skin. She was now nearly seven months pregnant and was mentally ready to have her baby. Nettie was exhausted from the humidity, but the constant noise of rain drops, and distant thunder made her relax a bit as she rested. Nettie was lying down on the soft couch in the sitting room with her feet up, when there came a knock at the front door.

"Don't get up, dear, I'll get it," Maggie said as she got up from her chair and put down her cup of tea.

A moment later, Nettie could hear the front door creak open, and a man's voice came from the porch. They had been expecting Hiserodt since yesterday but due to the constant rain, it made his travels slower, as part of the roadway outside Eldora had flooded, and he had to wait to leave.

Hiserodt walked into the room with his usual limp and saw Nettie struggling to sit up. He offered his help, which she took, and made her way upright. "Thank you, sir," she said and made a mock curtsey.

He tilted his hat to her as a gentleman would and sat down in the armchair that Maggie had extended to him. He removed his hat and apologized for getting rain water all over the rug. Nettie could see he looked nervous about something. The anxiety in his already nearly black eyes made her unsettled. She knew why he had come. He needed to know what was happening with Enoch.

"Tell me, Nettie, how are you and the baby doing? Do you need anything?" he asked in a calm tone.

This is all just formality, she thought. *He doesn't care and he sure is not normally this nice. He must be scared. I've seen him scare the life out of grown men a time or two. This is different.*

"I'm fine, thank you. I assume you want to know more about my father than the baby, so I'll get to it, Mr. Hiserodt," she said.

"Please, just call me Bill."

She nodded, then continued, "I already told Maggie, so I'll tell you now. They're letting the old man out. He made a deal, but I don't know what. All I can say is that he made one, and Frank, and Nate are on their way now to retrieve him. He should be here late tonight or early tomorrow morning. It may be slow going...I heard he is sick."

She thought about telling Maggie and Hiserodt that it was mostly due to her nagging her husband to bail her father out but decided against it. She had talked Frank and his brother, Nate, into mortgaging their farmland to pay for Enoch's release. As a result, Enoch would be turned over to Frank as his sole bondsman. All Nettie knew about the deal he made, was that Enoch was sick and had no other choice. She didn't yet trust Hiserodt in knowing that she was the reason Enoch would be home soon. What did that mean for her father? Surely, Bill wasn't going to welcome him back with open arms. Not after being caught and losing five hundred dollars.

There was a long silence. Nettie could see Maggie's lips get tighter the way they did when she was mad. Hiserodt clenched his hat tighter until Nettie asked, "Why have you been selling off all of your things? This house is about empty. You're going to leave him, aren't you?"

"He's obviously a traitor and no good will come from being with a man like that! Yes, I am leaving him! Come with me, Nettie! We can be happy, you, me, the baby, and Effie."

"And go where? We ain't got anywhere to go. At times I hate the old man for being the lowlife criminal that he is, but he is my father, and he's given us everything we have," Nettie said.

"He hasn't done anything! This house? Given to us by that man sitting next to you. The buggy we own? Same man, next to you. Your father has only ever given us heartache and grief!"

Hiserodt chimed in, "The counterfeiters may let him leave, but the fact is, if he made a deal, we could all be in trouble. We may need to put the old horse down."

Nettie immediately stood up, "For God's sake! Are you gonna kill my father?" she yelled.

Maggie then stood up and shouted, "Shut up, you damn little fool! You know what this business is! If he ain't got even half a mind to save himself after what he's done, then there's no helping him."

Hiserodt gestured for both women to take a seat, "Lets keep calm now, ladies," and in a soft calm voice he continued, "Enoch is like family to me, but the counterfeit leaders won't leave him around shaking snakes. Now, I *want* what's best for him, but what we *need...is* to do what's best for *everyone.* If he rolls over on us, if he hasn't already, then we're all done for."

Liar, Nettie thought. *You'd just rather he be dead so that the grip that fear has on your neck would leave and let you breathe. Those in charge will do the same to you, you liar.*

"You have to see this how we see it, Net. We could all lose everything. Including each other," Maggie said.

Hiserodt had gotten up while Maggie was speaking and now stood behind Nettie with his hands on her shoulders. She hated the way his touch felt to her. Cold, like a snake. She shuttered on the inside, but also felt something else. It was new, and exciting, and she didn't quite understand the feeling, given that this man just proposed her father's death. She began to feel disgusted.

"Look...in his letter he said he was sick and not getting any better. You may not have to do anything at all."

"And you might not, either," Hiserodt said.

He had leaned down and was now rubbing Nettie's shoulders, his mouth mere inches away from her ear. In a whisper that seemed seductive enough to entice even the most prude women, he said, "You only may need to lie a little bit. Find out what he said and what deal he made." He then brushed her hair behind her ear and came closer, "Then be a good little girl, and make it known to your stepmother here."

Nettie knew a threat when she heard one.

Maggie had come and sat down on the couch next to Nettie and leaned in close to the opposite ear as Bill. Placing her hand on Nettie's baby bump, she said, "Think of what could happen to your husband, Frank...what if something happened to the baby?"

II

At the Rainsbarger's family cabin, mid-April, 1884, just outside of Steamboat Rock...

The Rainsbarger homestead was located on the backside portion of nearly 160 acres of land and an additional 40 acres of farmland. Most of the area consisted of farmland and deep forest. The two-story family cabin was set back on the property only about 100 yards up from the Iowa River. The back of the cabin faced the river, and the front faced the thick green brush that blocked out the rest of the Hardin County citizens.

The forest was thick and untamed except for a small dirt road that tracked its way through the trees and eventually came out on the other side, about a half mile outside of Steamboat Rock. On either side of the small cabin lay the farm fields. The forest surrounded the home and fields like a shield, covering one end to the other, end capped by the river. There was no way to surround the cabin or sneak up on it from the rear, unless you came by boat up the open river.

It was near dusk now and the stars were out. The moon's glow could scarcely be seen through breaks in the tree line. Creatures of the night began to make their evening calls, and for the moment, the world sat still. Only the family who lived there stirred and dared to make any noticeable noise.

Tonight, the Rainsbarger brothers, and company, were all outside, seated, or standing around the wooden cabin's front porch. Finley sat next to Enoch Johnson on the two chairs just left of the front door. William, Nate, and Frank Rainsbarger leaned over the rail from the grass front yard and engaged in deep conversation with the others. Detective Norton and Henry Johns stood on the two steps leading to the front door. The evening air was silent and unmoving, unlike the men outside.

"Johnson, I have half a mind to arrest you right now, you stupid bastard. Not only did you miss your first court date, but the Judge knows the physician's note you sent was a fake!" yelled Norton.

"I know, but I really am sick, I couldn't go," he cried.

"If you miss this next court date you're going to prison for good! Frank here will lose the return of his mortgage, and then where is your daughter, and grand baby gonna live? In the cell next to you? You can't leave the county either! We'll find you and bring you back."

Henry Johns looked over at Frank, "I told you boys not to associate with this horsethief."

"Yea, yea, I know, Henry, but you can't choose who your wife is family with," Frank replied.

Henry looked over at Finley who was just sitting there sharpening his knife and chewing tobacco. He then looked back at Frank and said, "Tell me about it." Manse and William laughed at the comment as Finley smiled and threw his empty tobacco tin at Henry, who dodged it with ease.

"It's all fun until one of you is behind bars, I see," said Norton, "Johns is going to be the foreman for the federal grand jury once the trial goes to court and he knows the case better than anyone. You are all family here, and you need to make this work, or Johnson is done."

"I don't understand how you got caught in the first place, you old coot," Nate laughed.

"Getting caught was the easy part, getting loose is the hard part," Henry replied. "Martha and I went to visit Finley one evening for dinner and some members of the Boulder gang showed up quite inebriated, Enoch included. They bragged about getting paid in counterfeit money and were generous enough to give me some."

Nate laughed again, "What a dumb name, the Boulder gang."

"It's a fitting name," William interjected, "everyone of them was apparently as dumb as a rock, you included Finley."

Henry Johns and Detective Norton exchanged a glance that told the other one that none of these men were taking this seriously. Frank was the only one who seemed to be contemplating anything at all. Enoch noticed their exchange.

"Don't worry! I'll show up, but I still expect the leniency we talked about, Henry. Steadman reassured me it would be done."

Frank interjected, "You know the word is out about there being counterfeiting in Hardin County. It only took a couple of days, and now everyone is talking about it. They're also talking about the old man and why we're keeping him here. Some folks think that this land is some kind of fortress."

"We like privacy; what's so wrong about that?" Nate remarked.

William spoke up, "It's easy to pin petty crimes on people who act like petty thieves, but that ain't us. Are we going to become guilty by association, Henry? It seems like an easier way out than honest folks having to expose their neighbor."

It was Henry Johns' turn to speak. He paused for a moment, then said, "I like you boys enough, but maybe stop going to nearly *every* watering hole every night. Disappearances of people and property are easy to pin on lonely night riders, especially in Hardin County."

"People never liked us to begin with and now we are harboring a convicted counterfeiter," Finley added, "The folks of Steamboat and

Eldora are easily spooked by a pair of mischief makers, and look, there's five of us. We don't need any attention. Most people don't know us too well, but unless we are working, we are at the saloon or with friends. We're just normal folk, but the blind lead the blind, I suppose."

Norton, who was unable to get a word in for a while, interjected, "Can we get back on topic? I don't care if folks are afraid of a band of brothers, or a band of robbers. Right now, Johnson needs to be on a shorter leash, and not leave *Rainsbarger Country*, or whatever folks call this area."

"I ain't a dog to be leashed," Enoch sneered.

"You smell like one," Finley laughed.

Henry was getting angry now, and he nearly yelled, "Look, most folks have either had cattle stolen, or maimed, their fields burnt, or their living supplies stolen, and now ordinary folks are hearing about a counterfeit operation that's been right under their noses. They're just plain scared, even of their own neighbors. They want to know what Johnson knows and that's the names of those involved."

"As long as we are not involved and stay uninvolved," Frank said. "People are more stupid and timid than a wet pussycat. Net, Nate and myself are quiet enough people and would like to keep it that way. Enoch, you can stay here since Maggie kicked you out. Henry, you can come and speak with Enoch here when you need to. I don't want anyone else coming around who don't need to be. Come on now, old man, out with it. Tell Johns and Mr. Norton what you know."

III

The small cabin's front door slammed shut as the five men entered. Frank and Nate sat down together on one side of the kitchen table, Henry Johns, and Detective Norton sat on the other side, and Enoch sat down on the end, in between the men. The remaining brothers had gone on to William's house just a few rods down the way.

Nettie, hearing the men come in and sit down, entered the kitchen a moment after they did. She kissed Frank on the head as she passed him by and did the same to her father, Enoch. He briefly looked up at her with deep fatherly admiration. She was what he lived for. She was how he knew true love.

Nettie quickly set out cups and leaned over the stove to get the kettle of coffee. "Let me help you with that, Net," Frank began.

"I'm pregnant, Frank, not dying," she said as she smiled. Placing the drink ware on the table, she pulled up a chair in the corner of the kitchen, folded her arms and sat down.

Looking at her, Enoch said, "Dear, do you think it would be a wiser idea if perhaps you didn't hear this conversation? Perhaps, the less you know, the better. I don't wanna cause undue stress to you and the baby."

"It's too late for that, old man, you're sick, you were just in jail, and now you're facing a gang of counterfeiters, and brought all that mess under *my* roof. I'm staying," she said in a firm but polite tone.

Enoch chuckled. Nettie had always been a soft spoken, polite young girl, but at times he could see more to her than that. He thought he was seeing his own stubbornness in her, or maybe she had just grown up a little more, and he had missed it. Either way, a little callus was good for a young girl in this country.

"Are you ready to begin?" asked Norton.

Henry Johns had already pulled out of his small case, Enoch's signed statement and a fresh piece of paper to take down more names. "You've already told us about Marx and Rice. Who else do you know about?"

Enoch looked around, still thinking about Nettie. She rubbed her belly as she sat there listening. He knew he could give all the names they wanted but he'd still end up with some time in prison at some point, and would continue to miss out on her. He'd miss out on the baby, and it killed him inside. Tears came to his eyes and he became angry. No one came to visit him from the counterfeiters, no one tried to bail him out. Frank and Nate put up the money, but it was her doing.

She saved me, he thought.

"Johnson? Are you okay?" Henry asked.

Enoch turned to face the men and they could see the wet streaks on his cheeks that had cleared the dirt from his face. He swallowed hard and began to shake. "I can give you the names of about twenty or more men," he said at last through a groggy voice.

"Twenty or more? That would be more than enough for a secure indictment. What judge would say no to a case like that!? We're gonna clean out this whole counterfeit operation once and for all," Henry said.

"That's the plan," Enoch replied softly.

He had returned his gaze to his daughter and knew his only chance at providing a better life for her was to end an operation that would try to keep everyone in poverty, and possibly her more than most, as she was the daughter of the man who got caught, the infamous 'Horse-thief' Johnson. He once cherished the name, but now he only saw it as foolishness. Still staring at Nettie, his tears fell even more as he started telling Henry the names of the men.

"John and Milton Biggs, Foy, Wisner, Haines...Leverton...Popejoy..."

His voice trailed off as he listed the names one by one. Henry Johns wrote in a fury. Frank and Nate listened quietly. Nettie held her belly and sat listening. Everything was quiet except Enoch's voice. He could hear his heart beating. Racing. He wondered when it would stop. Maggie's words replayed on a loop in his mind.

"You're gonna die with your boots on..."

IV

The end of October, 1884, in Steamboat Rock...

Henry Johns once again stood on the curb just outside the Farmer's Exchange Bank. The crisp leaves crunched under his feet as he approached the bank's front doors. The roadway was painted with red, orange, and yellow foliage that had fallen from the trees. Some blew quickly inside the building with Henry as he entered.

Once he entered the bank, he noticed two distinct differences from his last visit. The first, was that due to public outcry over there being possible counterfeiters in the area, a number of guards were positioned inside the bank. One was posted by the doorway. There were two more on either ends of the long counter where the bank tellers stood, and one more at the bottom of the stairs that lead to the manager's upstairs office. Henry wondered what good they would be against counterfeiters. Then he wondered if some of them might be in the gang themselves and that's how they procured their positions. The second thing that was new was that Mr. Noyes was there. He had been avoiding Henry and was now no longer able to. Henry caught just a glimpse of him as he headed upstairs to the office, accompanied by two other men.

Standing at the bottom of the stairs, Henry looked for his courage. He remembered Martha's words about his incessant need for the truth, possibly becoming the reason for his death. Then he thought of his children. *What would they have if he lost everything to fools?*

As he put one foot on the bottom stair, the armed guard put a hand out and stopped Henry. "Whoa there, partner! Where do you think you're going?"

Henry wasn't sure what to say. Perhaps the truth? *I'm here to interrogate your boss and his friends.* That wouldn't work. As he was thinking, he noticed that the guard kept diverting his eyes to a woman at the teller counter furthest from him.

"You know, chap, that's a lovely looking lady over there. Wouldn't you say? Her name is Mrs. Clow. She's a lady of the night and dare I say a possible member of the counterfeiters," he said as he leaned in closer.

"Nooo? Her? You're pulling my leg, aren't you, mister?"

Henry kept a straight face, "I'm an informant for the Secret Service, and I never joke around! Now go! Go get her, chap," Henry said as he shoved the guard in her direction. Henry could barely hear the young man yell, "Ma'am, I need to see what's in your bag," as he entered the office door.

When Henry entered the room at the top of the stairs, the three men turned to look at him. It was a small room with only a desk and some books on a shelf behind it. Ash Noyes sat at the desk, Dan Turner stood leaning against the wall near the desk, and William Hiserodt sat in the chair against the wall facing the door. His face was red and he looked as if he had been yelling.

"Hello, gentlemen," Henry said, "Sorry for the intrusion, but I need to speak with Mr. Noyes."

"Yea, don't we all?" Hiserodt replied, clearly in an angry tone.

"You shouldn't be in here, Mr. Johns," Turner replied, "This conversation doesn't concern the likes of you."

Henry interrupted, "I rather think that it does." He pulled up another chair next to Hiserodt and sat down. "Who wants to tell me more about the fakes coming in and out of town. Should we start with you, Mr. Noyes? I have an indictment ready for you, sir, and I can have others ready for you two gentlemen as well. I want to know who's responsible for redistributing the money. *Now talk!*"

"We're in the middle of a financial conversation, and it may be best that you remove yourself until you can speak with Mr. Noyes privately. My transactions are private. Of course, a man such as yourself can understand that, right Henry?" Hiserodt replied.

Henry could tell by the tone that he said it, that it wasn't a request, but a statement. *Beat it!* Is what his tone said to Henry. "I think not, Bill, unfortunately, your transactions are interfering with mine, and this may involve all of you. This needs to be stopped."

"Be careful where you step, Johns. I take threats personally. I asked politely once, and I won't a second time."

"Maybe I should leave. I'm sure I could get more information out of a simpleton like Leverton," Henry replied as he pretended to know more than he did. Enoch had given him names and a few stories to validate his claims but not everything. He noticed Ash Noyes sit a little straighter, Dan Turner unfolded his arms, and Bill's black eyes twitched at the name.

"Listen here, you crazy bastard," Noyes began, "You don't know anything and Leverton don't know anything. So unless you have proof or a warrant to be here, I suggest you leave immediately."

Henry stood up and pushed back his chair. "That's fine, chaps...I'll be on my way to see another colleague of yours. My wife just made some delicious blueberry pie, and I heard homemade desserts may make the fat pig talk. I'll tell Wilcox you all said, 'hello'."

Before Henry could finish his statement and take a breath, Hiserodt had stood up, shoved Henry into the wall behind him, and pulled his knife from its place on his side. Henry could feel the cold blade against his skin, and wondered if Hiserodt buried it in his throat if it would hurt, or if it was sharp enough to do the job right.

"No more talking from you! Don't get yourself into things you don't understand! I'll kill you where you stand, Henry!" Hiserodt yelled.

The other two men had come around, about to hold either side of Henry to the wall, when the office door burst open. The guard whom Henry had swindled by using Rie Clow as a distraction entered the room with his gun drawn.

"Drop the knife!" he shouted as he shoved Hiserodt away from Henry Johns with his gun's barrel.

CHAPTER 5

DOLLARS AND CENTS

I

At Frank and Nettie's home, the beginning of November, 1884...

George Winnans rubbed his eyes and blinked hard. He had been staring at the tree line that was yards off and covered in darkness. He rubbed them again even harder as he continued to stare into the darkness. "I think I've had too much bitters to drink this evening, Frank," he said, "My eyes are playin' tricks on me."

For a while now, George had been sitting on the front porch with Henry Williams and Frank. They had a few drinks and throughout the evening George thought he had seen lights way off in the forest. *They were just small flickering flames*, or at least he thought. Standing up, he tried to squint his eyes to see.

"What is that, Frank? Is it a fire?"

"I don't see what you're talking about, George. Maybe you should go to bed. We have enough going on around here without you going crazy. Besides, I don't need you hollering and waking the baby. You'll have hell to pay with Net if you do," Frank replied as he took another drink.

"No, no, I think he sees something, Frank," Williams said as he now stood, squinting his eyes also.

"You two are losing it," Frank retorted as he stood up and leaned over the porch to look as well. Then he saw it, too. There were small lights flickering out at the edge of the woods. Without losing contact with them, he came down the porch steps and walked a little closer. He knew George liked to drink, but there was no way he drank so much they *all* saw twinkling lights. Frank then got a nauseous feeling and then began to sweat even in the cool night air as the lights began to move.

"Counterfeiters," he whispered.

"What?"

"It's the counterfeiters! It's their men, Henry," Frank replied in a panic, "They've come a time or two during the day to speak with Enoch, but this is different. I think they've come to *collect* him." He then turned and ran inside. Henry and George rushed to their horses that were tied up just below the front porch and drew their guns. Then the whistle blew and echoed through the land. Men on horses charged out of the brush with torches, and fired shots into the air, yelling as they went.

Frank had grabbed Nettie, Vina Fisher, and his baby, and hid them in the closet of his room. A moment later, he and Nate came back out onto the front porch with rifles. Enoch followed them out but wasn't holding a gun. Frank, and Nate stood together on one side, and George Winnans, and Henry Williams stood on another. Enoch stood at the top of the front steps. Within a minute, they were nearly surrounded by seven masked men with guns. The men came to a halt and lowered their guns. The horses stamped the ground and kicked up dust as they tried to calm their nerves. They seemed aware of the anxiety of their riders.

"Evening, men! We're only here for Enoch. His wife sent us to collect him," said the man in the middle as he tipped his hat.

"I don't think so, fellas," Nate replied.

"I wasn't asking. There's seven of us, and five of you, but we don't want any trouble. We're only covering our faces to hide who we are from *you* boys. Johnson knows us. We're friends, ain't we, Enoch? We just came to take our friend back to his wife is all."

"There's more of us than you might think, *Popejoy*," Enoch said.

The sound of rifles and revolvers being armed rang from each side of the cabin as William Rainsbarger, and Ed Johns came from the left, and William's sons, George and Joe, came from the right.

"Plus, there's two inside. I ain't going nowhere. At least, not with you."

At the sound of his name, Popejoy lowered his bandana that was covering his face, "We've come peacefully before, Johnson, and requested simply to know if you were still for us, or against us, and if so, what you told the detectives. There's a case being formed against us and you're in the center of it all. The boss isn't just going to lie under it."

"And neither am I, you fool. You all passed dollars while I merely passed cents. The detectives know it now, and they know it well. I told you all before when I was locked away, that if you deserted me, I wouldn't lend a helping hand. Where were you all when I got caught? No one came to me, except to pass threats by the mouth of my wife. I told you all not to leave me!" Enoch shook a little as he spoke, but his voice didn't waiver. He finally told the counterfeiters that he had deserted them and their cause. He felt liberated, yet afraid.

"Well shucks, I guess you'll be a dead man then, Johnson," Popejoy said calmly. He then reached for his gun and then stopped. He laughed hard as everyone took aim and prepared to fire. Still laughing, Popejoy continued, "Damn, you're *all* skittish. I'm just playing, Johnson. I ain't gonna shoot you. I ain't dying for a pathetic, no good horse thief, but I'm sure the boss would *love* to hear your reply."

He then spit on the ground, tipped his hat, and turned his horse around. The men behind him began to disperse and ride back to the single roadway back out of the woods. As they cleared, a lone rider stayed and stared at Enoch. He wore dark colored clothes, a bandana up to his eyes, and a hat, so that all that could be seen was his eyes. Enoch locked eyes with the man, and then a great fear overcame him. He knew the man was John Biggs, his wife's uncle who had brought him into this whole operation. Enoch trembled backwards a bit and then grabbed the wooden railing. The covered man looked a moment longer, then turned to follow the other men.

II

At the Johnson home in Gifford, November 16th, 1884...

John Tiser, the Johnson's hired hand, lay awake in his small cot at the Johnson's nearly empty home. All he had in the small room, was the cot and his clothes that he had hung up to dry. The rain had hit hard a few hours ago, but it was now slow, and constant. Thunder could be heard every so often and lightning would give a brief glimpse of his surroundings. As he lay there listening to the storm, he hoped it would be cold, and wet enough to start snowing soon, maybe even enough to provide a layer of ice. He hadn't yet finished the sled he was working on at Manse Rainsbarger's shop, but he was close, and was anxious for the first real snow.

Maggie Johnson was in the room adjacent to his and was sitting by the fire. The boy had gone to bed hours ago without saying anything. She knew that once he had finished with his work, that he wasn't going home due to the oncoming storm, but sitting in her silence, she forgot he was there.

She stood up and stoked the fire. Returning the stoker to its place next to the fireplace, she withdrew to the kitchen, and removed the kettle from the stove, when she heard the front door open, and several men enter her home. Tiser heard them enter as well. Moving to the doorway that was cracked ajar, he sat behind the door, and peered out into the kitchen, careful to remain in the room's darkness.

Three men had entered, only one of which John knew. The man with the limp was Hiserodt, and the two others kept their backs to Tiser as they sat at the table in the kitchen. Their faces stayed out of view. The storm began making noise again and the evening greetings were lost in the noise.

"What are we gonna do about that old hornswoggler now?" Maggie asked through gritted teeth. She was fidgeting her hands in her lap while she sat, and slowly rocked back and forth, not in a nervous way, but one that was anxious, nonetheless.

"Nettie's letter said he has a new trial coming up in January, he's been meeting with Johns, and Norton, and giving out more information.

Maybe he's too old and sick to run and made up his mind that leniency is his only option. From what John and Popejoy heard, it sounds like he isn't planning on going down alone. I don't see any other way around it...we're gonna have to kill him!" Hiserodt yelled.

Spit flew from his mouth as he said it, and he hammered the table with the drinking glass in his hand. Thunder struck just outside as he hit the tabletop, making his strike seem louder than it was. The glass shattered, cutting his thumb. He drew in a deep breath, took out his handkerchief, and wiped away the blood. More relaxed, he said, "He's your husband, Mag'. Tell me how you want it done. You want to be rid of him and I need him gone! Henry Johns is now the foreman of the grand jury for the indictment, and as soon as my men find that rat, the dogs will be licking their chops with his blood, too."

"I don't care how you do it," she said, "Just do it quick, and make it look like an accident. Perhaps his insurance will pay out and you'll have your money back." As she said this, she got up and went over to Hiserodt, and kneeling, she took his hands in hers. They were still dripping with his blood from the cut glass, even after having wiped at them. "Please," she cried.

He looked at her deeply, then took her face in his hands, smearing the remaining blood on her white skin. "These two gentlemen here have a plan, and I know they'd do anything for you, but their time and skills aren't cheap," Hiserodt said as he gestured towards the unknown men.

"A thousand dollars each! That's what I'll pay from the insurance, once I collect it! Just do it! Hell, do it here if you have to," Maggie cried, nearly yelling.

"We might be able to do it here," one of the men said, "If we can get him here! He's old and sick. We could make it look like an accident." He nodded to the man sitting with his back to Tiser's door. Even with the lightning strikes, John's face was hidden from their view when they looked at the man. John thought he knew the man's voice. "What do you think?"

Then came a voice John didn't recognize at all. "I think, out by the old road would be better. We simply need to wait for the celebration of the new president elect. It'll happen in two days, at least that's what the signs in town say. Get him to come here, Maggie, and we can catch him alone. You can conceal a man's screams a lot better under a crowd, than in the silence of his own home. Most of the folks should be closer to Steamboat and Eldora than way down here. You'll have to be the bait, Mag," said the man.

"You reckon you can get him to come?" Bill asked, still rubbing the blood on her face and getting closer.

She kissed him for a brief moment, then pulled back and nearly yelled, "I know how I'll do it! If it's me he wants, then I suppose I know just the thing. You see, darling, tonight is his, and my anniversary. I'll write the telegraph now, and beg him to come get me."

Hiserodt smiled a thin, evil smile that was barely visible through his beard, as Maggie wrote her telegraph frantically, even though it was straight to the point. She couldn't bear pretending to still love him, even through a letter. This is what she wrote:

Mr. Johnson,

As you may have come to know by now, I am not with my parents and not at the Ellsworth Hotel in Eldora. I am staying at our home in Gifford. You missed our anniversary. Come down and get me Tuesday night. Tell Nettie to send my shawl.

-Margaret

"So that no suspicion comes your way, and so that no one actually sees you with the letter, you need to have the Tiser boy send it out tomorrow morning," Bill said.

At the name, Maggie jumped up in a panic.

The Tiser boy! She forgot he was there! Did he hear them? What would he do? Would they have to murder a child now, too?

John Tiser saw her panic, and his heart beat hard in his chest from the conversation of murder. And now...she realized he was still there. Maggie and Hiserodt looked like two ferocious demons in the dim light. Hiserodt's hair was astray and his dark eyes pierced John's soul. Maggie was covered with blood on her soft skin. They both peered at the doorway's darkness.

Do they know I'm here, he wondered.

"Maggie, tell me you sent the boy home early! He's not still here, is he? Damn it!" Hiserodt yelled, and slammed his hand down again, spraying blood droplets across the tabletop.

He jumped up, and pushing Maggie aside, he removed the blade from its sheath on his side. Holding it underhand, he approached the bedroom door. He pushed it open and saw the boy lying there. Tiser's back was towards the door with his face against the wall. The blanket was pulled up over him. John Tiser held his breath and pretended to be asleep. He awaited in infuriating anticipation to see if he was done for.

Then he heard a whisper from the doorway, "He's been in here for hours now, Bill. He's most likely been sleeping the whole time. If he slept through thunder, he no doubt slept through you hitting the table," Maggie said.

John held his breath a little longer. The bedroom door then creaked all the way closed and he was left in darkness. The only thing that remained was the sound of rain and distant thunder.

CHAPTER 6

CANNON FIRE

I

November 18th, 1884, at the train station in Steamboat Rock...

The train station platform began to shake as the incoming train came screeching to a halt. Several train cars passed Enoch as he sat in his buggy near the back end of the platform. The train conductor blew the train's thick horn, and it echoed off the brick walls that made up the station booth.

He had gone to look for Maggie as he had hoped to catch her on her way to Eldora. She often took the train into Steamboat Rock, and he hoped she would today. Even if he did meet her, he wasn't sure what it would accomplish. Would she want him back? Would she consider running away with him and his children? He wasn't sure, but he was determined to find out. He wasn't happy about the argument he had with Maggie, and that she now spent her days at her parent's home, or at the Western House hotel in Steamboat Rock. At least that's what he'd heard. Even though he didn't like it, what could he do? He knew he had nothing left to offer her. Nonetheless, he intended to try to win her back, if not for his sake, then for Effie's.

He sat upon the buggy seat clad in dirty clothes and an even dirtier overcoat and scarf. The scarf was wrapped about his face, and he held the leather whip in one hand and the bridle in the other. The buggy's top was up to shield him from the wind, but it was still cold out. His breath could be slightly seen through the scarf and his hands were frozen in the gloves he wore. The wind had made the ride to the train station even more difficult to bear, but the sun would soon begin to rise, and would start to thaw the ground, and Enoch. It would make for a nicer ride back, especially if Mrs. Johnson returned with him.

He thought of her beauty and wondered what she would see in an old, used up man as himself. He wasn't optimistic about finding her, or that she would go with him, but for the first time since leaving the Sioux City prison, he started to feel like himself. His sickly body began to find its strength as he waited at the train station. He spoke to himself in a small quiet voice as he waited. After a while, his body welcomed the cold as it refreshed his spirit, and he stepped down from the horse and buggy onto the concrete platform.

Dozens of men, women, and children were pouring out of the train's open doors. The attendants were starting to remove their luggage from the storage compartments on one side, and more families were trying to board on the other. Enoch watched as all of the people swarmed the station like bees and he began to call Maggie's name. People started to run every which way, and Enoch couldn't keep up, until the station cleared. After about fifteen minutes, Enoch's hope had faded. Everyone on his side of the platform was gone, and the train began to pull away from the station now that the other families had boarded.

As the train inched forward, he could see the platform on the other side through the gaps in the train cars. At first, he thought he was seeing a dog that had been left behind, and then he realized it was something else. It was a man lying face down on the platform and he wasn't moving.

"Hey! Don't move, fella! I'm coming! I'm coming! You alright?" Enoch yelled.

He ran over to the back of the train as it passed and jumped the tracks over to the man. Reaching him, he rolled him over. The man was laughing when he was rolled over. His gums were black from chewing tobacco and swallowing the chew instead of spitting. His brown beard was covered in the dirt he had been lying in on the platform.

He reached up at Enoch, who was now leaning over him, grabbed him by the shoulder, and the back of the head, and head-butt Enoch in the nose. Blood gushed out and onto his scarf. Enoch grabbed his scarf, and clenched it over his nose, trying to stop the flow as he started to step backwards. It ran down his hands, onto his shoes, and onto the concrete flooring. He was taken back by the blow. His confidence and regained strength were still fading.

Two other men came running out of the underbrush behind the horse stall that was on that side of the track. Upon regaining his bearings, Enoch realized he knew who they were. It was James Rice and Albert Leverton, two of Black Bill's hired confederates. Enoch had seen them a number of times in his dealings with the counterfeiters. The man who was face down and attacked him, he recognized after a second glance. It was Henry Finster, the man who owned the large cave by the river that they used to hide stolen horses in.

The other two men were clothed in a long duster, boots, and had a knife on one hip. Rice held a shotgun in one hand that was aimed up, resting on his shoulder. His boots were dirty and faded. He had a short brim hat on, and a long mustache that curled on the end. Leverton had his hand on the revolver on his hip. His hair was slicked back and had long thick sideburns. Albert was the shorter of the two.

"Well, well, it looks like we caught the weasel sleepin' boys," Rice laughed.

Enoch tried to keep his front towards them and not let them surround him. His bad knee locked, prohibiting him from running. They managed to surround him anyway and then he heard a loud noise like a whip. Then he felt searing pain. Hiserodt had approached Enoch from behind and drove a cane into the back of his bad knee, and hard. Enoch fell to the ground when he felt it. Before he knew it, Henry Finster wrapped his legs around Enoch's, and grabbed his arms. The two gunmen rolled them over and Leverton punched Enoch hard in the gut. Henry held him tight. Enoch gasped for air, trying not to choke on the blood running from his nose.

"Hold still, old man! We just want to talk! Besides, there's no running now," said Rice. He pulled out a pair of iron Billy tongs and grabbed Enoch's face near the chin.

"Calm down, you old coot," yelled Leverton, "We need to know what you told them feds! Tell us what you said, and Mr. Hiserodt here may let you live!"

At these words, Enoch sucked in as much blood as he could from his upper lip, and spit it back into Leverton's face. He reeled back, loosening his grip, and clawed at his pocket for his handkerchief to wipe his face.

"Now don't get your dander up, you old cuss! Just tell us what they know and who knows what! What did you tell Johns? I'm not just gonna stay quiet and lay under this," Hiserodt yelled as Rice sat on Enoch's chest. Rice opened and closed the iron tongs as he got closer to Enoch's face.

Enoch finally caught his breath and said, "I ain't gonna lie under it either! When they locked me up, no one came to me! You all left me there to rot. I didn't have no choice but to make a deal, and even then, that was the only way for them to allow bail! If I'm set to go back to the penitentiary then I ain't goin' alone! I told your boys once, and now I'll tell you! You passed dollars while I passed cents and the feds know it! I ain't saying no more about it, so do what you're gonna do!"

There on the station platform, outside of ear shot, they beat the old man. With Henry on his back he was unable to cover the blows. Once exhaustion set in, Leverton took the iron tongs from Rice, and sat on Enoch. Prying open his mouth, he gripped Enoch's tongue with the clamps, and pulled it just outside of his mouth.

"If you aren't gonna say anything more to us about it, then you won't be saying anything more to them feds about it, either," Leverton yelled.

Enoch struggled under the weight of the men, but he no longer had any real strength to make any progress. As he fought to break free, Rice took his knife out, and slid it into Leverton's open, outstretched hand. He brought it to Enoch's tongue and prepared to make his cut. Before he had time to start his first slice, a nearby tree cracked, and splintered near the horse stall. They were being shot at. The revolver slug buried itself deep within the tree, smoking at the entry point.

Two station guards had come around the brick station booth on the far side, and saw the men attacking Enoch, and opened fire. The men struggled to their feet and prepared to fire back. Another shot went through Rice's hat and it soon caught fire. They aimlessly returned fire, not sure what to do with Enoch.

In a scramble, they made their way over to their horses that were loosely tied to the hitching posts near the stalls. Leverton and Rice climbed on, with Leverton driving the horse. When Henry tried to jump on, he nearly knocked Rice off the back. On his second attempt, Rice was ready, and he kicked Henry in the teeth mid jump. Leverton whipped the reins in his hands quickly as they retreated into the brush. Henry scrambled into the woods just as a loud charge of buckshot went off. Hiserodt had escaped to his own horse and buggy on the other side of the tracks as his men returned fire.

Enoch lay there on the hard floor panting, trying to get up. He turned to his side to see who had shot at the confederates. Looking up, he saw the two guards approaching. The shorter guard was reliving his shot at James Rice when they came around the bend.

"Did you see that shot!? If my aim would have been a few inches lower I would have shot that old mudsill straight in the face, and his teeth would have popped out the back of his neck!" he cried.

As they reached Enoch, he gave a simple smile, and waved at them. The man's voice became distant and then Enoch fainted. They put the old horse thief in the back of his own buggy and covered him with a blanket. When he awoke, he returned home without Mrs. Johnson.

II

Late afternoon, November 18th, 1884, at the Rainsbarger's cabin...

Frank sat on the wooden bench just outside the old barn and watched the sun start to set. He had his hair slicked over to one side with a neatly groomed mustache. He was holding his hat in his hands in front of him as he was looking down at his boots. On the outside he was ready for the festivities of that evening, but on the inside, he was discouraged by his wife's actions towards him. She now acted cold to him and accused him of several petty crimes. He supposed she would try to do the same about tonight, but it would be different. Tonight, he would be with his brothers, and in Cleves, having a simple celebration. Even though he asked, Nettie wouldn't go with him. Nettie knew Vina was there to watch their baby girl, Zella, but she still refused. Lifting up his head, he saw an old man limping towards him.

Enoch was now sicker than he was before, and he dragged his foot a bit as he walked over to Frank from the cabin. His bad knee was still bruised and ached from the encounter earlier that day. He was afraid his time was up, and now couldn't afford, financially, or physically, to make a run for it.

Nate came running from the front door, and upon reaching Enoch, took his arm, and helped him along. Nate was wearing his black hat and dark gray suit with a black vest. His hair was also slicked to one side. His mustache, that was longer than Frank's, ran past his chin. Enoch was for once, dressed in clean clothes, even though he still smelt of his usual self. He was wearing two shirts, a vest, a coat, and in one hand he held the overcoat that Nate had gifted him when he arrived to make permanent residence at their homestead.

Once they reached the bench, Enoch dropped down next to Frank. He reached into his vest pocket, and pulled out a small flask of gin, and took a drink. After a few gulps, he spoke, "Well, boys, I think I'll be going to Eldora again after all, then perhaps to Gifford, assuming she's telling the truth. I didn't see Maggie in Eldora a few weeks back and I don't think I'll find her there again today. I don't feel right about going the journey alone, but I can't help it...I need to find her."

"I don't think you should be going until we can convince Nettie to go with you, but I suppose tonight might be as good a night as any if you're determined to go. There'll be plenty of folks around," Nate replied.

"Folks who want me dead," Enoch grumbled, "The men running the whole thing, I'm sure will have me killed!" He shook his head in disappointment at whom he'd become and took another swig of the gin. "Supposin' I don't find her, I'll be staying at Mr. Taylor's place, and return in the mornin', assuming I don't get gunned down."

"You should take this," Frank replied as he handed Enoch a small side hammer revolver. "You may need it, and even if you can't aim true, you may scare off anything, or *anyone* you need to. Hopefully it gives you some comfort, old man."

Enoch took the gun and tucked it into the side of his boot. He was afraid, and being so, he choked up. He swallowed back tears and said, "You ain't no choir boys, but you're goodfellas. Frank, I didn't take kindly to you just before you married Net, but I'm determined to change my mind. You boys bailed me out, put up your own money for my clothes, food, shelter—," he trailed off as he recalled it all, still holding back tears. "And now I think I'm fixing to return to the dust. Boys, you best take care of them girls, especially Zella. No more late nights doin' God knows what. You keep yourselves armed to the tooth and on watch. I don't think anyone will come for you, but they may come for Nettie before all's said, and done. Frank, seein' as you used to go with Nettie to church, I take you for a prayin' man. You best be sayin' them for me now."

Frank simply nodded his head in agreement, looked up at Nate, put his hands on his knees, and stood up, "We better say bye to the girls and make sure there's enough firewood for them to last until we get home," Frank said quietly.

He shook Enoch's hand, wished him well, and then left the old man sitting there. Frank wasn't happy about the situation, and even though it was a day to celebrate the election of President Grover, he had other matters to attend to besides joining in on the celebration.

Enoch sat there a moment longer and then made his way to his buggy which was luckily close at hand. He put on his overcoat, wrapped himself in his blood-matted scarf, threw his whip in the buggy seat, and took a deep breath. As he stood there with his hands on the horse's reins, Nettie came up to him and put her hand on his. She had tears in her eyes as she said goodbye under her breath. She gave him a brief hug, then lifted her dress off the ground and ran towards the house.

"This old man will be back for his girls, don't you worry," he yelled after her. He then mounted his buggy and drove off towards Eldora. He rode through the tree-lined dirt road in silence and with a watchful eye. Every so often he would reach down and pull the side hammer pistol out of his boot, make sure it was ready to be used, and then tuck it back in.

Once he reached the main thoroughfare, his nerves started to settle. There were dozens of folks out getting ready for the bonfires. Almost no one seemed to even notice him. They were closing up their shops, putting up banners, and splitting wood for the fires. Some folks were boarding up their windows in anticipation that things might not end in a celebratory manner. Old men sat on their porches, eyeing the rough young folks, and cleaning their lever action rifles. This election was a big win for Hardin County. Everyone would be either celebrating, or at home, guarding their possessions.

Enoch's horse was starting to get even more nervous around all of the partygoers, and he thought it best to move out of that area, and onto the main road. After some time searching Eldora, he decided it was no use looking for her there. There was so much commotion about, that he wouldn't be able to see her in the crowds, anyway. It was time to go down to Gifford.

It was already getting dark, and he wanted to be closer to town before it was too late. He thought of Nettie and Maggie as he was on his way. He thought even more about baby Zella, and it made him smile. He had a thousand questions in his mind and not an answer in sight.

The continual sips of gin relaxed his body but not his mind. It wasn't right that he should have to go find his wife under threat of death by the man she was possibly sleeping with. If anyone was out to get him that evening, then he would need a plan to throw them off.

Who would it be this time?

As he rode along through Eldora, he noticed that the bonfires were beginning to be lit. Dark was settling fast, and he was nowhere near Gifford. He rode a little faster. The buggy bumped up and down on the hard dirt road, the front wheel hit hard and began to splinter in the middle. Enoch hadn't noticed as he was now slipping into the gin's warmth. He wrapped his scarf around his face, pulled his overcoat shut, cracked the whip, and rode on.

It was now dark, and as far as he could see, there were patches of light along the long road leading downward towards Gifford. The lights were bonfires spaced out evenly along the road. To Enoch, they seemed like way stations along the way. They were a place to be seen, and a place to see others he might want to know are about. Albeit, some partygoers were wearing party masks, and their identities were concealed. Others wore bandanas around their faces to shield the cold, and some wore scarfs. Even with such obstacles, he knew almost everyone, and thought he was still better off near the light of the fires. The bonfire groups were filled with thundering laughter, the clinking sound of glass, and tin as folks cheered, and the occasional argument that had already started.

As Enoch was approaching his third fire on the long route, a thick knot in a log cracked, and startled his horse. He tried to bolt, but Enoch tugged the reins hard towards himself. The bad front wheel began to splinter even more. The excessive relationship with his gin aided in his continued blind eye at the wheel's health.

As the horse kicked, someone grabbed the bit and yelled, "Whoa there! Calm down, calm down!" Enoch recognized the voice at once. It was Ralph Surles, his old horse thieving friend. He climbed down from the buggy and shook Ralph's hand.

"Hey, ya old hard case, come warm yourself a bit by the fire, and have a beer," Ralph said as he handed Enoch a dark tinted bottle. "You remember Mrs. Kennedy, Mr. Cramer, Nate Thompson, Thomas Nott, my brother Benjamin, and of course John Blair!"

Enoch shook all of their hands and felt a small twinge of disgust as he shook John's hand. Panic started to rise within him. The men were all old horse thieving friends, but he was never fond of John Blair. What worried him even more now, was John was dressed as one of Black Bill's confederate gunmen.

Enoch again swallowed hard after he shook John's hand to greet him. John stood opposite of Enoch on the other side of the fire, sipping his beer, never taking his eyes off Enoch. Taking a drink, John asked, "So...how is your case coming along? I heard you got caught real good by them feds. You got a trial coming up, when? January? What do you think they do to ya?"

He's baiting me, Enoch thought.

Enoch knew in his heart that Blair was in Hiserodt's pocket by the way he asked the question. He didn't want to answer him. While Enoch was thinking of a response, Thomas butted in, "You're gonna plead guilty and hope for a lighter sentence aren't cha? You already told em' what they needed to know."

Thomas was clearly unaware of the growing tension between Blair and Johnson. He slapped Enoch on the back and gave a small snort and laugh. At this, John's mouth became a snarl, barely visible through the flickering flames that reached for his face and made the shadows on it dance.

"Hobble your lip, you old gull," Enoch barked, trying to play his harsh remark off as a joke, "Nothing is settled just yet and we don't know who's listening out here!" As he said this, a loud group of men ran by yelling to their friends at the nearest bonfire. They were followed by a smaller group of kids wearing masks and dirty coon skinned caps. They were sword fighting with sticks they had found and were chasing each other.

"No, no! We're all friends here, ain't we, Johnson?" replied Blair. "Tell us all about it. What's that fella's name you've been working with? Johns? Norton? Oh, no it was your son-in-law, Frank, right? He got you bailed out oh' Sioux I hear! Say...what ever happened to Milton Biggs? Ain't nobody seen him since. You didn't give him up, did ya?"

Enoch only gave a nervous laugh, then finished his beer. He threw the bottle and looked around, trying to hide his fear that something was at work against him. He looked from bonfire to bonfire and saw all of the large groups of people celebrating and having a good time. He thought he saw glimpses of Black Bill's men in the crowds but couldn't be sure. He looked back at Blair, then down at his feet. Thomas had started a conversation with Nate Thompson, who was standing next to Enoch on the other side.

Surely he knew Milton had died. This was a mistake.

Looking back at the other groups, he answered John the best he knew how, with a lie. "No, I don't think the feds will get what they want from me. I plan on *'obtaining'* some steers this evening. I'll get a bit to move on towards the border. I'll be meetin' a few men around Seth Tash's Hill in a bit. I should probably get to movin'."

He looked back at John Blair, but he was gone. Enoch's gut sank. In a panic, he looked around, and then tripped over Ralph's boot as he turned to climb up onto his buggy. He grabbed the reins, sent the whip flying through the air, and was off as Ralph called after him. A quarter mile down the road, he heard it. A whistle blew sharp into the cool air, and pierced his ears, even over the crowds. Then a second blew, then a third. The appointed watchmen were calling out his position and declaring to all that he was heading to Gifford. He reached down for the gun in his boot and discovered it was gone. He cursed as he assumed he lost it when he tripped over Ralph's boot.

Enoch was almost out of the alignment of bonfires and into the thick brush just before Gifford. Looking back over his shoulder, he saw them. One by one, silhouettes of men in dusters stepped out on the road away from the fires. He now knew there was a plan against him as he suspected. The confederates kept blowing their whistles, as he passed. They could barely be seen through an orange glow from the fires. It was truly dark now.

He was now at the beginning of the thick brush, and out of the area of celebration. He whipped the horse again, hard. Sweat was running down his face, even through the cold winter air. He was standing as he drove the horse and buggy at full drive. His heart was racing. All was silent except for Enoch's heavy breathing and the horse's steps on the hardpan. Then he heard it; a loud crack in the sky. He recognized the sound immediately.

Cannon fire had begun.

III

Earlier that day, on November 18th, 1884...

"We better say bye to the girls and make sure there's enough firewood for them to last until we get home," Frank said quietly.

He shook Enoch's hand, wished him well, and then left the old man sitting there. Frank wasn't happy about the situation, and even though it was a day to celebrate the election of President Grover, he had other matters to attend to besides joining in on the celebration.

Nate leaned in towards Frank as they walked towards the house. "I heard Net say she wasn't gonna go with us. She seemed madder than an old wet hen earlier. Is she upset that we ain't goin' with the old man?" Nate asked. He nudged Frank's arm as he said it. Frank didn't seem to show any playful mood now, and was annoyed by Nate's question, but still, he smiled a little.

"Well, she simply don't understand that we can't keep working the fields, and the thresher without any help, and now's the time to find some. Even though it's a night of celebration, she doesn't want to leave the baby, and she definitely doesn't want to see Fin. I don't understand why they don't get along. He never worked for Hiserodt, and he sure as spit ain't gonna' shovel Enoch's grave himself," Frank replied. "I know Finley can be an ornery son of a gun but he's family," he continued.

"I still think about last Christmas when you told Net' she needed to bury the hatchet with him, and she threw that pot at your head. She clean missed and took out the window. I still laugh about that and I even duck whenever I hear you two arguin'."

"Sometimes I see you all bent over, running past our doorway as we argue. It makes me laugh, and then I get into even more trouble," said Frank. They both laughed a small chuckle as they approached the front porch. They tried to keep it quiet so as not to disturb Nettie and have her asking what was so gosh darn funny.

Nettie was outside the cabin by the door with her arms crossed. She leaned up against the post and stared at Frank. She had just returned from saying her goodbyes to her father. They saw her grab the bottom of her dress and run back as they slowly walked back towards the house. Enoch yelled, and Nettie looked back, unable to hear what he had said.

Frank grabbed the outside of her arms, gave her a small kiss on the head and looked at her. "You know, Vina can take care of the baby. Why don't you come with us? I'll make Nate sit in the back. We can talk about our favorite scriptures together like we used to," Frank suggested.

What could she say? She knew her father may be going to his death, and she couldn't do anything about it. She felt sick and angry.

In a soft voice she replied, "Why won't you go with the old man? He needed Nate earlier, and he may need you both now. He's a slippery worm at times and can even deceive those closest to him. Frank, you know how he lied and tricked you into hauling that box full of money back in your buggy. I hope Hiserodt never knows that you were the one that helped Henry Johns in the first place. The old man needs someone to keep him on the straight and narrow, and I'm afraid you do, too. If he ain't in much trouble now, he will be. I'm afraid for his life, and I'm afraid for yours."

Nate butted in, "Excuse me for saying, Net', but if the old man is fixed to lay in the bed he made, why would you want Frank anywhere near such distasteful folk? Wouldn't that incriminate him even more? Who's to say what they would think?"

"Nathaniel Rainsbarger! You know that I look at you like my own brother, but you stay that tongue before I do it for you! Who's one to talk about distasteful folks when you made this home a brothel, harboring Rie Clow and Eliza Williams! Whores! They're both whores and I want them out, but that ain't gonna change, is it? They're both inside right now, watching over your niece, like they know how to raise a child better than her own mother," Nettie barked. "To answer your question though, no. I don't want Frank around such folk, and I don't really want him around my Pa' either. Albeit, two young men, such as yourselves, might have more of a say against ruffians than an old man."

"Maybe, and maybe not," said Frank. "I know folks around here like seeing our heels more than our toes, but we ain't bad people, and becoming outlaws isn't exactly what I have in mind. I'm just a farmer, Net. I'm doing my best to try to take care of our family. I know we seem like harsh folk at times, but none more so than anyone else. We may drink bitters, or chew from time to time, but what man doesn't these days? We're no different than even an old man like Mr. Geottles."

Nettie bowed her head low and shook it up and down, demonstrating she understood the world, and how Frank had come to view it. Maybe she had just been hoping for something more. She desperately wanted to tell Frank the truth, but then they may all be taken care of. Folks disappeared around here too often. Wiping away a tear, she leaned upward, and kissed him, and said, "I'll give Zella a kiss for you if she wakes. Be safe and don't go out partying, either. You come home in one piece. You too, Nate!"

Nettie then went inside, and Frank, and Nate headed towards Frank's horse, and buggy team. "Well, that was a rare form to see her in, wasn't it, Frank?" Nate asked. "I thought she was going to be mad still, but I think something has got her scared." Frank considered it as they approached the horse and buggy. He knew Nettie to have a soft side, but he also knew she could be tough at the same time; but scared? That was new. What did she know that he didn't?

He knew Enoch was in a bad place with Black Bill, and that he never wanted Enoch to get out of prison. Did that make him a target in Hiserodt's eyes for paying for his release? What about Nate? He had put up his portion of the mortgage for Mr. Johnson as well. He knew that Margaret and the old man had had their issues before he had even gotten arrested, but it was never serious, or at least it didn't seem like it to Frank. Enoch could cut a deal with Mr. Hiserodt and pay back the money or leave the country. Of course, he and Nate wouldn't get their money back if he did. Still, his death wasn't warranted, right? It sure seemed that Enoch and Nettie thought otherwise. Sure, Enoch was scared that the counterfeiters wanted him quiet, but they couldn't be seen in the public eye, which murder would certainly put them in view of if they were caught. Frank realized his heart was racing, and he needed answers.

"I know we set plans for the evening, but I think it may be best that we stop by Henry Johns' place and see what exactly Enoch has been telling him. I wanna make sure that the indictment is going well," he said to Nate.

"I don't mind adding the Johns' place to our evening haunts. It may be best to find out what the odd fish said to Henry. It would be good to find out if he's gonna show up to court, and if we'll get our money back," Nate replied.

They continued talking as they hitched the two horses to the carriage and prepared for their journey north. The preparation took longer than either expected as one of Frank's driving horses had dropsy all summer and hadn't gotten any better. "Frank, you may need to put this old man down. He looks like he's been rode hard and put up wet," Nate laughed.

"He may be an old-timer, but he's still got some piss and vinegar in him yet. He'll do fine tonight, it might just take a bit longer to get where we need to go," Frank answered.

Nate laughed again, and then they were off. They talked while on their way, but never about what folks thought of them and the family. As they came out of the dense woods that surrounded their homestead, and onto the main road, they met Mr. Smith, and John Bunger. They invited them to join them in their evening's journeys. Both men declined the offer. The two men used to be friends with the brothers, but now refused to be seen with them in public. They claimed they would come by the farm sometime next week for a drink and to catch up.

Frank and Nate moved on, ashamed by the interaction. They used to go out on late nights with the two men. Neither one of them said it, but they knew in their hearts that they wouldn't see either man come next week. They rode on, and in silence after that. Frank wondered what they had done to deserve such avoidances. This wasn't the first time since Enoch's return from prison that their familiars avoided him and Nate.

As they drove through town, they watched people gather wood for the fires and some had already been lit. Young kids had party masks on and chased each other through the streets. The two brothers watched everyone prepare for the evening in silence. Some people looked at them with disgust. Frank knew some folks accused them of being a gang, but he never saw the talk as serious. As folks made a point to stay clear of them as they drove on, he suspected that there was more to it, and planned on asking Henry if he knew anything about it.

While they carried on towards Abbott and Cleves, they continued to watch the partygoers. Some folks were ready for the celebration, and others seemed anxious. There were large groups of men huddled around bonfires, and few women, and children out. The majority of the crowds were talking about what the election meant for the future of Hardin County. Most were pleased but others seemed less convinced that any real change would come. Some folks thought Cleveland was an honest man, while others swore, he would be another source of political corruption. He was the father of an illegitimate child, and some felt that he wasn't to be trusted in his personal life, and therefore couldn't be trusted in public office. However, Grover had won the election, in part due to his honesty, and some celebrants had banners with his slogan, *Tell the Truth*.

Nate wondered if Enoch would see similar banners on his travels and consider the idea. Frank wondered if the folks of Steamboat Rock would learn to do the same about the Rainsbarger family.

Both men pondered the slogan.

CHAPTER 7

THE REVERE HOUSE

Late evening on November 18th, 1884, in Ackley...

The bedroom door made a dull click and thud as it came to a close. It was a typical room with a bed, a nightstand on either end, a small liquor counter, and bathroom in the corner. It was dimly lit and very welcoming to the ideas that Joshua West had in mind. He and Maggie Johnson had taken the evening train into Ackley and had signed into the Revere House Hotel under the names Si Kidder, and *Wife*. The name change only served the purpose of protecting Mr. West from being accused of spending the night with a married woman. Maggie worried that if she needed an alibi, that there wouldn't be anything linking her here to her time with this *pig*.

On the way there, Maggie had been extremely flirtatious, and hands-on with Mr. West, but now her mood had changed. She seemed nervous and paced the room back and forth as he threw their bags down. He then began to take off his shoes and undo his pants. Maggie saw him in the corner of her eye and pretended not to. She snuck into the washroom as he was climbing into the bed. She wasn't ready for what he had in mind and couldn't help but let her emotions show. She tried clearing her mind and decided to try anyway. She had never said no to a man before.

What would he do if she said no?

After some time, Maggie came back out in a robe. To Joshua West, she seemed more nervous than before, and he was even more irritated than before.

Still pacing, she asked, "Why wasn't there a telegraph at the front desk like we expected?"

Mr. West shrugged and said, "I don't know but I'm sure everything is fine, Mrs. Johnson."

She cringed, "Ugh, please don't call me that! Can we just talk a bit, please? I don't know if I'm ready yet. Do you think everything went alright?" she said all in one breath.

Joshua thought the trip to Ackley was short but thought the trip to *crazy* was even shorter for Maggie. He then got up, only wearing his underwear and socks, and poured her a drink which she downed in one go.

"Another!" she nearly barked.

"Not to be too rude, miss," he began as he handed her another drink, "but we've both done this before and there usually isn't this much talkin'."

"They're killing him. They're killing the old man right now. Don't you get it?" she began to cry.

"Surely, ma'am, I understand that I'm an alibi so-to-speak, but I'm also a paying customer," he replied as he placed his hand on her shoulder.

If he touches me again I may have him killed next, she thought.

She couldn't hold it in any longer. She wretched her arm away from him and threw the glass against the wall. It shattered into dozens of pieces after making a small hole. Falling into a pile onto the floor, she burst into tears, then slammed her fist into the floor, and threw her head down.

"Mrs. Johnson, if you're this distressed about your husband's death, then surely you loved him. Why are you here with me?"

She wiped away tears and a small bit of snot from her face. She looked up, and locked eyes with Joshua West. She laughed a small laugh and said, "I'm not crying because he'll *be* killed. I'm crying because we haven't heard that that rat *is* dead yet!"

CHAPTER 8

PEACE TO HIS ASHES

I

Just outside Gifford, Iowa, early morning on November 19th, 1884...

Although the sun was rising, the treetops covered that area outside of Gifford in a thick overlapping pattern that created a canopy that didn't let the sun's heat reach the ground. The ice on the grass crunched with each step as James Hamilton drew closer to the blood stains. The man began to feel cold, and sick as he looked over at the mangled mess on the ground. He had found a body earlier that morning, and had already sent his companion, Van Voorhis, to notify the proper authorities. He had looked over the scene several times while he waited for their arrival and thought he had understood what had happened. Now that the sheriff had arrived, he wished to be gone from this place.

Two teams had arrived by buggy. The first team consisted of Sheriff Wilcox, Deputy Boylan, Mr. Rood, and Mr. Streeter, Mayor Hadley, and the two doctors: Nathan Morse, and Myron Underwood. The second team was a group of men charged with the task of keeping the returning partygoers out of the area of the accident. When they arrived, several men stepped down from the covered wagon and started a watch post around the area.

Upon arrival, Wilcox and the men who came with him began noting the scene of the accident and murmuring amongst themselves.

James Hamilton had gone and sat on his buggy that was parked out of the scene, and on the road leading up into Gifford. It was a cold morning and the new sheet of ice helped preserve what the scene had to tell.

"Mr. Hamilton, if you wouldn't mind, just stick around for a little while longer," Wilcox said. "I'll need to have a word with you in a moment."

Mr. Hamilton simply sat and watched as the men combed over the area that he had outlined to them, again, and again. It was never fun finding a dead body, but waiting around while it was still lying face down a few feet from you, was even worse. He waited in agonizing anticipation to find out who the man was, as he had not rolled the body over yet to check. Even so, he wished he was on his way away from the body, and often looked back at the road to catch a glimpse of Van's return.

After some time, Wilcox called the men together with whom he had arrived with, to hear their reports. He leaned his heavy body up against the buggy's side and it sank a little under his weight. Removing his hat, he spit, and asked, "Well, what does it look like, boys? I think the poor son of a gun had a nasty accident."

Dr. Morse spoke up, "Well, a few of us examined the body and the horse. That skittish fellow does get a little nervous when you get close enough to him to see anything, but he held still enough to see he has some blood on his back legs. There is sand in the man's wounds as well. He may have been dragged by the skittish horse. Your deputy found a party mask about a rod away, or so." He pointed behind him, some distance away and continued, "The peculiar thing is, there are two single horse tracks imprinted in the hardpan."

"What are you saying, doc? That the poor fellow wasn't alone?" Wilcox asked.

"Perhaps not. They could be older tracks, but they look like they were made about the same time, Sheriff," Morse answered.

Wilcox leaned in close to the doctor instead of the buggy, and placing a hand on his shoulder, he pointed over to Mayor Hadley, who had not rejoined them. "You see that man over there? He's the humble mayor of this podunk place, and he's dealing with a lot more than you even know about," he said in a rough tone. He squeezed Dr. Morses' shoulder slightly, and then looked at the doctor, "If you're gonna suggest what I think you're suggesting, then you better be *damn* sure." He then let go of Nathan's shoulder and resumed leaning up against the buggy. He took out a cigar and let out a cloud of smoke in Morse's direction. Looking at Dr. Underwood, he barked, "What else?"

Underwood gave Morse a small sideways glance and stated, "I studied the horse, and his tracks, and can say with *confidence* that the tracks are consistent with the horse's hooves."

"Good. What else? It's cold and I want to get this over with. Speak up, men!"

Mr. Rood stumbled over his words and then began, "It looks to me, and judging by the broken wheel, that the fellow had an accident as his front wheel split. He then decided to ride the horse the rest of the way but since it may have been a bit nervous, it may have trampled, and dragged him. Looking at the blood trail outlined by Mr. Hamilton, I'd say about a third of a mile. There are two single horse tracks, however...they may not be from the same time. Along with the mask, there is a broken bottle just near the fence. The label looks old, but it appears to be a bitter bottle, which is only sold in a few stores in the county; two I believe."

His words came rushing out as one continuous sentence, and Wilcox chuckled as he finished. "Is that all?" he asked.

Morse dared to speak again, "You saw the body, Sheriff. The left side is torn up, it has dozens of lacerations to the head and face, and two large indents in the skull. He has bruises everywhere. What do you think?" As Nathan Morse spoke, Mayor Hadley had joined the group and whispered into Wilcox's ear.

"Well I'll be," he said, "The poor fool is *'Horse Thief'* Johnson. What do I think? I think someone should tell his family he's dead." He then tipped his hat and remarked, "Give me a moment, gentlemen," as he left them standing there and casually walked over to James Hamilton, who was still waiting with his buggy. Wilcox leaned up against the buggy rail, took his last puff of his cigar, dropped it, and stepped on it. He sighed deep and his breath could be faintly seen in the air.

"Well, what do you need from me, Sheriff?" Hamilton asked. "Who is it?"

"I need you to tell Mr. West to send a telegraph for me. Have him tell Maggie Johnson her husband is dead, and to come at once."

"Why does it need to be sent from Joshua?"

"Don't ask me about things you don't understand, James," he replied while holding in a laugh, "That stupid son of a gun won't be able to be a part of any indictments now; and hey, who knows? Now that Maggie's a single lady, you might have a shot, Hamilton," Wilcox said while still stifling a laugh.

II

At the Rainsbarger's cabin, around 8am, the morning of November 19th, 1884...

The morning frost had not yet worn off of the cabin's windows, even though the sun had beat down upon them for several hours. The small fireplace in the sitting room was lit and at full roar. Frank and Nettie sat on the long couch together. Nettie was under a blanket, holding their baby girl, Zella, in her arms while she slept. Nate was seated in the chair next to the fireplace and yawned wide as he placed another log on the already over-zealous fire. Henry Williams was still asleep in Nate's room and wouldn't be up for some time. Vina was asleep in the room next to his. All was silent, except for the crackling warmth of the timber as it burned. As they watched the flames dance, a knock at the door rattled them from their thoughts that they were lost in.

"Who in their right mind would be knocking at this hour? Especially all the way out here! Maybe it's Manse, he's supposed to come by later," Nate said as he got up from his seat to see who was at their door.

Nettie could hear the door creak open and Nate greet whomever was at the door with a simple, *"good morning, come on in"*. A moment later,

Maggie Johnson entered through the entryway to the sitting room, and took a seat in the chair Nate had just been sitting in, to warm herself by the fire. She said nothing.

"Good morning, Mag," Frank said. "Not that we don't like seeing you, but we weren't aware we would be seeing you today, especially not so early. Is everything alright?"

She turned to look at them all staring at her. She smiled slightly and said, "Why yes, I had taken the early train in from Eldora is all! I thought I would come and see the baby! Can I hold her?"

Nettie looked uneasy. The last she had seen Maggie, she had spoken of killing her father and if she didn't keep quiet she suggested she may harm her baby. *Why was Maggie here? Did they kill her father already? Did he escape? George Winnans had asked Enoch to run, even offered him money...but did he go? Where was he now?* She had so many questions. She had expected the next time she saw Maggie, she would be with her father.

"Of course you can hold her," she said at last, and made her way over to Maggie. She leaned down, kissed Maggie's cheek, and handed her the baby. They locked eyes for a moment in the exchange and Maggie's look told her nothing. Her eyes were blank. She only had a thin smile on her lips.

"Have you seen your husband, Mrs. Johnson?" Nate asked nervously. He also wondered where Enoch was and why she was there. *What had happened?*

Nettie had returned to her place next to Frank as Maggie was staring at the sleeping baby in her arms. Nate was standing against the entryway when he asked.

"No, no...I haven't seen him since we had our *disagreement.* Why?"

"Well, he went to go look for you last night, and said if he didn't see you, he would stay at the Taylors' place. He never returned. Have you heard from him at all?" Nate questioned.

"Not at all, dear," she said, never looking away from the baby.

"Well, you can wait for him here if you would like. Can I get you anything?" Frank asked.

"No, no, I'm fine right here, thank you."

They all sat in silence for some time before another knock came at the door. This time, it sounded frantic, and before anyone could get up to answer it, they could hear the door open, and slam shut. Manse came rushing into the sitting room with a letter in his hand.

"I have a telegraph for you! It came in early this morning into Eldora. Here, –" he said as he shoved the letter into Frank's hand.

"That's from Joshua West," Maggie said, still not taking her eyes off of the baby.

Frank opened the letter and read it slowly. Tears began to build in the corner of his eyes as he read it again. He looked up at Nettie, brushed her hair away from her face, and said, "It's about your Pa...it's bad, Net."

They didn't hear Vina Fisher come into the room when she did. She had been woken up by the sound of Manse slamming the door. When she saw Frank begin to cry, she cried, too.

Nate snatched the letter from Frank, and read it over. "Enoch's dead," is all he said as the letter fell from his hands and onto the floor.

Manse put his hand around Nate's and Vina's shoulders and held them close as they cried together. Frank held Nettie to him with her head buried in his chest. He could hear her deep sobs over the roaring fire. Frank kissed the top of her head.

"I know, Net, I wish I were dead, too," he said as he choked back more tears. They all cried together, except Maggie. She just kept staring at Zella, who was now awake and making baby noises. Maggie made ridiculous-sounding baby noises back, the way adults do when they speak to infants.

They all began to collect their emotions as time passed. The initial news of Enoch's death burned slower, like the log in the fireplace. It still burned, and would hurt to the touch, but it was no longer over-whelming. Manse offered to make their morning coffee, and to stay around for a while. Frank and Nate retreated to the kitchen with him, and Vina took the baby for her morning bath. Nettie and Maggie sat in silence opposite of each other in the sitting room. As the log began to extinguish, the room started to become cold again.

"How did you know the letter was from Joshua West?" Nettie asked.

"Let's not act coy now, Nettie, you know damn well how I knew. It was a slip for sure, but I don't think anyone else heard. Besides...the deed is done. You can rest easy now, and stop worrying about that old man. You'll have a simple, happy life here if you choose," Maggie replied matter-of-factly.

Nettie felt nauseous at the news. She knew the counterfeiters wouldn't just let her father go, not after her meeting with Maggie and Hiserodt. She thought of begging for his life or even telling him, but it would have only brought them all trouble. After all, she wasn't truly convinced at the time that they would kill him. They wouldn't get away with it, anyways. She also wanted to hate Maggie and Hiserodt for not doing anything, but the counterfeit higher-ups weren't to be trifled with. They might kill them all if they retaliated. As far as Nettie knew, Maggie and Black Bill had no other choice, either.

"They were never going to let him live, were they? Are they going to come for me, or will they leave me alone?" she asked.

"Who? Oh, the men in charge! No, of course not, to both of your questions!"

"Who are they?"

"You are a damn little fool, aren't you? Not even I know who they are, dear, and there's no changing what's been done. Besides, your father left you money...insurance money! You need to collect it!"

"I think I'm going to be sick," Nettie replied. She leaned forward, grabbed the ash pale next to the fireplace, and threw up into it. *How could I keep this a secret that I knew? Frank can't ever know.*

"Goodness, dear, get it together," Maggie sneered. She then went over and sat next to Nettie, holding her hair back, she whispered into her ear, "It's all done now. Keep your mouth shut, and nothing will come your way. Now if you'll excuse me, I must get a ride to go collect your father."

Maggie stood up, and kissed the palm of her hand, and blew it at Nettie. She then left the room and Nettie was alone with her troubled thoughts.

What have I done?

III

After Maggie arrived at the scene of the accident that morning, she had a farm boy, a local neighbor, and Sheriff Boylan remove Enoch's body from the scene. They loaded it into the back of Dr. Underwood's wagon, and took it to Gifford. Thousands of citizens had come to see his body but refused to move it; instead they celebrated his death. Over the next year and a half, his body would be exhumed several times.

That morning's newspaper from the Eldora Herald wrote a eulogy stating that Johnson was once a respected harness-maker, but after the death of his first wife, he gained a checkered past. They wrote, 'Peace to his Ashes'. The town suggested another bonfire to celebrate Enoch's death and vacancy in the community.

CHAPTER 9

THOSE THEY FEAR

I

Saturday, November 22nd, 1884...

Sheriff Wilcox had shown up early to the Rainsbarger cabin in a manner that was just as surprising as Maggie's early visit. Frank and Nate were just heading out the door to go work in the fields when he reached the front porch.

"Good morning, men," he said in a polite tone, "I hope I didn't startle you. I just came to speak with Frank. Do you have a moment?"

"Good morning, Sheriff! We were just heading out to work on the farm, but I could spare a minute or two. What's on your mind?" Frank asked.

Nate took a seat on the front porch and finished his apple as he waited for Frank. He acted disinterested in why Wilcox was there but assumed that it had to do with Enoch. *Even though he's gone he's still gonna cause us trouble,* he thought.

"Well, this is going to take more than a minute. I need you to go with me to the hill outside of Gifford where Mr. Johnson passed."

"Why?" Frank asked.

"It may be best if we discussed that on the way there. Grab your coat if you need it, Rainsbarger, and let's go," he said as he turned towards his buggy and climbed in.

Frank turned to Nate, "Tell Nettie that I'll be back later, I guess. Don't worry about the work right now, Nate."

He turned and threw his coat on while he climbed into the sheriff's wagon. Nate sat on the front porch and watched as they faded out of sight and into the thick forest. Frank and Nate exchanged nervous glances as the wagon pulled away.

After they cleared the underbrush from the forest and came out on the main road, Wilcox finally spoke up, "Dr. Nathan Morse held the first inquest for Enoch, and found that his wounds didn't seem an accident. Dr. Underwood held a second inquest recently, and while he cleaned and examined the body, he also discovered this may not have been an accident."

"You mean, they think the old man was killed?" Frank replied.

"Exactly. At first, Underwood said that the horse tracks were consistent with Enoch's horse, and that he could have been killed by him, but now…," he shook his head side to side and shrugged, "It seems the doc likes to meddle in things. His report came back that the wounds in Johnson's skull were not consistent with a horse hoof, and neither were the dozen, or so other gashes."

"You think it was the counterfeiters Enoch was helping Henry Johns indict?"

"I don't know anything about any indictment, Frank, so it's hard to say," he lied.

"So, why are you bringing me?"

"Well, it was your horse and buggy that Enoch was driving that evening and I need to know if there's anything out of the ordinary about them. That, and what you want to do with them. It would be helpful if you could look at the tracks as well. I'd like to go over the whole area with you. *I* think it was an accident, but the *doctor* suspects a murder. To tell you the truth, we heard that Enoch left your house and had spoken with you, and Nate last. It would be a *shame* if either of you were ever labeled as a suspect."

Why would we be suspects? What an odd thing to say. "Are we suspects?" Frank asked, a little irritated. "Why would we be?"

"No, not that I'm aware of, but you coming along should help me clear things up," Wilcox lied again.

By the time they arrived, Frank's hands were frozen, and so was his face. Wilcox seemed not to participate in the acknowledgment of it being so cold. His heavy body didn't seem hindered by the chill that had crept in, and he moved with ease. It took Frank a moment or two to get down from the high buggy seat. The two men made their way through the thick brush and towards the buggy that was still there. At the sight of it, Wilcox let out a curse and ran over to it.

"It's been moved. It was a ways over there," he said, while pointing closer to the hill that went up into town. "It wasn't right on top of the roadway, but it wasn't this far over, either."

"Well, at least we know one thing is for sure. He did lose control of the buggy at one point. Look, there's slide marks at the top of the hill, and they drag out a way," Frank remarked while showing Wilcox what he meant.

"Now where is that darn horse? Maybe someone took it?" Wilcox asked.

"Over there, in the thicker part of the brush, near the fence, I see him."

They ran over to the horse and Wilcox leaned in to look at him more closely. "Be careful; he may try to kick," Frank remarked.

Wilcox leaned in closer as the horse stood still. He then found his next problem. "Someone cleaned the blood off of his back legs, Frank. The buggy has been moved, the horse has been cleaned and look, over near the buggy. Someone sat the wheel upright." He stood up and leaned against the post to the barbed wire fence that the horse was caught in. He took out some chew, tucked it into his lip, sighed and spit. Frank was looking around on the ground at the horse tracks. "Someone has definitely been here....and now it definitely doesn't look good," Wilcox said as he sucked in more tobacco spit. "Even the bitters bottle ain't in the same place."

"Perhaps this was more than an accident, Sheriff. I don't know for sure, but either way, you need to go slow, and catch them all...anyone that may have been involved, all of them."

"Tell me about the horse and buggy, Frank."

"There's not much to tell. Both are old and fragile. The horse always was a queer fellow, and I never could straight saddle him. The broken wheel had been going bad for some time and made a peculiar noise when it was driven. It sounded like a part of it was going out. I must have told Enoch about it half a dozen times. Hell, most of Hardin County probably had."

"I remember the buggy noise. Can you prove in any way that the horse was one not to be ridden?" he asked.

"Are you accusing me now? I'm not going to try to ride him for you and show you, but you're more than welcome to try yourself. Besides, I do have something back home that may answer that for you."

The two men rode back in silence and when they had arrived, Frank directed Wilcox to pull the buggy over near the barn. Nate and Nettie had seen them coming out of the forest road and had caught up to them. The three Rainsbargers outlined to the Sheriff where the horse had a seizing fit and had fallen and broken some shafts a few days before Enoch's death. They all stated that the horse was easily spooked, was very unpredictable, and had seizing fits.

"It seems like that horse may be an ornery bugger, Frank. Thanks for your time. We'll be in touch," he said as he tilted his hat and rode away.

Wilcox's work was done. He did what Hiserodt had asked...

"That damn fool, Underwood, is stirring the pot when he ought not to be," Hiserodt had yelled.

"What do you want me to do, boss?"

"I want you to play the game, Sheriff. Ask the questions, investigate, accuse if you have to! We can't have everyone out there shaking snakes, but it's the sheriff's job to do that! If you're out there doing it, then no one else will be, so handle it, Wilcox!"

"If the townsfolk hear it may be murder, then what?" Wilcox replied.

"If? Thanks to Underwood, they already are claiming murder! Some folks are already asking questions. Thousands came to see the body. If we have to frame someone, then we frame those they fear. You frame someone who is easy for everyone to get behind and blame. Now who do you think that may be?" Hiserodt asked condescendingly.

"There's a handful of names I could pick from, but you're thinking of Rainsbarger, aren't you? Most of them haven't been arrested for jack squat, boss."

"And yet the people fear them! People fear those they don't understand."

"Well, maybe about half the folks do, but the other half are divided on their involvement in any crime," Wilcox replied.

"Look, there's a few ways this plays out. Either nothing comes of the idea of murder, and we continue on with smooth sailing, or we take action. Henry Johns can't possibly think he'll win in court against anyone with his star witness being dead. If everyone screams murder, then we have to play that game," Hiserodt sneered.

"I'll do what I can."

"You'll do what you're told! Take that Rainsbarger boy to see the accident and see what you can find out. If we have to pin this on anyone, he's the best target. He put up the bail money, and has the most to profit from his death, especially if the town thinks the Rainsbargers are running the counterfeit operation. He also housed Johnson and hid him away in their overgrown hole. He harbored a horsethief, and a counterfeiter, and the people know it."

"I still don't see the point in taking him to the scene, and outlining that it may have been murder," Wilcox said sheepishly.

"Several reasons, mainly so he doesn't go around asking anyone else to investigate. He's bound to hear from the folks in Steamboat Rock and Eldora that Enoch may have been murdered. If he thinks you're investigating, he may not go to anyone else."

"What about the girl?"

Hiserodt chuckled, "She's a stupid little girl, and will keep her mouth shut. If not, then we'll get her to join us, and we can keep her out of the way."

"Seems like you have it all covered, boss...how do we get the remaining folks to join the cause?"

"With vigilance, Mr. Wilcox...with vigilance. I need honest men to believe a lie, and I need a liar to tell it. Maybe we should make a 'donation' to the Eldora Herald to help persuade their cooperation."

II

Dr. Myron Underwood's office was small and quaint. Upon entering the office, you found yourself in a small room that had a desk, chairs, coat rack, and two small bookshelves. To the left was another door that led into a larger room where patients would be seen. Frank Rainsbarger and Justice of the Peace, Mr. Cunningham, were seated opposite of the doctor as he took his place behind his desk.

Underwood was a taller man with a large forehead and an even larger dark beard. His hands were folded with his fingers interlocking up at his mouth, with his elbows on the desk. You couldn't see his mouth as he spoke, but rather his mustache would simply twitch as you heard him.

"What can I help you with, gentlemen?" he asked as they all took a seat.

"Thank you for your time, doctor, this should only take a minute. I'm the county Justice of the Peace and I'm simply here as a witness today. I'm also here to help Mr. Rainsbarger settle on the insurance policy on Mr. Johnson. We just need you to sign over the death certificate and any and all relevant paperwork," Cunningham said in a cheerful manner.

Underwood didn't say anything or move. He just sighed and twitched his mustache.

"It's my understanding that you are the Johnson and Rainsbarger family physicians and as such, you know the parties, and have the aforementioned papers ready, yes?" Cunningham asked.

"I am, and I do," was all Underwood replied.

"Was it really murder, doc? We were told that it was an accident, but Sheriff Wilcox said you think differently," Frank said.

Underwood sighed again, and said, "Unfortunately, I can't divulge such information."

"Not even to his family? My wife wants to know how her Pa' died is all, doc. Surely, you understand," Frank said in an annoyed disbelieving tone.

"These fine folks have been through a lot these last few years," Cunningham said with a bashfulness that acted as a ploy to get him to answer, "Can't you humor the man and answer the question?"

"I will do no such thing, as it is in the law's hands now. It's up to them to resolve that issue," Underwood replied.

There was a ringing silence for a moment and Cunningham began to look angry. Frank seemed confused at the statement and sat in silence. He finally looked over at Cunningham in a way that said, *now what?*

"What are you saying? Any investigation has nothing to do with an insurance policy, and even if it did, it would be up to the insurance company to deny the claim, and not up to a simple-minded coroner…"

Underwood then aimed the palm of his hand at Mr. Cunningham as a gesture to stop talking. "Let's be clear then…Mr. Rainsbarger is a suspect, and as such, I will withhold the certificate for now. Furthermore, it is odd, that *you*, Mr. Rainsbarger, would come to collect the certificate for an insurance policy that *isn't even in your name*!"

Cunningham hit the desk, and standing up, yelled, "I read your report before coming today, and it seems like you can't keep simple facts straight, doc! Frank and his family are innocent!"

Underwood seemed to ignore Cunningham and merely shook his head in disapproval. "Where were you the night of the murder, Rainsbarger?" he asked. "Murder is on everyone's mind now; you know?"

"Are you a detective now, Myron?" Frank replied coldly.

"Why drop the formalities of doctor, and sir, and call me by my first name? Perhaps I touched a nerve?"

"I use those terms for gentlemen and respectable folks, and you are neither. Nothing more than a snot-nosed child. I was in Cleves with my brothers. Where were you?"

"Are you threatening me, boy?" asked the doctor as he then also stood up, placing the palms of his hands down flat on the wooden top.

Frank decided to stand as well, as he began his reply, "I'm only asking what you're asking, but I think we're done here; like you said...it's in the law's hands now." He headed to the door and glanced back to see the doctor sweating and trying to keep calm. "I'll leave the insurance to Nettie. I didn't want to be a part of it, anyways," Frank finished.

As he opened the door to exit the small office, Underwood replied, "Actually, boy, I have, after a thorough autopsy, summoned a jury to investigate the death as well. She will need to be questioned regarding the matter also."

Frank looked back for a moment. It wasn't a hard look, but the doctor seemed shaken by it and stumbled back into his seat.

"Let's just go, Frank," Cunningham said as he gently shoved him out the front door.

III

At the end of November, Maggie and Nettie tried to claim the $16,000 life insurance policy from the Union Mutual Aid Association. Authorities thought that it was too much money for a horsethief and refused to pay it out. They then brought Maggie in for questioning after the autopsy revealed the most likely cause of death was not an accident. They said they would continue to fully investigate the matter, even though she brought with her, Joshua West, her alibi, who confirmed they were together the night of the murder. She claimed that they went to meet a man about helping Enoch escape the counterfeit gang, but she wouldn't say who.

Nettie was also questioned about her and Frank. She stated that Frank was in Cleves that night and came home with groceries. He and Nate had gone to their brother, Manse's house, and then to Mr. Geottle's store. They continued their evening with a few of their nephews, and later went to Finley Rainsbarger's house. She stayed home with the baby.

After the word spread that Enoch was most likely murdered, and that Maggie had been questioned, she became a suspect, and she feared a mob would try to lynch her. She then moved to the Ellsworth hotel in Eldora and remained in service to the counterfeit ring. After Dr. Underwood's inquest was held, several minutes of testimony went missing.

Enoch Johnson was finally laid to rest on November 25th, 1884.

CHAPTER 10

NETTIE RAINSBARGER

I

December 25th, 1884...

It was late afternoon as the holiday dinner came to a close at her Uncle Doud's residence. Frank and Nettie had spent the day there and enjoyed the quiet gathering. It was a day of calm all around as the snow fell in a mesmerizing way. The only thing that wasn't as calm as it would seem, was Nettie's heart. She often wondered what an uneducated, nineteen-year-old girl could do against a gang of counterfeiters and outlaws, hellbent on their own idea of frontier justice. Nettie thought that to blame someone who was a known criminal was easy, but to place blame on those who are innocent, was pure hate. The more the winter barreled on, the more her own devices made her understand that hate.

As she stood there gazing out the frosted cabin window, she watched Frank, and Zella play outside in the newly untouched snow, and contemplated the secrets she had kept. There were more than a few. She loved Frank, and yet she hated him as well. Nettie knew he worked hard on the farm and the thresher to provide. The only problem was that nothing was being provided. They had food and clothes and a small home, but they would have nothing for their children if this was the life they'd live. At least, that's what she told herself. The truth was, she wanted more than this life would give, and she now resented herself for marrying a simple man.

A coldness grew in her heart as she watched Frank play with their daughter. The love he showed Zella was unlike what Nettie felt she received. He'd do anything for her, and she was barely half a year old. Deep desperation clawed its way to her mind and anxiety filled her lungs as she continued to watch.

Murder had become the word on nearly everyone's lips in Steamboat Rock and Eldora. Gifford itself was tainted with the idea and couldn't see past it. As a result, Maggie was being considered a suspect, and the selling off of her home only aided people's suspicions. However, her new life at the Ellsworth hotel suited her extravagant nature. Maggie had visited Nettie several times over the past few weeks on late night visits. They would talk by the fireplace quietly, and Maggie would impress upon her the luxuries of her new home that Nettie could have as well. All the rich men that would come through, and would fawn over her, and give her riches, and money, and anything else she could want. All she had to do was give herself to them each night; that, and help clear Maggie's name.

The indictment and murder rumors had caused such an uproar that Maggie no longer felt safe, and she would rarely leave the Ellsworth hotel anymore. She needed a new name to throw to the folks that had become as ravenous as hungry wolves for a name to lay blame to. Nothing ever happened in small towns and now there was a scandal to rival any old tale people told around a fire.

Maggie needed Nettie's help, and in exchange, her family would never lack. She had also impressed upon Nettie that the only other name people would cling to would be Rainsbarger. Frank and Nate had harbored the old man and would be easy to blame.

Maggie's words rang clear in Nettie's mind as she still stood there at the window watching...

"They're petty criminals, Net, and people know it. You said it yourself that them boys take what they want. You know how it could look...Frank and Nate ran the counterfeit operation with their brothers out on their

*secret farmland, and that's easy enough to believe! No one goes to Rains-
barger country and sees their simple life. Finley is known to harbor, and
associate with horse thieves and liars, anyways! It's easy to think that
Enoch got caught, they rescued him from jail so he wouldn't talk, then
when he gave just enough information to Henry Johns, they decided he
needed to be silenced."*

"But Henry Johns doesn't fear them and is their friend," Nettie replied.

*"Well, damn girl, these folks don't know that! This is going to have to
happen if we're going to survive! You don't have any other choice! Besides,
do you want those two whores who live in your house raising your daughter
to grow up and become like them? Frank should have given them the
boot long ago, Net. Rainsbarger has a bad reputation and look how they
live…you won't ever survive as a young woman. I beg you to think of Zella,
and Effie."*

Nettie gripped the windowsill and leaned forward, resting her head
against the cold glass, she understood that her life was nothing that
she thought it would be. Frank was going to have to provide for his
family, even if he didn't know it yet. Hiserodt had already summoned
the townsmen for a meeting next week and there was no stopping the
cruelty he would use to betray innocent men.

II

At the schoolhouse in Steamboat Rock, January, 1885…

The crowded room at the southeastern end of the building over-
flowed with dozens, if not hundreds, of men from Eldora, and the
surrounding areas. Hiserodt's gun-toting-confederates surrounded the
outside of the building, keeping outsiders from the evening's secret
meeting. There had been a few meetings here before of this kind, but
not to this extent. The rumors of counterfeiters and murder had stirred
all of the people into a state of fear and they wanted answers. With the
need for preservation of their well-beings, Sheriff Wilcox called together
an order of men.

Wilcox stood on a small platform in the middle of the room surrounded by men who were up in arms, and acting belligerent on their fears. These were just the type of men whom he, and Hiserodt had a need for, and with the flames of oil lanterns, and moonlight illuminating the room, he called the meeting to order. He remembered what Hiserodt had said...

"Rile them up and keep them in anticipation! If you tell a lie loud enough and often enough, they may believe it!"

"Good evening, gentlemen!" he yelled over the shouts of men. "We gather tonight to lay out the facts as they've been revealed!" All the men gave a hearty shout in reply, and it echoed through the empty school. Wilcox continued, "Horses have been maimed, haystacks burnt, and property stolen, or damaged! Worst of all, people have gone missing! Who's to blame?" He looked around the room at all of the rowdy men standing shoulder to shoulder. They looked like cornered dogs ready to bite. "I'll tell you who! Only one name comes to mind when mischief strikes our towns! The Rainsbargers!! They've terrorized our communities, and haven't let up, men! We've all got a story to tell about one of them or know a feller who does!"

Angry shouting continued as he named the ones to blame. He could already see the rise of a mob in his mind and felt eased by his persuasion of these men. They would most likely do and believe anything they were told.

A man in the crowd named William Haines shouted, "They stole my sheep and little lambs a year or so ago!"

Mr. Heidlebrink yelled, "Frank stole four of my cattle also!"

Another random man in the back stated, "I heard they were the ones that robbed Mr. Goothaus' store! They dang near cleared it out!"

Wilcox put his hand up to interrupt their accusations. "Exactly men! What's to be done? You've all heard the stories and know them to be true! They've housed outlaws, and notorious desperadoes like Jesse James, and Jack Reed!"

Henry Eisner then interjected, "That's when those bastards stole mine and William Ayer's horses!"

Mr. Fenton jumped up behind the taller men in front of him, and nearly screamed, "That's probably when I lost my whole buggy and harness! Is there no justice in this county?"

Another wave of shouts of approval came from all men. They were in a frenzy now and were becoming more and more unstable. Wilcox remained calm, and with joy, looked over the room. "I'm here tonight to put justice into *your* hands! Anyone who wishes to become deputized will get free whiskey at the Western House Hotel and Saloon, courtesy of Mr. Hiserodt!" Wilcox stated. There were even more shouts of joy and men whistling approval of the meeting's outcome thus far. Many men clapped Hiserodt on the shoulder or back to demonstrate their agreement with his endorsement.

A lonely voice in the back bashfully spoke up, "These are mere accusations, Sheriff, where's the evidence against the Rainsbargers?"

Several men shouted back in anger and fear. Another man threw an empty bottle in the direction of the voice, and it shattered against the wall. Hiserodt then addressed the men in a loud deep voice, "Men, please listen to Sheriff Wilcox! He has a sworn statement that the brothers are running the counterfeit operation out in their lonely land by the river! They've stolen your goods and your money! They harbored Enoch Johnson until his death, and how did he die out there on Johnson's Hill?"

They all shouted, "MURDER!"

"And who murdered him, gentlemen?" Hiserodt asked. They all agreed to the name, Rainsbarger.

Wilcox answered, "A case is being built against them, and the state now believes the Rainsbarger gang planned out an elaborate insurance scheme that they are now trying to escape! When Johnson got caught with their money, and it was confiscated by the U.S. agents, they were determined to get their money back!"

A man near the left wall shouted, "I ain't never heard them boys talk about hurting nobody! Only one of them has killed someone, and even *he* was let go!"

Another man on the opposite wall argued, "I heard one of them just last week start yelling in the saloon that he wanted booze or blood!"

"Enough!" Wilcox yelled. "Frank Rainsbarger's wife gave us incriminating evidence. She claims that she found blood on Frank and Nate Rainsbarger's clothes the morning after Johnson's murder! We need to protect ourselves until the law deals with such scum! The state is working on the case, and a way to quietly remove the girl, and her baby from Rainsbarger country. This stays here for now, men! Their arrest will be called for by myself on her behalf once we get a statement. We must, for our preservation, stand together. Stay together!"

"Stay vigilant!" they shouted back in unison.

"Meeting adjourned!"

The group of men quickly dispersed, and the sound of their buggies and horses on the school yard front lawn could be heard from inside the room. The men raced towards the Western House for their free whiskey, as promised. Only Sheriff Wilcox and William Hiserodt remained in the school room. The two men shook hands as they exchanged a laugh.

The war against the Rainsbarger family had begun.

III

At the Ellsworth Hotel, January 14th, 1885...

Maggie rushed Nettie through the front doors of the hotel with her arm around her shoulders. She was complimenting Nettie's dress, and acting nicer than usual when they reached a room with large double doors called The Den. The hotel itself was fairly small, but large enough to house a dozen-or-so patrons and even more in the downstairs saloon. It was a quiet morning in Eldora and not many folks were at the Ellsworth hotel at the time.

An armed man stood just outside the doors with a bandana over his face. Nettie thought the fellow was an odd fish, covering up his face in the daytime with no one around. It seemed the counterfeiting gang feared more than she knew. Upon seeing Maggie, he pushed open the doors and closed them behind them once they entered. The man joined them in the room, grabbed Nettie hard at the elbow, and squeezed it to guide her to her chair into which he shoved her. After which, he grabbed baby Zella from Nettie's arms, and took the screaming child away. Nettie looked furious but didn't say a word.

She had been placed at a large round table at which Bill Hiserodt sat on the other end, eating his food like he had been starved for days. Next to his plate was his revolver, which he then turned to face Nettie where she sat. Without looking up, and with a mouth full of food that was being washed down with coffee, he said, "We need you, Nettie. I can see the doors of the penitentiary opening wide, ready to devour me. We all need each other, or we're done for."

She could see now that he was shaking while he ate. In a soft voice that could be heard easily in the quiet space, she replied, "I know, I'll do what I need to, just please...don't hurt my girls."

Hiserodt stopped eating and looked up at Nettie. Still chewing his food, he looked over at Maggie, who was seated next to Nettie. He smiled and asked, "Girls?"

"Effie isn't my child, Bill, she's Nettie's. About three years ago, she had the girl and I claimed the baby, as you see, our little tramp was only fifteen," Maggie said in a proud tone.

"I see," he replied as he went back to eating. "Well, the coroner has the town's folk here and a county over talking about murder. He claims that your father died from blunt trauma to his head. I can't stress this enough, Nettie, we need something to that effect to really stick the conviction to them boys." He made a face as if he had just eaten something rotten and said, "Rainsbarger? *Rainsbarger?* What the hell kind of name is that? They're no good white trash, and a meddling gang to be sure. They need to be drowned like rats, and this is the perfect opportunity to do so."

"I know what you need and can get it...what's going to happen to me and the baby? What about Effie?" Nettie asked plainly.

Hiserodt laughed, "You're still a young girl! Full of life and curiosity! You'll stay here, and have everything you could want or need, of course!

I've already spoken to the hotel proprietor, Mr. Deyo, about it. It's all been settled."

Maggie grabbed Nettie by the chin, underhand, and said, "She has such a pretty face; doesn't she? She can work, Bill! The little hussy knows her way around a man! Don't you, girl?"

Hiserodt was now leaning back in his chair drinking his coffee and looking at the morning sun coming through the windows in elegant rays. "It's settled then, she can show me her *skills* when we're done here," he said at last.

Nettie shuttered at the thought, and then remembered the way she felt when he had been with her at Maggie's house before. "What about protection? The boys may try to come for me like my Pa' did for Maggie," she asked.

Hiserodt laughed again, a bit more nervous, "No one's coming for you, dear. Those boys will be behind bars in a matter of days. I'll have the affidavit ready for you."

Maggie spoke up, "We can't wait days. You'll need to do it tonight. Get what you need, and then leave for Mrs. Williams' house. I'll be there in the morning to collect you; so be ready."

"I need to know you won't run or tell the boys about the plan. The whole county is fixed against them! We can't go back now! Your girls will stay here until you arrive with Maggie tomorrow," Bill said.

"Tonight? What if Frank sees me? Why can't I go when he's working? If he sees me, he'll know, and then you'll both have trouble! Those boys aren't any rebel gunslingers, but they aren't known to miss, either!" she cried.

"Go when he's asleep or cause a distraction. Kill him, if you have to! I don't care which but do as you're told so your girls don't end up on the wrong end of a thresher!" Then looking at Maggie, Hiserodt said, "If you wouldn't mind, Nettie and I have other business to attend to now."

He motioned for the door as he stood up and undid his belt.

IV

That same night...

Nettie laid awake in her small bed next to Frank, listening to the wind howl outside. A snowstorm had hit just after supper and hadn't let up. With the sound of the storm and Frank's snoring, there was no hope of sleep on any normal night. Tonight was different. Frank's arm was still draped over Nettie as she lay there awake, contemplating her escape. He may be asleep enough to move his arm, but the whole bed would creak and crack as she snuck out from under the covers. Her heart was heavy and pounded in her chest. She turned her head to look at Frank. He was a handsome man, and she did love him, but there was no turning back now. She had to get back to Zella, by any means. She had told Frank that Zella had stayed the night with her aunt and uncle so they could have some time together, which Frank took full advantage of. She enjoyed their time together, knowing it would be the last time. Her heart began to break. With a single tear escaping her eyes towards her pillow, she turned away from him.

She couldn't hear anything stirring in the house, only the sound of wind whistling through the thin cracks and creases around the windows, and doors. As delicately as she could muster, holding back a cavalry of emotion, and more tears, she slowly slid Frank's arm off of her, and onto the soft bedding. He snored louder than normal, and in a hurried movement, he turned over, facing the wall. Nettie used Frank's movement against him. Pulling the covers off in one quick motion, and standing up, she disguised her noises under his loud snores, and creaks that he had made as he turned over. She sighed heavily and brushed her tears off onto her sleeve. She had thought about this moment all day, and still wasn't sure of herself, or her plan. She would need to get dressed, get the object Hiserodt needed, open the door, and go out the front. All while not getting caught. She looked back over at her sleeping husband and her tears turned to anger. Not at him, but rather the situation she was now faced with.

Catching her breath and a calmer state of mind, she slowly began to slide open the dresser drawer. It creaked loudly and Frank stirred as it did. Nettie held her breath and tried to squeeze the drawer in such a way to silence its telling call. Standing there in her nightgown, she slid her hand inside the half open drawer, and searched blindly for the object Hiserodt needed. Even though it was cold outside, she was sweating, and was partially blinded by her tears. In her frantic state, she didn't hear Frank wake and sit up.

"What are you doing, Net?" he asked while yawning.

At his voice, she jumped and slammed her hand in the drawer. "Jeez, Frank! You scared me half to death," she said, trying to quickly think of a lie.

He smiled, "Well, gosh, I didn't mean to scare you, but I can't help but notice that you're not lying next to me...what are you doing in my drawer?"

"Oh...," she said in a guilty tone, "I was just looking for some socks to wear." She pretended to shiver as she spoke, without realizing that there was no lantern on, and Frank could barely see her, anyways.

"You know your socks are in your drawer, silly women," he said with a charming laugh.

"Oh, right...I know, dear! I just wanted to wear a pair of your long socks; they keep me warmer."

Frank then got up and stretched. Nettie panicked as he came over. Standing behind her, he kissed her neck, opened the drawer, and gave her a pair. In the brief moment the drawer was open, Nettie could barely see the object she needed.

"Here you go, darling," he said as he hugged her from behind. "Why don't we go back to bed? It has to be the middle of the night."

Nettie tried not to shake as Frank touched her or let him hear that she was crying. *What would she do? She needed to be gone, and now!*

"That sounds like a good idea, Frank, but could you please do me a favor first? Can you please go get the oil lantern from Nate and George, so we can have a little heat?" She knew Nate and George Winnans were out in the barn drinking to their heart's content near an open fire. If she could get Frank to go all the way out there, she may have a chance to escape, but only just. "Please?" she said in a begging tone that Frank knew wasn't really a request. It was more of a tone that said, *do this for me and I'll do something for you.*

Frank smiled again and replied, "Oh, silly woman, you stay here. I'll be right back." He squeezed her gently and kissed her neck again. Letting go, he left the room.

Once he was gone, Nettie waited to hear Frank put on his clothes he had draped over a chair in the hall. When she heard the front door swing shut, she dropped the socks, and ransacked the small dresser drawer. Pure adrenaline entered her veins, and her bones shook with panic. Her fingers clawed at the small object, and she brought it out, inspected it in the moonlight, and smiled at her craftiness.

Looking out the small bedroom window, she could see Frank was now approaching the barn and the two men seated outside by a small fire. She didn't have long. As fear overcame her, she ran barefoot out of the room and quietly opened the cabin's front door and closed it behind her.

The wind was chilled with the icy snow, and it took her breath away as her bare feet struck the powdered ground. The ice crunched under her feet as she ran to the opposite side of the cabin as the barn. Running at full strides, the cool air filled her lungs, and her breath became sharp. In a flood of tears, hate, and panic, Nettie reached the tree-line, and tripped into the dense timber. She fell face first and caught herself with the palms of her hands. A small branch scraped her cheek and blood met the salty tears. Her palms took in shards of jagged rock and splintered timber. Rolling over onto her back, covered by the woods, and snow, Nettie laid there, and listened to Frank call her name. With every bit of infuriating desperation, she stifled her overwhelming screams.

V

January 15th, 1885...

Nettie sat in the hotel room all day, waiting for Maggie to come back. Effie and Zella played in the corner of the large room with Zella's wooden blocks. Effie was trying to help Zella stack them all on top of each other, but they all kept falling down at the last block. Nettie sat on the floor opposite of the two girls with her back against the wall, watching them play. She had felt like crying all day as she watched them. Zella would never know Effie was her big sister, and Effie would never know how much Nettie loved her.

"Sissy, I think baby 'Ella's hungry, and I am, too," Effie said to Nettie as she tugged on her sleeve to get her attention.

"I'm sorry, dear, I don't have any food, and I can't leave you two alone up here. Maggie—I mean, your mother," she stuttered, "should be back soon, love," Nettie replied. Not a moment later, a knock came at the door, and Maggie Johnson entered the room with four men. One of the men was the hotel operator, Mr. Deyo, who had a tray of food that he placed on the small table. Effie ran over to the table, lifted the tray cover, and snuck a piece. Maggie looked at her, and Effie smiled, and pretended to be innocent as she went back over to where Zella sat.

Nettie knew Dr. Underwood and Mr. Deyo but wasn't familiar with the other men. She stood up to greet them as they entered the room, and Maggie introduced them to her. "Nettie, dear, these two men are the state's attorneys, Henry Huff, and John Stevens!"

Underwood removed his hat, and greeted her with, "Ma'am, it's a pleasure to see you again. I am the man who discovered your father had not had an accident, and I am sorry that we now find ourselves here."

"I know, sir. I remember you from the inquest last year. It's a pleasure—," she trailed off.

The men looked around nervously as if they'd been invited into a stranger's home and didn't know where to sit. Maggie had gone over to help Effie get her food, and Nettie now sat on the end of the bed waiting for someone to talk. They didn't expect a young girl to know the plan, did they? She could tell they wanted to ask about the cuts on her cheek and hands. Her face and knees were also bruised. Finally, Mr. Deyo cleared his throat and spoke, "I understand it's been a hard day;

shoot, a hard couple of months for you...but eh, these men have a few questions for you."

Dr. Underwood went, and sat down next to Nettie, and putting a hand on her shoulder said, "I hear you're a brave girl. Hiserodt told me about your cooperation with him, and in relation, Sheriff Wilcox. He said that you have something for me."

She looked over at Maggie who was still helping the toddler eat her food. This was it. This was the moment she would destroy her marriage, and two men's lives forever. She reached into her nightgown's front pocket, brought out a small shiny object, and handed it over to the doctor. "I believe this is what you are looking for," she said.

Underwood undid his clenched hand and looked down at a pair of iron knuckles. He looked back up at Nettie and smiled. "That's exactly what I've been looking for, and unfortunately, is most likely what killed your father. This would be consistent with Johnson's markings," he replied as he handed them over to Mr. Huff.

Nettie looked over at the attorney with a single tear on her face and said, "I believe my husband, Frank, and his brother, Nate, killed my father. Please...," she said as her voice cracked, "I need to know. Please find out!"

John Stevens had taken a small piece of paper and a pen out of his bag and handed them to Nettie as he knelt down in front of her. "We were advised about your escape, and we do need a statement, ma'am. Can you please read and sign this?"

Nettie never looked down at the paper. There was no point. She couldn't read it through the onset of tears that flooded her eyes and had yet to start their descent upon her face. Zella saw Nettie's face and heard her begin to cry. The small baby began to cry also and put her face into the floor. Nettie then signed the paper as her tears scarred it while Maggie tended to the little girl.

Henry Huff spoke up as Nettie handed the paper back to Stevens, "Mr. Hiserodt told us your other brother-in-law, William Rainsbarger, threatened you, and told you not to speak. He said this is all your fault. What you've done tonight is admirable. It must've been extremely difficult to leave your husband, knowing he's a killer, especially having a baby so young. We don't need threats coming your way. Hiserodt agreed and has ordered two guards to be with you at all times. They're just outside this door, right now, if you need them."

"What happens now?" Nettie asked.

"We arrest them, ma'am!" Huff replied.

VI

On January 16th, 1885, Frank and Nate Rainsbarger were arrested for the murder of Enoch Johnson by Sheriff William Vance Wilcox. It was the state's theory that the brothers had conspired to take out a life insurance policy on Johnson, dress a cadaver in his clothes, and stage a runaway horse and buggy accident, during which, the cadaver would be thrown into the river.

When the body would be recovered, it would be so decomposed, that it would be unrecognizable. They would be able to collect the insurance money and start over somewhere else. But at the last minute, they had decided to actually kill Johnson, as they could not obtain a cadaver. This contradicted their original theory that they wanted Enoch killed for exposing their counterfeit operation.

On the day Frank and Nate were arrested, it was recorded that Nettie hid in a closet, and wouldn't come out until she was convinced by Maggie that they were in custody. Whether she hid out of fear, or shame for having them arrested, we do not know.

Afterwards, Nettie was paraded around town and adored by the townspeople. They believed that she was a young naive girl who had been duped into marrying a criminal and should be helped. The Eldora Herald claimed, "*The dashing and defiant Frank had captivated the innocent maiden.*"

The town's view of the Rainsbargers changed and an all-out movement to eradicate Hardin County of them was even more prominent. The Vigilance Society worked even harder to aim their own brand of justice towards the family.

CHAPTER 11

THE RAINSBARGER 'GANG'

I

At the jailhouse in Eldora, January, 1885...

The jailhouse was exactly that. It was a thin two-story wooden house with a front door and windows. The inside had a front desk, and the cells weren't open-barred walls. Instead, it had solid wooden doors like an ordinary home. The bottom floor is where the inmates were kept in the small, enclosed rooms. The second story of the jailhouse was a small living quarter for the deputy on watch.

"You've got five minutes. Their room is just around the corner, Mr. Johns," said Deputy Barnes as he pointed to the hall behind him.

Henry Johns shook off the flurries of snow that clung to his hat and coat as he approached a solid wooden door. It had a lock on the outside, but no window in the center of it in which to view any occupants. He placed his ear to the door and listened. He heard nothing. Henry waited and listened another moment longer before he gave a single knock. Then he heard the creaking of springs from an old cot and the shuffle of feet.

"Yes, boss?" came the voice of Frank Rainsbarger.

"It's me, Frank! It's Henry! How are you two lads holding up?" he asked.

"Henry! It's great to see you, uh, well, you know what I mean," Frank replied. Henry could hear Nate chuckle a little at Frank's statement.

Henry Johns looked to his right and out the window at the snow falling in a peaceful manner. Unlike his heart, which was anything but calm. He hung his head low and slumped forward until his forehead rested on the door. "It's good to see you chaps, too," he said in a defeated tone. "I'm sorry you boys are in here. I fear this may be my fault. It seems while I was busy with my own ambitions, a great many folks were busy working against us. I'm afraid they have the upper hand now," he trailed off with a sigh. "It's not over yet, though, boys! There was a meeting today at the town square, and I told them all, that I know you couldn't be guilty of this crime, and that I knew where you were the night Johnson was killed!"

"He was my friend," Nate said in a quiet voice.

"I know, chap, but they don't know that. They only know what Nettie tells them," Henry added.

At her name, Frank asked, "Nettie? What do you mean?"

Henry's gut sank as he knew no one had told Frank, or Nate who told the police they killed Enoch Johnson. "By god, Frank! You don't know, do you? She gave the state's attorneys your knuckles from your clothes drawer, and claimed you boys beat her old man to death. It was her doing...rather the counterfeiters using her most likely." There was a long silence and only the wind could be heard in the distance. Frank didn't speak again after that.

"So, what do we do now?" Nate asked.

Henry cleared his throat, and removing his head from the door, he said, "Well, I know Enoch was most likely killed to prevent him from exposing anyone, however, as you know, I already have a list of names. I'll go forward with the indictment and hopefully you boys will be out of here in no time! Be of good cheer, boys, I already told everyone I'd spend over fifty-thousand dollars to free you and bring the real criminals to justice!"

"Thank you, Henry, but you know that makes you a target now, don't you? Are they really calling us a gang?" Nate replied.

"Everyone is either scared, angry, or both. Whoever has a hold on Nettie has gotten under everyone's skin pretty good. But...the real gang of thieves is scared even worse as they know they'll hang if they're caught. The hangman's noose is calling their names, and they hear it loud and clear."

A voice from the front of the building called out, "Time's up, Johns. It's time to get moving before the storm gets any worse, and you have to stay in a cell yourself."

"Well...we'll wait on you then for the next step towards our freedom. Be careful, Henry. Tell Martha we love her, and hope to see her soon," Nate said in a small voice.

Henry Johns then left the two men, and rode home in silence, wondering if the next time he saw them they would become free men.

II

January 20th, 1885, at the Ellsworth Hotel...

There were several patrons inside the dining hall of the hotel. It had snowed for several days prior, and many folks didn't want to make the trip out of Eldora in bad weather. They could take the train nearly anywhere but most still refused to endure the harshness of the cold. Many families were sitting down to eat and to be warmed by the large fireplace in the dining area.

Snow continued to bombard the byways, and other than the sound of wind, it was a quiet night. Even the talk amongst the patrons was at a dull roar as nearly everyone was talking about the Rainsbargers arrest, and spoke in hurried whispers, as if no one else around them knew what was happening. The hotel kitchen sat at the back of the hotel, separated from the eating area by just a thin wall.

Hiserodt and Mr. Huff sat inside the kitchen against the back wall and watched Mr. Deyo boil several pots of water. The steam was welcomed by the two men as there was nothing else heating the kitchen at the moment. Henry Huff wasn't sure why he was there, but he had been asked by Hiserodt to accompany him to the hotel kitchen that evening, and to bring along the knuckles that Nettie had given him. He fumbled with them in his pocket as he waited for Hiserodt to speak.

"Damn, gentlemen, can't one of y'all hold the door while we bring this in? It's heavier than Popejoy's mama," said Amos Bannigan as he and Popejoy burst through the kitchen's back double doors. They were carrying a large wooden box on one end, and the other end was being carried by Henry Finster, and George Edgington. The box was covered in frozen dirt, and ice, and was several feet long. It had a thin lid that had been nailed closed. The nails were aided by the frost in keeping the top in its place. Hiserodt, and Huff stood up and helped the men slide the box into the kitchen, and onto the hardwood floor in between the prep table, and the large wood burning stove.

"Is it supposed to smell that bad?" Popejoy asked as he dropped his end.

"It wouldn't have smelt any better beforehand," Amos replied.

When everyone let go of their end, dirt, and ice broke free from the box, and worms scattered, and crawled under the kitchen appliances. Mr. Deyo, the hotel owner, saw it, and shuddered at the idea of worms getting into food, forgetting what was inside the box itself.

"Would you two stop complaining and get the top off?" Hiserodt barked.

Henry Finster and Edgington removed themselves from the area of the stench and backed out slowly through the doors they had entered. Hiserodt handed Bannigan a crowbar and nodded towards the box.

"Bring over the water first," Popejoy called to Mr. Deyo.

He removed the pot from the stove top with both hands and slowly poured the boiling water onto the fresh ice. It made a hissing noise as it melted, as if the water was branding the wood itself. Fresh steam arose from the air and an intense smell came with it. Amos dropped the crowbar he had been given and vomited onto the newly cleaned prep table. Henry Huff threw up into his coffee cup he had been holding. It made a deep *glup* sound as it went into the coffee and the noise almost made him vomit again.

"Damn it, men! Get it together!" Hiserodt said as he knelt down to the box and began breaking away frozen chunks of dirt.

When it was mostly defrosted, and void of any worms, Popejoy took the crowbar, and began to pry. "What the hell is it?" Huff asked, holding a handkerchief to his mouth and nose.

"Well, seeing as Nettie has now joined the party the ladies of the night have been throwing here every night, we got her a party favor," Popejoy said.

Amos chucked and then gagged. Huff gave a disturbed look and Hiserodt smiled. "What maggot infested cave did you crawl out of, to have such rotten humor?" Hiserodt laughed.

"That would be Finster's cave, sir! Now someone help me get this off," Popejoy said, still laughing at his own joke. With a few more attempts at the lid, it finally broke open, and the stench was much worse. Amos and Mr. Huff resumed their gagging and stomach lurches in separate corners. Deyo walked back over with watery eyes and was holding his breath. He then dumped the second pot of heated water onto the object inside the box.

"It smells like rotten feet," Popejoy said through a stifled laugh, "No, no it's worse than that."

Still leaning over the box, Hiserodt breathed in deep and made an *ahh* sound as he exhaled, "It's much better than the smell of war, boys," he said.

After some time, the smell of rotten meat subsided enough for Popejoy, and Bannigan to reach in, and lift out the object inside. Mr. Deyo grabbed an end, "This way, men, I've prepared a table in the other room. Should be an easy clean up."

They then rushed through another set of double doors to the right and found a small room with a long table and an old sheet covering it. The only thing on the table besides the sheet, was a hammer. Upon entering the room, Hiserodt said to Huff, "I need the object now, Henry." He put out his hand and waited. The man fumbled with the knuckles again and handed them over, wrapped in a dirty cloth. Hiserodt dropped the cloth and grabbed the hammer. "If anyone wants to leave, now's the time. This may make a mess," Hiserodt said. "Remember, men, Dr. Underwood is still investigating the matter and we need to make sure he finds the evidence we need him to find."

He lowered the knuckles to the defrosting rotten meat and brought up the hammer to strike it. He had just leaned back when the door burst open. Maggie ran in with a scarf over her nose and without looking around she asked, "What is going on? What's that stench? All of the hotel guests can smell it and it's making everyone sick—."

She stopped when she saw what the men were doing as she then understood. Hiserodt and the other men were huddled around a table with the corpse of Enoch Johnson. They had dug up his body, defrosted it from the harsh winter ground, and were now about to imprint Frank Rainsbarger's knuckle indents into his skull. They all looked at her, and she straightened up, and smiled. She then removed her cloth from her nose and laughed a small laugh. "If you're going to beat the old man a second time, at least let me do it," she said as she took the hammer from Hiserodt.

III

A few days after his arrest, Frank wrote Nettie a letter that said he once considered her his friend, but he couldn't call her that anymore. He also asked for a photo of Zella. On February 3rd, Nettie wrote a four-page letter in return and accused the entire Rainbarger family of murdering her father. She claimed that they beat her father to death, and then she quoted the Bible about God's judgment. Her letter was printed by the Des Moines Daily News and was used to continue to fool the community at large. Nettie then continued to be clothed and adored by prominent men in the community. It seemed she was starting to believe the claim that her husband killed her father.

Her letter even claimed that her father came to her in a dream and said, "Nettie, don't worry about how I was killed, but I will tell you who did it. Frank and Nate killed me." Those who knew Nettie best didn't believe she even wrote the reply to Frank's letter. Throughout

February, the Eldora Herald would continue to incite the people against the brothers, while Henry Johns tried to convict the counterfeiters. It seemed that no one was in search of Enoch's true cause of death.

IV

Late night, March 10th, 1885, at the home of James S. Ross...

James had been asleep for some time when the rain started. After being woken up by the storm, he laid there awake, and listened to the noise, breathing in the cool air. He began to think about the next morning's paper, and wondered what he should print next. Normally he already had it ready, but his constant writing of the murder, and Rainsbarger brothers had begun to cloud his mind.

After some time, he rolled over and sat up on the edge of the bed. He couldn't sleep anymore as he had a paper to prepare, and had to have it ready by morning, anyways. Scratching his head, and yawning, he got up, and decided to get started. Everything was silent, except the soft rain outside. It was cold and dark, and he knew that it would turn to snow by early morning. The need to prepare the paper and get to his office before it turned to slush hurried his steps.

James entered his kitchen and then poured a cup of water from the pitcher on the counter. He began to become lost in thought about what Wilcox had told him. The people of Eldora and Steamboat Rock already thought the Rainsbargers were criminals, and now they *for sure knew* it, or at least that's what he thought. He could continue to cover any developments on the case, but what would tomorrow's paper say?

He contemplated this, and many other bothersome questions for another minute or so, until he heard someone clear their throat. James jumped, and nearly dropped his cup in the process, spilling water on his clothes. "Dang nabbit! Who's there?" he yelled as he turned to the direction of the noise and lifted the cup above his head to use as a weapon.

"Calm down, Ross, it's just us," said the voice.

His eyes adjusted to the dark room as he squinted, and he then saw Sheriff Wilcox seated in his armchair, and Deputy Amos Bannigan standing next to him holding a bag. They had snuck into his house and he didn't even hear them. Hell, he walked right past them, and into the kitchen, and didn't even see them.

"Geez, men! You could knock and wake me up properly instead of sneaking in. What do you need, Sheriff, that couldn't wait until morning, anyways?" he asked.

"Your skills, Ross. We need your skills, and your press. I need you to print a story in tomorrow's paper. Those two boys' coffins have been built, but we need someone to help drive in the nails, so-to-speak. For them, and the remaining family," Wilcox said.

"I've been doing my job and doing it well. Everyone is in a frenzy now and they'll believe anything I write. Besides, folks are about as fond of the two Rainsbarger boys as they are of finding a snake in their bedroll," James replied.

Bannigan spoke up, "Then make them believe the whole family are criminals. It should be easy for you!"

"That's right," Wilcox interrupted, "Tell them William Rainsbarger has been threatening witnesses and his boys have been playing 'outlaw' as if they were Jesse James himself! Reprint the story about the other one, Manse, being involved in the bank robbery in Steamboat Rock! Make them tear this family apart until they're all good and gone!"

"The Society is counting on you to do your part in running those rat-bags out of this county, but we know you can do more than that," said Amos. He then threw the bag at James' feet, and said, "Here's some motivation for you, courtesy of the Society members. You may own the press, but now we own you. That's twelve thousand in newly printed bills. Are you catching on yet, boy?"

Ross bent down and opened the bag. He then took out a fresh bundle of bills and thumbed the end as he took a deep breath. To him it smelt like freedom. He smiled and asked, "What do you want me to print?"

V

On March 11th, the Eldora Herald printed an article that asked for the community to band together against the entire Rainsbarger family. They printed a fake story about the family and lied about their history. They outlined them all as outlaws who had escaped the law in Ohio by moving to Iowa, and stated that they were planning to run from the law again.

"The Rainsbarger crowd are seeking a new location. The people, with the cooperation of the county press, have them on the run and there should be no let up until all are in the penitentiary."

After the paper printed its story, rumors spread far, and wide about the remaining free brothers planning to murder several leaders in the community.

Henry Johns began to feel guilty about Frank, and Nate being used as scapegoats, as *he* was the one to get Enoch Johnson to confess the names of the counterfeiters. They were simply caught in the cross-fire. After being denied bail by Judge Miracle, Henry Johns then had Frank, and Nate removed from Hardin County, and taken to the jail in Marshalltown to avoid any mob violence, as a group of twenty armed men came to Eldora from Steamboat Rock.

He feared a *gang war* was on the horizon.

CHAPTER 12

THE GANG WAR BEGINS

I

April 1st, 1885...

By the light of the moon, Finley Rainsbarger swayed back and forth on the back of an old horse. It was a clear night, and the chorus of crickets, and other insects could be heard. The clinking of the metal from the horse's gear played a harmony with the insects as it moved slowly through the grass. He then dismounted his horse by a tree that was near the worn-down road. He drank some of his water, and offered a drink to his horse, who was desperate for a break. They both had a long day, and night spent meeting with Henry Johns, and Finley knew they needed to rest. He sat down under the tree for a while, and listened to the breeze, and the sound of the grass move. He took the knife from his boot, began to sharpen it on a stone, and whistled while he sat. The night rolled on and the sound of crickets faded. He may have dozed off for a while but wasn't sure. Time wasn't a concern when the moon was still the only light in the sky.

When he regained himself, he could hear horse hooves a short distance off, and men yelling. Finley then realized this was what woke him. His eyes had adjusted to the night enough that he could see two men in the distance riding hard towards him on the grassy hills. He wasn't worried about other riders on the road, at least not until he heard a gunshot, and the bullet enter the grass near his feet. Fin jumped up and drew his own revolver as he saddled up onto his horse, who was now spooked. He whipped the reins in one hand and was off. He was being shot at by two men who had sworn to uphold the law in Hardin County: Deputy Cady Swain, and Deputy Amos Bannigan.

"Come on, Swain! Don't hold back on your shots! This Rainsbarger is the nastiest of them all! You've got a date at the marble orchard, Rainsbarger!" Bannigan yelled.

Finley rode the horse hard across the path, and shot over his shoulder without looking back. A few more stray bullets grazed past his head and the horse's left side. The horse neighed loud and kept going.

"The path curves and leads back this way a bit. Cut him off, Amos!" Swain yelled back. His voice echoed across the land. It made Finley feel like they were closer than they were. The path did lean back towards the men a way, but not all the way. Instead of taking the path to them, Finley decided to veer off and into the brush. He was too far from Henry Johns' home to turn around, and too far from his own home to go there.

Horse hooves pounding the grass, yelling, and an occasional shot being fired, was all that could be heard. There were no other options. Finley pulled hard and turned the horse around towards the men. He was in the underbrush of a large tree when he turned and wasn't fully visible to the men. He fired back, and waited to see what he'd hit, if anything at all. Knowing he now needed to reload, he holstered his revolver, and removed his rifle from the saddle's side, and brought the gun to his eye. He heard another shot from the assailants, and in an instant, his horse's face hit the dirt, and slumped forward. Finley lost his balance and caught himself on the ground with his gun barrel, which twisted his wrist backwards.

His horse was dead. By the time he regained his footing, the two men were fleeing down the path in the direction that they came. Finley looked in the opposite direction of the men and saw that a group of three other riders were firing into the air, scaring away his would-be assassins. The folks of Hardin County always spoke a lot against the Rainsbarger brothers, but an attempted murder was new.

II

April 6th, 1885...

William Rainsbarger stood in his open field of crops, inspecting them as the sun beat down. There was still cooler weather in Iowa, but the sun made him sweat, nonetheless. The grain wouldn't be ready for a few more months, but the fields were well on their way to being threshed. He rolled some of the wheat in his hands to feel its development. A few yards out in the adjacent field, stood two of William's sons, George and John. George was the oldest, but both were still just boys. He admired them as he watched them examine the fields. A few more yards to his right stood his home.

Williams' daughter, Rosa, sat on the front porch, tying her shoes, and getting ready for the day ahead. He smiled at her beauty, and with everything surrounding his brother's arrest, the hope he saw in her eyes, returned some hope to him. He smiled again, and looked back at his boys who were slowly making their way to him. As he watched them, he suddenly went deaf for a moment, and then heard an echo ring though the trees. He spun around to see a cloud of gunpowder smoke near where his left ear had been before he turned.

"You know, I really hate to do this, Bill, but it's got to be done!" a voice yelled near the tree-line by the river.

The running water was a few yards off and someone was approaching from that direction. William could hear the sound of a rifle being reloaded, and realized, whoever it was, meant to shoot him. As he heard the rifle's bolt slide into place, he dropped to the ground as another shot went off and shattered the heads of wheat just above him. Frantically, William began to crawl through the fields towards his home. "Boys! Get down, and fire back! Midline of the crops!" he shouted.

He had not taken his gun to the fields that morning as he had only gone out to inspect the crops and was planning on returning to the cabin for breakfast. A scream came from the front of the cabin, and Rosa yelled, "Boys, help! Pa's being shot at!"

The front door screen burst open as William's oldest daughter, Mary Ellen, came out holding a rifle she could barely lift. Immediately behind her, was his wife, Elizabeth. She grabbed the rifle from her daughter and yelled, "Give me that, girl, and both of you, get back inside!"

Gun fire rang through the field as George and John returned fire. Whoever had shot at William was waiting for a clear shot. "I can't see the bastard!" George cried. He shot in another direction and only birds scattered. Everything was quiet once the echo stopped.

"Pa?" John whispered loudly. "Where are you?"

There was no reply, but he could hear footsteps approaching from his right. The steps became faster and faster until William plowed through the tall crops, tackling both his sons to the ground as a third rifle shot went off just left of them. Another shot went off in reply to the previous one, from the front porch of their home. William, and his two boys took the opportunity to duck, and run back toward their home as the crops shattered behind them. George and John shot two more times each, firing behind them as they ran.

"Mary Ellen! Bring your Pa' his gun, now!" Elizabeth screamed.

Within a moment, her arm reached out of the cabin's front door with a revolver in her hand as the boys spun the wooden chairs around and took cover to reload. "Everyone fire at once!" William bellowed.

A hail of gunfire and smoke emerged from the front of the small house and into the field of crops. The entire family was sweating and shaken by the sudden barrage of gunshots on a rather quiet morning, that they didn't hold back. Crops twisted through the air in pieces, and the occasional shot that got away ricocheted off a few boulders. When they had all emptied their rounds, they sat in silence and listened. All they could hear was faint footsteps in the distance pounding the ground as someone ran towards the river.

When Deputy Amos Bannigan reached the water, he nearly jumped into the small boat Sheriff Wilcox was waiting with. "I almost had him! Damn it!" he said through gritted teeth. "His pigeon-livered rat-infested boys were there and armed to the tooth! They need to go, too!"

"Perhaps I should have sent Deputy Swain to do the job," is all Wilcox replied. He didn't say anything more as they returned quietly down the river from where they came.

III

April 7th, 1885...

It had been nearly three months since Frank, and Nate Rainsbarger had been arrested, and their family cabin lay empty by the Iowa River. Spiders, and other insects had made their homes in the cracks, and crevices undisturbed. Maggots had nearly devoured the food that was left behind, and the smell of mildew, and rot had filled the air. The cold wind blew the dry leaves into the cabin as the door opened. Ash Noyes and James Rice began to raid the forgotten home, as John Bunger entered with a container of kerosene, and a lantern. Deputies Swain and Bannigan entered behind him, dragging a heavy object in a wrapped up cloth.

"Remember, boys, you ain't here to smash every plate and loot every tiny object you think might add value to your pathetic lives," sneered Bannigan.

"We need evidence that can be used in the Rainsbarger case, so spread out and find what you can! Look for the husband's mittens, and the brother's coat. We were told they had blood on them, and they may be the biggest help," Swain added.

"Hell, I'll find any old mittens or coat and put my own blood on them, if ya need me to," Bunger said as he casually knocked the family's keepsakes off of their place on the shelves. They crashed to the floor, and he crushed them under his boot, pressing them into the floor.

Swain smacked his arm, "Get to pouring the kerosene so we can get out of here, or I'll do it, and you can help move this body!"

"Poor girl won't get a proper burial. You think anyone in Chicago will miss her?" Bannigan asked as a joke.

"Does it matter?" Swain replied. "She's dead!"

James Rice could be heard in the other room, smashing objects, and going through drawers while the other men stood in the living room with the body of a dead girl. Ash Noyes was in the other room doing the same, but in a much quieter fashion. Rice stuck his head out of the bedroom doorway a moment later, and asked quietly, "Were the Society members really going to use the poor girl to fake Nettie's death?"

"Oh, now you're worried about being quiet?" Swain remarked.

"I don't know why; there ain't nobody out here," Rice said.

"To answer your question," Bunger interrupted, "I thought it was a foolish idea. I can't believe they talked me into digging the hole in the first place."

Noyes called from the other room, "What are we doing with the body here anyways?"

"We're getting rid of it, you dope," Bannigan laughed.

"Well, bring it in here then, here's as good a place as any!"

The two deputies dragged the body from the sitting room into the bedroom from where Noyes had yelled from. Upon entering the room, they found him lying in the empty bed, wearing one of Nettie's dresses which was much too small for him, over his regular clothes. He laughed and jumped up. "Put her in the bed, boys," he laughed again, as the dress tore in the back. It then slid off of him and onto the dusty floor.

The three men stifled their laughter, and then unwrapped the sheet, hoisted the dead girl's body into the bed, and pulled the sheet over her. Bunger had set down the lantern and followed with a trail of kerosene from the front entry to the bedroom. All men were glad the smell of the kerosene mostly masked the smell of the body. They all stared at the girl lying there in Nettie's bed.

"She don't even look like Net," Rice said.

"She won't look like anything here in a moment," Swain replied.

Albert Leverton then entered the house's open front door, knocked on the hardwood wall closest to it, and yelled, "We didn't find anything in the barn, boys, but let's get this done."

"Let's exterminate these rodents, men," Bunger said.

One by one, the men cleared the house out into the cold night air. Their breaths could be seen in the moonlight as they watched Bunger add more kerosene to the outside of the cabin, then string a line through the grass to the small barn. James Rice held the burning lantern in front of him to watch. He looked around and saw a dozen or so other men with torches. They outlined the forest near its one road. In the distance, a whistle blew, and the men gave a loud shout. Rice could see them throw their torches into the fields of crops, the barn, and forest. Bunger took the lantern from Rice's cold hands and threw it overhead into the front window of the Rainsbarger's cabin, igniting it immediately.

The men shouted again in unison, "For life and property!" It echoed through the grassy hills and into the tree-line. Another whistle blew, and the men began to return from that area. As they traveled along the worn-out road onto the main thoroughfare, they burned down all of 'Rainsbarger country'.

IV

April 9th, 1885, at the home of Henry and Martha Johns...

'The Rainsbargers, who have been running everything with a high hand and terrorizing everyone, find themselves with a little of the same kind of sauce. We hope they enjoy it.'

-The Eldora Herald

Manse threw down the paper when he finished reading it and cursed. He looked around the room at all of them seated at the table. They all looked defeated, except Henry Johns. He looked angry yet determined at the same time. Martha was standing in the open kitchen, and she began to cry when Manse threw the paper down. She had kept it together until then, but now she couldn't hold it back as she saw her husband, brothers, and children in fear for their lives. Yet, hadn't she known it would come to this? Seated at the table was Manse, Finley, and William Rainsbarger on one side, and on the other was Henry, Ed, and Lincoln Johns. Their hired man, Henry Wikert, stood leaning against the kitchen wall.

"I can't believe you boys were all shot at! I suppose they're coming for me next," Manse said as he sat back down and folded his arms.

"We were *all* shot at? You, too, Henry?" William asked, concerned.

"Yesterday, on my way home," he said in a short manner, "Wikert met the men out near the road with the boys and opened fire. They ran them poor bastards off."

"What do we do now?" William asked.

Henry Johns threw back his drink and gently placed the cup down. He had resolved in his mind what needed to be done. "We go to war, gentlemen. This is only bound to get worse. This county is on the verge of a gang war, and it may not let up for decades, two or three perhaps. The way the indictment is going...it wouldn't surprise me if it took that long," Henry said, and sighed.

Finley looked around at the men across from him and saw what Henry meant. Henry and each boy were now equipped with a knife, bullet belt, and sidearm revolver, which was neatly placed at drawing length on the hip. Wikert was arrayed the same way. This isn't what Finely wanted for his brother's, and nephews, and he sure as hell knew this wasn't what Henry wanted for Martha. Fin looked over at her being comforted by Wikert with tears on his shirt. Finley's heart began to break.

"Well...you all sure look ready for war. Where did you get all of the guns and ammo?" Finley asked.

"I spoke with my attorney, John Roberts, about protecting myself and this was the solution. We have no other choice. The Vigilance Society isn't working to keep us, and our property safe, and neither is local law enforcement. I had to...I had to arm my boys, hired men, and detectives. I armed them all," he said while choking back his true feelings.

Wikert picked up when Henry couldn't speak, "We have more for you, boys, too. We don't know the relationship between the counterfeiters and the society, but they both seem to hate you all."

"What else is new?" Finley asked.

Ed and Lincoln chuckled a little, and Finley smiled. It was enough to ease the tension for a moment, and then nearly everyone gave a small laugh, even Martha, as she wiped away her tears. William was the only one who didn't laugh at all.

"They burned down the family cabin and farmland. Two nights ago, apparently—," he trailed off in a defeated tone as he looked down at his hands, "I could see the smoke and flames all the way from my fields!" His tone sobered the occupants of the room once again. "Do you really think it will be twenty years, or more, Henry? What about Frank and Nate? We can't let them sit as innocent men in prison for thirty years," William continued; his voice sounding as if it hurt him to say it. The thought of his younger brothers rotting away for decades, made him feel sick.

Henry finally spoke again, "I've already hired the best attorneys in the state. They should be meeting with the boys soon in Marshalltown, and hopefully we'll move forward. In about a week's time, I will meet the men in Eldora, and learn more. My attorney says this county's prominent banker, William Wiemer, knows about the counterfeit money, and is willing to meet with us. I'll keep you updated. All will know the truth."

Martha stared at them all in an empty gaze as they continued to talk of war, and justice. She considered a question that had plagued her since this all began.

What is truth?

CHAPTER 13

HENRY JOHNS

I

April, 1885, at the Schoolhouse in Steamboat Rock...

Outside the schoolhouse, the wind howled, and the trees bent, and creaked under the weight of the oncoming storm, much like the men inside, bending to their own will. More masked men were scattered upon the schoolyard property, armed to tooth, and nail, ready to disband any intruder, or threat. One of Henry Johns' detectives had tried to attend the meeting but was already turned away under threat by the mob outside. The glow of the torches made the school look like it was on fire. Nearly everyone who was a part of the Vigilance committee had shown up in an uproar. This meeting would be anything but calm as the men inside were pursuing the mind of a mob. Rainsbarger was no longer a name to be feared but had become one to be destroyed. The men who had arrived acted upon this idea with cowardice that was masked as justice and Wilcox knew it.

Inside, the men were shouting over each other and *at* each other. Some argued they were the ones who took the shots at Finley, and William, and bragged about it. Farmers, and lawyers had turned into lying gunslingers, and outlaws at the mention of the Rainsbarger name. Wilcox lifted his hands to stop the shouting and to arouse the mob's attention. They took no notice as they continued their desperate shouts.

Their need for praise and approval from their neighbors was an incessant fever that would only keep burning. The sound of a gunshot rang out, and nearly everyone ducked low, or behind a child's desk. Some men drew their own guns, until they all noticed that it was Wilcox who had fired a shot into the ceiling above him. Small splinters of wood were riding the air to his shoulder.

"Now that I have everyone's attention, I would like to call this meeting to order," he shouted as he brushed the dust from his shoulder. "Good evening, distinguished businessmen, and deputized men of vigilance! Tonight, I know that you are all aware that Frank and Nate Rainsbarger have been arrested, and that the girl and child are safe!"

All men gave a loud cheer, and raised their gun, or torch into the air. Wilcox raised his hands again, and this time to his success. He continued, "You are all aware by now that there have been some recent shootings going on in the county, and we're proud to say it's in the name of honor, and preservation! Those desperadoes are shaking in their boots, or so we thought!"

"That's right," Hiserodt added, "The remaining free brothers have since been armed, and have started strengthening their numbers! They've hired men for their criminal gang! Their wealthy brother-in-law, Henry Johns, is their sole beneficiary, and dare I say, the leader of their crimes!"

All men shouted again and began to chant, "Death to Henry Johns." Hiserodt continued in a loud deep voice that penetrated their murder cry. "He has promised to spend upwards of fifty thousand dollars to free the two criminal brothers that have been arrested! He has hired them the best lawyers the state of Iowa has ever known, but his money can't buy your blind eye, can it, men?"

They shouted in unison a resounding "*no*" that echoed through the school. Wilcox held up a folded newspaper, and shouted again, "The Waterloo Courier printed John's statement in which he said he would have enough armed men ready to rescue those white trash boys! Our deputies have scouted the area near John's home in Abbott, and have seen hoards of men, and guns being transported to the residence!"

He paused to look over the waves of men, who now said nothing. They didn't speak, or move, or show anything at all. They just stared into Wilcox's eyes, fixed on his every word. Everything he said was fuel to their frantic state.

Finally, he spoke again, "It's time to arm yourselves, and your families...war is upon us!"

II

The night of April 16th, 1885, at the train station in Abbott...

The train's whistle blew loud and echoed through the station platform. Henry Johns could feel the train start to leave the station as the ground began to shake, and feel unsettled, much like his feelings about his journey home. He had just returned from Eldora after having met with the attorneys he had hired for Frank and Nate. The brothers were to be transferred back to Eldora for their preliminary trials shortly, and he needed an update, which he had promised to the remaining free Rainsbarger brothers. He had also given over the list of names he received from Enoch to the Department of Secret Services.

It was a cold night with the wind blowing hard against him. Henry wanted desperately to climb into his covered buggy and shield his face from the harsh winds. He thought about making Mr. Wikert drive the two-horse team back, so he could sleep the short distance home. His youngest son, Frank Johns, who was barely sixteen, had come with Wikert to pick him up at the station, and would no doubt have something warm to drink waiting for him.

The train's smoke cleared as it pounded the tracks in the opposite direction, and another fainter whistle could be heard. Wikert had whistled at Henry and was flagging him down on the other side of the platform. Upon reaching the two men, Frank handed his father his side arm, then embraced him.

"I'm glad to see you in one piece," Frank said as he looked Henry over.

"Me too, lad," he replied as he looked over at Wikert and asked, "Did anyone follow you?"

Wikert removed his hat, and while twisting its brim answered, "Not that we've seen...it's especially quiet out tonight. If I'm being honest, it makes me nervous, boss."

"It makes me anxious, too. There were several men carrying guns about the train station before I left," Henry remarked as he looked around at the empty station. The wind was the only noise that could be heard. Even the train had moved far enough away to conceal its loud pace along the tracks. With the train noise gone, Henry thought he could still feel its constant rhythm in his chest. His heart was beginning to beat faster, and his palms started to sweat the more they stood there in the open.

Frank spoke up in almost a whisper, "We should probably get moving...I brought the buggy instead of just the horses so we could all ride together with some cover and comfort."

"Good thinking, chap! Let's get moving," Henry said at last. The men quickened their steps as they left the boarding area for the trains and moved out into the open. Once they stepped out of the station, the wind was much colder but not as violent in its movements. Wikert led the way to where the horses were tied up with the buggy, just outside the horse stall near the roadway. They walked down the open dirt road and past two small buildings as they went. When he turned the corner of one, Henry and Frank saw Wikert draw his gun, cuss, and start running.

"What's wrong?" Henry yelled as he drew his own gun and ran after him. Upon turning the corner of the nearest building, he saw what Wikert saw.

"The horses are gone! Someone must have untied them from the buggy! Something doesn't feel right, boss!" Wikert yelled.

"I feel the same! Frank, lad, take cover in the buggy. Wikert and I will be back. If you hear, or see someone coming that isn't either of us, you hide, or run. I *will* find you, now go!" Henry said in a firm but quiet voice into his son's ear.

The boy nodded his compliance, ran towards the buggy, and climbed inside. As he ran, Henry did a double take. Frank may be just a boy, but in that moment, Henry felt he had raised a man. When he regained his thoughts, he noticed Wikert had grabbed his rifle from the back of the buggy, and was now staring down its barrel, walking next to Henry. The two men stayed side by side as they roamed the empty roadways and approached the station.

The depot's attendant booth was empty, and Henry's gut sank at the sight. "Someone should be posted," he said to Wikert as he nodded to the booth. Wikert didn't acknowledge him, but kept his rifle aimed in front of him, listening for any movement against the wind's cry. There were no noises indicating that a horse may be near.

"We might be apt to find someone looking to harm us if we keep looking in places we ought to find men and not horses. I say, we move out to the woods behind the station and see if they ain't roaming around out there. Perhaps whoever let them off the buggy hitch stole them and didn't leave them behind at all. What's our move if we don't find them, boss?" he nearly shouted over the sudden gust of wind.

"We either wait for the last train back to Eldora, or we walk the mile home. I don't really like either option, to tell you the truth."

"I don't either. It may be best we head to the buggy, check on the boy, and have him help us search the woods since the timber is back that way anyhow. The bays may be closer to the wagon," Wikert suggested, having already turned back.

"Let's go then," Henry said as he glanced at the station booth again. Henry did agree they wouldn't find the horses in a train station waiting to catch a ride. They had simply gone back to see if they were followed, but now he wasn't sure if he wanted to know the answer.

He watched a moment longer until he decided to move. As he watched, a man dressed in a vest, and tie came strolling towards the booth, unlocked the door, and went inside. Henry's heart felt lighter at the sight, and he sighed in relief. Turning, he ran after Wikert with his gun still drawn. With a few quick paces he had caught up to him. Wikert had lowered his gun as he approached the covered wagon so as to not accidentally shoot his boss's son when he inevitably came popping up from under cover.

"We need to find those horses and get out of here, boss," he said as he reached the buggy and leaned against it, lighting a cigarette.

Henry reached the buggy just after Wikert had and smacked the side of it hard. "Come on, Frank, let's get to looking for those horses; we need your young eyes to help in the dark," he said calmly, taking a drink from the water jug Wikert handed him. There was no reply. He hit the side again hard and yelled for him to come out. There was still no response. Leaning over the side, Henry and Wikert rummaged through the blankets that were thrown across the back storage area, assuming the boy may have fallen asleep.

"He's not here, boss!" Wikert said as he threw down his half-smoked cigarette and cursed.

Panic struck both men and they raised their guns again, this time on high alert. "Let's check the brush! We haven't seen anyone on the roadways!" Henry yelled.

They ran past the horse stable near the roadway and out into the swaying branches of the overgrown woods. They pushed past the initial low branches and into a less dense part. Their breathing became heavy, and labored as they continued on, having already ran to the train station, and back. They yelled Frank's name as they ran, and stopped every so often to listen for a reply. The wind had begun to settle, but was still strong enough to whip their shoulders, and sides with low-hanging branches. The branches left minor cuts on Henry's cheek but his jacket took most of the abuse.

"Boss, wait! I think I hear something," Wikert said in a loud whisper as he fought against the wind to listen. Both men lifted one side of their head to the air as if they were pressing them against a door to hear who was on the other side. They held their breath in unison in anticipation of what they might hear. Finally, rising on the rush of wind, they heard two noises; a horse neigh, and a faint voice yell for help.

"By god, let's go, Wikert," Henry Johns yelled as he rushed forward towards the noise.

They were nearly out of breath, gasping for air as they drew near to the noise. They had stopped yelling Frank's name as they approached. A large bush stood in the center of their path and blocked the view of whomever had been yelling. Henry hoped it was his boy, but the wind made it hard to tell when they first heard it. They crouched behind the bush and listened to the horse neigh again. With guns ready, they rushed out on either side, and entered the scene. Frank was standing there, tugging on the reins of both horses as they stamped the ground.

"Whoa! Whoa!" he yelled at the two bays as he looked over and saw his father standing there with his gun aimed at him. "Look! I found them! I heard them once you two left, and I rushed to grab them. The ornery one kept pulling me further into the woods," Frank said in a cheerful manner.

Wikert took the reins from the boy, and worked to settle the horses as Henry returned his gun to his hip and grabbed his son. Even more exhausted, and ready for the cover of his buggy, Henry Johns and the two boys made their way back to the wagon with the missing horses.

III

A quarter mile down the road, the wind subsided in tandem with their fears, and anxiety. They only had about a half mile ride to the Johns' homestead, so they began to relax. Henry decided to drive the two-horse team back himself. Mr. Wikert was seated next to him and had placed his rifle behind him in the buggy. Even further back, Frank was falling asleep, and waiting for the journey to be over.

"Do you think we've been jumpy for no reason, or do you think we're being followed, and don't know it?" Wikert asked.

"Horses don't just come untied by themselves, chap. Someone definitely untied them, but I don't know why," Henry replied.

"Then why are we going so slow? It makes me nervous!"

"I am aware of your nerves by the constant tapping of your foot, but...I don't think we're being followed. It's an open road for the most part and we'd see someone coming. We're going through Mr. Deemer's farm now. That's our marker for home. We should be fine."

"I know that, sir, it's the hills on either side of us that's got me worried," Wikert answered.

"I don't think now's the time to—!"

Henry's words were muted as he spoke. A rifle gunshot could be heard echoing through the grassy hills, and the horse tied on the left side of the buggy dropped dead, jerking both the other horse, and the buggy to a complete stop. It took a moment for the two men to realize what was happening as a storm of bullets found their place in the grass near the horse's feet or in the buggy itself. Frank was now awake as well, and in full panic.

"Run, boys! There's no telling how many there are! Go into the cornfield, and weave! Don't let them get you!" Henry shouted as a bullet entered the seat cushion between him and Wikert. Another struck the already dead horse, which only scared the one that was alive even more.

Wikert slid out from the seat as Henry tried to return fire but fumbled with his gun. Frank jumped, and Wikert caught him as he stumbled. The two men ran with heads low into the cornfield. Only the tops of the corn could be seen swaying back and forth. More bullets sprayed the corn where they had entered, and Henry hoped they had gotten further away from the fusillade.

As Henry watched the two men run away, he paused from jumping out of the wagon himself. A loud shot ran through the air, and in an instant, he lost his breath. The shot had come from the hill near the roadway and entered his side. It seared through his flesh, and settled in his lung, making it begin to fill with blood. Immediately, it was getting hard to breathe and he knew he had to move quickly. Gunfire was still all around him as he positioned himself to jump. The wooden post near Henry's elbow splintered and shards flew into every direction. Henry's elbow was violently jerked inward as he jumped from the high seat and warm blood ran down his arm. He held in a scream and looked down at the small shreds of meat that hung from his left arm. A few more rounds of buckshot went off and sprayed the air around him. One bullet grazed his chest, and several blew past his cheek, making several cuts along his face.

Henry then fell into the muddy roadway and began to crawl. He thought laying low would be the best way to escape the war above, but his lung was done for, and his elbow hurt like hell. He lay there motionless, blood streaming down his face, side, arm and chest. The gunfire had ceased, and he yelled as loud as he could with one good lung, "You killed me!" and then laid there motionless.

There was no moon out, but light shone upon his face as two men stood over him. He tried his hardest not to blink. Twice, he coughed up a small amount of blood as the two men stood staring at him. About fifteen other men now stood behind these two with a few torches lit.

"Look, Stevenson got him right in the side! There's no way it missed his lung," Hiserodt cried with laughter in his voice.

"And Rice's shot was just as clean! Killed that horse in one shot," said the voice of Deputy Amos Bannigan.

"You would have gotten a cleaner shot, and more than just his elbow if this bastard hadn't jumped," Hiserodt replied, "This son of a gun is either dead, or soon will be! His lung is filling up with blood and will drown this mangy rat! I told you, Henry...I take threats personally," Hiserodt said as he leaned over Henry. He then stood up and turned and whistled, "Let's go, boys!"

Hiserodt, and the dozen or more men snuffed out their torches, mounted up, and galloped away. Henry Johns stayed there for only a moment longer. He knew if he died, no one would be able to free Frank, and Nate, and no one would be able to stop the counterfeiters.

What happened to Frank and Wikert?

He choked on his blood, turned to his good side, and spit it up onto the damp grass. The wind began to blow again and the cool breeze stung his mangled arm.

I have to make it to Sam Deemer's farmhouse, he thought.

Rolling over onto his stomach hurt, but it was the best way to crawl that didn't make him feel like he was drowning. It took every ounce of him to keep going. About every two or three feet, he stopped, and prayed that Frank, or Wikert would double back, and find him. He had no such luck. Leaving behind a trail of blood, he crawled through the open field, and approached the small house. Henry fainted at the doorstep after managing one small knock at the door.

IV

Sam Deemer then found Henry Johns, and took him inside to care for him. The next morning, he returned Johns to his home, where he was cared for by Dr. Potter. The local newspaper wrote an article that they later used to try and frame Finley Rainsbarger, by saying he shot Henry Johns for not helping his brothers, Frank and Nate;

'The shooting, whoever it was done by, was cowardly in the extreme. The fact that Henry Johns is a brother-in-law of the Rainsbargers, is furnishing them money to defend themselves, has said he would clear them if it costs $50,000, had bought and armed them with Winchester rifles, and has said this war has just commenced, and will not end for twenty or thirty years yet, does not warrant men in turning highwaymen, and shooting him down when in the peaceable pursuit of his own business. Let the shooting stop or some parties will find themselves in a tighter box than Frank and Nate Rainsbarger are in.'

-The Eldora Herald

At that time, the remaining Rainsbargers, and their family friends, moved to Henry Johns' farm, and camped in the woods around it for mutual protection. Henry's brother, David Johns, took his wife, Emma, and moved to Cherokee County, near Aurelia, Iowa. Unlike Henry, he feared the Rainsbargers. His children were members of the Vigilance Society and would later testify against Frank and Nate in their upcoming trial.

CHAPTER 14

DETECTIVE MARTIN

I

April 21st, 1885, at the Ellsworth hotel in Eldora, Iowa...

Henry Martin, Federal Agent, and Secret Service detective to the United States Treasury, stood in the gravel of the large roadway, and watched as unsuspecting patrons came, and went in and out of the Ellsworth Hotel. The storm around Eldora was creeping in for the evening, and Detective Martin was already soaked as he stood there and watched dozens of citizens either run into the Ellsworth for shelter, or into a nearby buggy.

Thunder could be heard in the distance and started closing in as he waited. His overcoat hadn't kept the rain out, and his clothes underneath were wet as well. Henry Martin hoped everything in his briefcase was still dry, including the list of names of counterfeiters he had been given by Henry Johns. He knew at least one thing in his case didn't matter if it was wet or not, and he nearly smiled at the thought.

Rain ran off the end of the brim of his hat and the ends of his long mustache. Thunder cracked loudly near the hotel, which made the folks on the road scatter like roaches. The rumble only made Henry stand even more firm. As he watched, two armed men opened the doors to the hotel, and held them open for two women. Under the small canopy near the entry, the women huddled together as an enclosed buggy pulled up, and both women climbed inside. Henry smiled as he watched them leave, a cold, determined smile.

The perfect scene for his plan had panned out before him, and he wasn't going to waste it. Henry gripped his briefcase tighter in his left hand, and made his way to the hotel entrance, which he held open for a man with black hair, and even blacker eyes. The man thanked him for holding the door and walked briskly with a limp towards the direction that the enclosed buggy had come from. Henry watched him for a moment, and then turned to enter the hotel, which had now been turned into a brothel.

Upon entering, there were men, and women both drunk in nearly every corner, and seat. The women were no doubt prostitutes who flooded in from a county over. Nearly everyone had a drink, was gambling, and causing a commotion. Henry Martin didn't seem to mind. The added noise and bothersome patrons would be useful for his intended purpose. He wore a thin smile on his face as he turned from the crowd and headed to the front counter. For the most part, his demeanor was cold, and unwelcoming.

Still dripping wet from the rain, he took his soggy hat off, and after dropping it onto the counter, he said, "F. P. Suydam, checking in ma'am."

At the counter stood a woman who had a few gray hairs in her otherwise dark-toned hair and wore a nice clean dress. Her lips were pressed in as if they were sewn together and she was shaking ever so slightly. She looked up at Henry Martin briefly, but her gaze kept snapping to her right. She was clearly in a rage on the inside about a certain man in the corner who was talking extensively, to whom Henry Martin could only assume, was one of the top prostitutes staying at the Ellsworth hotel.

"Ma'am?" Henry said as a question.

Her gaze snapped back at him, "What kind of name is Suydam? It sounds like a made-up name," she replied sharply. "Are you here for the hussies, too?"

"All names are made up, Mrs...?"

"Deyo," she added, "My husband and I run the Ellsworth," she said as she relaxed a little and shook his hand, "Let me check the reservations, Mr. Suydam."

She then reached under the counter and brought out a large torn-up leather book and slammed it onto the counter. She opened the book where the cloth marker was set and scanned the page for names. While she searched, she asked without looking up, "What brings you to Eldora?"

Henry Martin had brushed back his wet hair and wiped the rain-water on his already-wet pants legs. Standing up straight, he cleared his throat, and answered, "I work for an insurance provider. I'm here to speak with Mrs. Johnson and Mrs. Rainsbarger about the late Enoch Johnson. Are they around?" Of course, he knew they weren't as he had watched the two women moments ago climb into a buggy and ride away, but any reassurance was welcomed.

"You just missed them. Oh, here's your reservation," she said as she scratched off the name and threw the book back to the counter below. She then pulled a bundle of keys out of her dress front pocket and fumbled with them. She kept glaring over at the gentleman talking to the sensual prostitute and cursed under her breath something about the man being a cheating bastard, and something worse about whores. Henry Martin determined that the man must be her husband, Mr. Deyo.

"Uh, ma'am, would it at all be possible to get a room near theirs? It sure would help me a lot. That way I'd be sure not to miss them," he asked, his voice now sounding a little sheepish. "My boss sure would be upset if I didn't get this taken care of in time."

She sighed deep and cursed again under her breath. This time Henry was sure it was in reference to his request. "I have a room available in between theirs. It just became vacant this morning," she replied as she began to run through the key ring to a new set of keys attached to it. Mrs. Deyo then slammed the key down onto the counter top, and slid it over to Henry. It made a light scratch in the wooden top, but she didn't seem to care. Glancing back over at her husband, she did a double-take as this time, he was now seated, and the lady of the night was rubbing his shoulders.

"What in Sam Hill is this? That whore's fixen' to get two black eyes in one night!" she yelled as she stormed away toward them.

Henry Martin didn't wait to see if Mr. Deyo or the woman got the spit beat out of them. He reached over the counter, picked up the remaining keys on the key ring, threw them into his hat, and tossed it back onto its place on his head. With the keys sitting safely on top of his head hidden by his hat, he walked up the thin rickety staircase to the rooms above the saloon. Henry palmed the key Mrs. Deyo had given him and stood facing his room door. The handle and door creaked as he pushed them open. Unnoticed, he entered his room and closed the door behind him. All that could be heard was the noise of the storm and the drunk whoremongers below.

He then walked over to the small wooden table and set his briefcase down. Slowly unhinging the latches, he peeled back the top to see if there was any water damage. He removed his dry clothes from the top and set them aside. All of his papers underneath seemed to be untouched. Shifting some of them to the side, he took out a small hand crank hole auger, and set it down next to the case, then began getting undressed. After he dried himself, he redressed into his dry clothes, but kept his shoes off. Searching for the correct keys for the rooms on either side of him, he found them, tucked them into his shirt pocket, grabbed the auger, and a handkerchief, and placed his ear against the wall that divided his, and one of the women's rooms. He heard nothing from either room.

Martin then peeled back his room door. Peering out into the hallway, he only heard the commotion, and the storm. No one was around. Creeping out of his room, he moved silently to the room to his left. Finding the correct key from his shirt pocket, he quickly opened the door, then entered the room.

There was a single light on in which he could barely see. There was a bed on the opposite wall of the one his room shared, and on the wall that the two rooms *did* share, was an old oil painting with a tear at the bottom corner. Henry walked silently over to the painting and knelt down near the tear. There was no need to be quiet with all of the noise inside and outside of the hotel, but he was used to being a detective; and a good one at that. Silence and discretion were a part of him now.

The tear at the bottom of the painting was rotten by black mold which had created a dark stain in the small corner. Henry thought it was a perfect spot, and taking out his handkerchief, he placed it on the floor below the torn corner. He then removed the small hole auger and set the sharp point into the center of the dark mass of rotten black that filled the tear. With a few quick turns of the hand crank, the auger drilled through the wall flawlessly so that he could see a dim light through it from his room on the other side. Placing the small auger into the handkerchief with the debris from the wall, he then wrapped them up, and exited the room. Moving onto the room to his right, he did the same thing behind a small vase of flowers that was placed on the desk in that room.

Once he had returned to his own domicile, he closed the door, and locked it. Henry then found where the two spy holes were on his side of the walls. One was just above the desk, and another was above his bed. Having poured himself a glass of whiskey, he extinguished the lights in his room, and sat at the desk with his dominant eye pressed against the hole. He could see the bed in the other room perfectly through the auger-made spy hole. Detective Henry Martin sat in the dark and listened to the noises around him. Peering into an empty room, he waited for Nettie to return.

II

April 25th, 1885...

The Den was a large common room inside the Ellsworth hotel that many non-inebriated folks retired to in order to avoid the drunken fights in the barroom. It was a long skinny room with several round tables and chairs, and was brightly lit. Many folks used to bring their families here for a quieter evening dinner, but there were hardly any families left at the Ellsworth. Most folks who came and went were either there for their fix of liquid courage, time with one of the prostitutes, or both. The hotel had become a holding cell for the explicitly deranged. Men, drunk with power, became drunk with the lust of women, and most often than not, it was either with desire for Maggie Johnson, or Nettie Rainsbarger. Tonight was no exception to the usual belligerence.

The Den became the speakeasy for several men at the Ellsworth. Bill Hiserodt, Sheriff Wilcox, Deputy Swain, and Dr. Rittenour entered the room with a drunk man's sway, followed by Mr. Deyo who closed the double doors behind them. Hiserodt limped even more exaggerated than usual to the table in the far corner against the back wall. Mr. Deyo, still holding his drink, plowed his way through the maze of tables, and chairs to join the men, knocking several over on his way. He laughed as he went, unable to even attempt to pick them up. The remaining men chuckled at his demeanor as they embraced their drink of choice and lit their cigars.

"Tonight's the night, men! I think I'll get my evening alone with one of the girls! Of course, they've been had a few times tonight already," Deyo laughed.

"That nosy wife of yours is always around! It'll never happen," Rittenour remarked, taking a sip as he spoke.

Deyo reached into his pocket and took out his room key. Nearly falling over as he reached for it, he threw it over to Dr. Rittenour. "You take the prude tonight, then!" They all laughed a bit, cheersed each other, and settled into their private saloon for the evening. Rittenour never took the key from Deyo as he was not keen on entertaining Deyo's nefarious desires. Cigar smoke began to fill the room as their drinks started to empty.

"Well," Wilcox began, "let's focus on what's at hand before the evening becomes even later. If the Rainsbarger or Johns' cases go to trial, what's the play?"

Hiserodt snuffed out the end of his cigar, and sighed, "If they go to trial, then we go, too. Play the long game, gentlemen! As of this moment, we are not suspected of having a part in anything in the Rainsbarger case. As far as Henry Johns goes...he may meet his end before anyone takes the stand."

Rittenour laughed, "It wasn't hard to get Dr. Potter's kids on board with the Society. He doesn't have a choice now but to ride for the brand. He'll keep us updated on Johns' health."

Wilcox interjected roughly, "Henry Johns is a stubborn mule! He survived the shooting against nearly fifteen men! He may say more than we like. But...reckon we do go to trial for the Rainsbarger boys, who do we have Huff put on the jury? I know it's not up to him, but he knows who to pay off."

After pouring another drink, Hiserodt replied, "Lathrop and Palmer will be on the jury for sure, that much we know."

"I can see to it that Huff does as he's told," Swain added. They all laughed, and cheered again.

"Of that, we all have no doubt," Wilcox said as he slapped Swain on the back, spilling his drink in the process.

The men all downed the rest of their glasses in one go and slammed them on the table. Looking the men over, one by one, Rittenour leaned in and loudly whispered, "I want to know...who *actually* killed Enoch Johnson?"

Hiserodt smiled a small smile behind his black beard, and glanced over to Wilcox, who looked like he knew a secret. Hiserodt leaned in and mimicking Rittenour's whisper said, "Why, who else but Frank, and Nate Rainsbarger, of course!"

The men erupted with laughter and stood up to join the men of less wickedness than themselves back in the barroom. Mr. Deyo grabbed his room key and threw it across the empty room. "I'm going to go find Maggie," he said as he swayed towards the doors, a little less than before.

Hiserodt called after him, "See about finding Nettie, she has a little more life in her!"

The sounds of the men's laughter dissipated as they all exited the Den and closed the doors behind them. The sounds of the evening's debauchery were the only thing left that Henry Martin could hear through the vent at the lower end of the wall. He had heard and notated the conversation from the small room on the other side of the vent that was near the table the men had been seated at. He had several other entries pertaining to Nettie's letter in the newspaper, the Rainsbargers being a gang, and local terrorists, that they killed Enoch Johnson, and that they shot Henry Johns.

Henry Martin looked down at his brief notes of the conversation he just heard.

'Deyo Wilcox Swane Hisroudt Rittenour in a conference room known as the den. Lathrop and Palmer to be on the grand jury; cigars and whiskey in quantities; conversation low; the names of Johns and Rainsbarger often repeated'

III

April 27th, 1885...

Detective Martin held his breath as he lay on his chest on his bed, face pressed against the wall, and the hole that was in it. He could see Ash Noyes, and the state's attorney, Mr. Huff, on the other side speaking quietly with Maggie Johnson. Martin froze as Maggie had picked up and moved the flowers that were obstructing the view of the auger hole. Now he risked exposure. He couldn't hear what they were discussing, but decided he'd wait and try to listen anyway. After a few minutes, Huff opened the room door, and he, and Mr. Noyes exited. Henry waited a few seconds before exiting his room as well with a newspaper in hand. He pretended to read it as he followed a few paces behind the men, down the stairs, and towards the hotel's front doors.

The doors were propped open to let in the cool morning air, which was quiet, and refreshing. There weren't many folks out on the road even though several people were migrating to Eldora for the Rainsbarger's hearing. Many folks were still asleep, fighting off whatever damage they had done to themselves the night before. The sun was barely up and hadn't even begun to thaw the cool air. Noyes leaned up against one door and folded his arms as he looked out at the near empty street. Huff leaned up against the other one, finishing his coffee out of a small tin cup. Both men sighed and seemed nervous to Martin, who was now seated at the counter near the entrance, still pretending to read his paper.

"You know, this all would go a little easier for us if we could get ahold of the statement Enoch had made to them federal agents, but damn! I can't even get a copy of it," Huff said in a calm, yet irritated voice.

Noyes laughed a little as he turned to see a two-horse team buggy approach the hotel, "Damn the statement! We can break down all statements," he said as the buggy came to a halt.

"Good morning, gentlemen," Hiserodt said from the buggy seat as he pretended to tip his hat.

"Mornin', Bill," Huff replied. There was a pause as they both looked at Ash Noyes. He hadn't answered him. Instead, he was now in the roadway, and staring down towards the other end of the street. Three single horse riders had entered town with the sun at their backs, making them appear as silhouettes on the horizon.

Noyes brought a hand up to his forehead to shield his eyes from the rising sun, "Well I'll be damned. Take a look at this," he said as he pointed towards the riders. Noyes had begun to walk quickly towards the men who were now off their horses and hitching them to the post out front of the City Hotel, which was only six buildings down from the Ellsworth. Huff had climbed into the buggy with Black Bill, and they kept an even pace behind Noyes.

Two men had already entered the hotel, but the one remaining outside made Noyes' ears red, and caused his hand to clench the butt of his gun. What he saw was a thin, fairly short man, with matted oily hair. He had a large hat on that hid most of it. He was dressed in an array of objects that made him look every bit as an outlaw, and leader of the scum world of petty gangs. The most notable gear of a desperado he wore was his gun and large dirk on either side of him.

Huff leaned in closer to Hiserodt in the buggy and asked, "Who's that fellow who looks ready for a shootout?"

Hiserodt gritted his teeth, and replied, "That's Finley *f**king* Rainsbarger, and he's as savage as a meataxe! The worst of the Rainsbarger renegades!"

Finley noticed them briefly, just watching him. He didn't acknowledge the men. He simply watched them back, and then entered the hotel with one hand on his gun, and the other on his knife hilt. His gaze made Huff shudder, and Hiserodt curse under his breath, teeth still gritted together.

"What do we do now? Who is he with?" Noyes asked to no one in particular.

Hiserodt jumped down from his buggy seat and in a panic replied, "There's only one way to find out! Stay here with the buggy, Mr. Huff! Noyes, come with me!"

"Mr. Hiserodt," Huff called, "I know the two men! The taller one is Justice Harrington, and the other is Detective S. T. Waterman, but why they're here, I haven't got the faintest idea. They're not a part of the trial."

Hiserodt nodded in acknowledgement, and then the two men ran the rest of the way down the road to the front of the hotel. Peering into the front glass, they could see the men had already checked in, and were most likely in their rooms. "I wonder what they are doing here," Bill said, sucking in gulps of cool air, and rubbing his bad knee.

"You think it has anything to do with Henry Johns?" Noyes asked.

Hiserodt spat and replied, "If that's the case, then the jaws of the penitentiary are opening wider than I thought. Let's go and see if something can't be done about their stay."

The two men entered the hotel into the small main lobby. A tiny bell rang above their heads as they entered, which drew the attention of the man at the counter. "Good morning, gentlemen–," the man began.

"Stow it! I don't give a spit about who you are or your formalities. Three men! They just entered here for a stay! One of them looked like he would scare the scalp off of Jesse James himself! They need to hitch their wagon, and head for the border, if you catch what I mean," Hiserodt sneered, placing his revolver on the counter top, aimed at the heavyset man on the other side.

Noyes stepped up with his knife out, and demanded, "Throw them out, you mangy mudsill! They're only here to cause trouble for the courts!"

"That's right! They aren't a part of this case! Throw them out! If not, you'll go down with them!" Bill finished.

"Well, that's going to be a problem, gentleman," the man said as he wiped sweat from his forehead. Being overweight made the man wheeze in a normal conversation, but now he was being threatened, and wheezed even deeper. As Hiserodt and Noyes exchanged glances, the man pulled his hand up from the counter underneath, pulling out a double-barrel shotgun. Aiming it at the two men, he replied, still wheezing through each breath, "I saw you two boys peeking your heads about my window before you entered. I figured you'd be trouble! I already agreed to board them, and there's no getting out of it! Now, beat it, you yellow belly maggots!"

He held the gun firm on them as they backed out of the hotel like two dogs that had been scolded by their owner for pissing on the floor. As they were nearly out of the hotel, Hiserodt spotted Finley leaning over the upstairs rail near his room. He was smiling as he watched. Hiserodt became infuriated, and even more so when Finley, with his thumb pointed up and his index finger out, mimicked shooting Hiserodt with a gun, over and over.

Back at the buggy, halfway up the road where they left it, and Huff, Hiserodt kicked the dirt, and yelled. His hat fell off, and he nearly fell on his rear as he did it. His bad knee told him his tantrum was too much for it. He regained himself and climbed back into the buggy seat.

"Rumor is, Finley already threatened Maggie, and Nettie. We need to keep him away," Noyes said after a long moment of silence.

"We can't get him kicked out of the City Hotel, but we sure as hell can keep him out of the Ellsworth," Bill remarked as he whipped the horse's reins and turned the buggy back towards the Ellsworth hotel.

He looked back at Huff and barked, "We need to settle this once and for all! Get me the doctor and Wilcox!"

None of them saw Henry Martin seated on the bench across from the City Hotel.

IV

Unknown to the counterfeiters at the time, Henry Johns had hired the two men, and requested both men to come from Marshalltown to meet him while he was recovering. He hired Detective Stanton Waterman to look into the counterfeit gang to help free Frank, and Nate, and had requested Justice Harrington to come, and take his statement on who shot him.

After seeing the three men enter town, Hiserodt placed one of his gunmen at the Ellsworth hotel's front doors with orders to *'shoot any strangers seen prowling around the Ellsworth at night.'*

V

On April 28th, Agent Martin heard Hiserodt tell Leyman Wisner in the hall at the Ellsworth hotel, "We have to get those god d**n son of a b**ches one way or another."

Wisner replied, "We can't let this go on this way; money is no object if that will do it. If not, we will take the law into our own hands."

Wisner was the first real banker in Hardin County and owned most of the land there. He had used dishonest means and people's misfortunes who were displaced by the war, to gain ownership of the land. History will try to show Leyman Wisner as a reputable man with honor who helped build Hardin County, but the reality is that he was a thief, and a liar who used people for his benefit.

His dishonest gain of the land earned him the nickname the 'Land Pirate'. Since the war with the Rainsbargers, he was losing money, as he wasn't able to sell any land. No one wanted to move to Hardin county.

On April 29th, 1885, Henry Martin saw the judge for the Rainsbarg-ers trial, Judge Henderson, having sex with Maggie Johnson through the carved hole in the wall. That same day, the Eldora Herald printed an article mocking the situation Eldora faced...

'Eldora is just now being honored by the presence of two detectives. They are stopping at the City Hotel and are registered as No.s 1 and 2. You fellows who shot the horse Fin Rainsbarger was riding on better fess up and ask the leniency of the court. You who scared poor Bill Rainsbarger out of his boots better do like Judas and go hang yourselves; and you follow-ers of Jesse James who filled poor Henry Johns cuticle full of buckshot better deliver yourselves up at once, for there are two detectives on your track.

The boys about town will please not do any shooting near town or along the roads over which the gang may pass, for their nerves are not very strong.'

On April 30th, Martin wrote a brief entry into his notebook, "*The gang had a rousing time in the rooms of Net and Mag.*"

By the end of April, the Eldora Herald said that there were hun-dreds of vigilantes thirsting for Rainsbarger blood. At that time, Frank and Nate were brought back to Eldora to be officially indicted for the murder of Enoch Johnson. Henry Johns, still recovering from his wounds, hired four detectives to ride to and from Marshalltown with them for protection.

VI

May 1st, 1885...

Seated next to the kitchen's double doors that led into the Den, Henry Martin sat alone reading over his notes, and drinking his morn-ing coffee. He had several pages of conversations he had overheard, most of which pertained to the Rainsbarger family, and not the counterfeit-ers. His guise, while at the Ellsworth, was an insurance consultant for Nettie and Maggie, both of whom he had yet to speak with. Unknown to all he did meet, he was actually there to gain information to convict the counterfeit members. So far, he had gained little to no evidence. The talk amongst those in Eldora was about the arrival of the two brothers arrested for murder, and their upcoming trial. Counterfeiters, murderers, a society up in arms; all of it sounded like a tall tale, and yet it was unfolding around Henry every day. He was still making sense of the connections between them all, and felt unsettled, wondering if he should ever find the truth.

Were the men truly murderers? He thought not, but he could see how many folks would believe it. One of the oldest Rainsbarger brothers, Finley, had a picture taken of himself holding his gun and large dirk. Henry thought he must have been proud of the intimidation that his presence brought as he then sent the photo to witnesses who were to testify in the upcoming trial. Henry Martin shook his head, letting out a small laugh as he thought about the ridiculous picture.

While he was still smirking, he heard a loud crash behind the double doors that led into the kitchen, and shortly after, three women erupted from the door, and into the Den. Mrs. Deyo was the first through the door, followed by two younger women. Her face was buried in her hands, and she was sobbing uncontrollably.

"My god, Eva, what will happen next? They have made this a den of murder and now they have turned it into a whore house! God deliver me from this!" Mrs. Deyo cried, nearly screaming.

She then turned and ran away from the two women out the two doors that led back into the barroom portion of the hotel. Eva ran after her crying, "Mrs. Deyo! Mrs. Deyo, wait!"

The remaining woman stared at the double doors as they swung closed and settled back into their resting position. She wore a long apron that was riddled with small food stains. She brushed her hair back from her face and turned to return to the kitchen from which she had just rushed out of. As she turned, she viewed Henry sitting by himself watching her. She smiled a smile that said, *I hope he didn't see all of that.* She then approached Henry and said, "My apologies for the commotion, Mr...?"

"Suydam," Henry replied as he reached out his hand to shake hers.

"It's nice to meet you! I am the hotel's cook, Mrs. Alice Finley," she replied. "Is there anything else I can get you?"

He leaned in a little, and said, "Can I ask, if you don't mind, what is wrong with Mrs. Deyo?"

Alice bit her lower lip, and looked around a little nervously, "It may not be the best idea if I speak on her behalf."

"Well," Henry began, leaning in closer, "if it has anything to do with Maggie or Nettie, I'd sure like to know. I'm here for insurance purposes for the family. Please tell me, and don't try to stretch the blanket," he finished jokingly.

Looking at Alice, he could tell she was confused by his statement, but also intrigued. She knelt down on the other side of the two-seat table and put her chin in the palms of her hands to listen to him. He chuckled briefly, and she smiled back, "It means don't lie."

Alice made a face that said, *I would never!* Henry could tell she liked to gossip, and hoped she would be of some help. "I know Maggie Johnson! I went to school with Net. She was an awful liar! She's the one that was in bed with Mr. Stevens last night! Mag was in the room with the judge last night and broke down the bed," she snickered.

"So, you're saying that Nettie is sleeping with her attorney, and Maggie is sleeping with the judge for the case?" Henry asked.

"They're sleeping with them, and about half of Hardin County!"

"I suppose that's what I heard last night. My room shares a wall with Maggie's," he said, trying to act as if he didn't *see* the bed break through the hole in the wall.

"I and Eva have seen some awful things in this house in the past few months. I would not stay here an hour, but for Mrs. Deyo, I am sorry for her! She can't help herself...," she trailed off.

"I've heard a good number of things myself. Is it all bad?" he asked in a tone that said to Alice, *tell me more.*

Alice's face became that of an overzealous girl, ready to embrace her wild nature but unsure of how to do so. She leaned in a little closer to Henry, and whispered, "I and Eva had lots of fun watching the Den.

When the bunch would be here night after night, drinking and smoking, seeing them all tip toe in and out of Mag's room," she said as she walked her two fingers across the tabletop to demonstrate tip toeing.

"I see. Anyone in particular?" he asked.

"Just the usuals...all the big bugs of the town," she said with a smile.

Henry smiled, and leaned back into his chair, "Well, thank you for sharing, Mrs. Finley," he said as he thought about all that she had just shared. "That certainly clears a few things up for me."

She then stood up, gave her appreciation for his time, and headed back towards the kitchen. When she reached the two doors, she paused, "Are you going to be here long? I never see you go into either of their rooms," she asked.

Henry Martin laughed at her comment and replied, "No, I'll be leaving as soon as possible. I try to be an honest man in a rather dishonest time." He then stood up, collected his things, tilted his hat to her, thanked her again, and left her alone in the Den.

VII

That same day, Henry Martin met with Enoch Johnson's old horse thief friend, Nate Thompson, in the town square. He told Martin, "*We don't hear anymore about Johnson turning state's evidence and accusing of the leading businessmen here and Steamboat Rock of being in with him in that counterfeit deal at Goldfield. The vigilant gang is now trying to stick the Rainsbarger boys for murder.*"

Henry Martin then packed his belongings and left town. Frank and Nate were then transferred back to Marshalltown to await a change in venue, since Eldora was steeped in prejudice against them. Several threats had been made to capture them and lynch them before a trial could take place.

CHAPTER 15

HANG THEM HIGH, HANG THEM ALL

I

Beginning of May, 1885, at the home of Henry Johns...

The weather was cool enough in the evening to bring about a sense of refreshment to those encamped around the Johns' homestead. The days were starting to become warmer, but not enough to be considered hot. There was barely anyone left encamped around the property to feel the change. Most folks now sided with the riotous voice of the real criminals of Hardin County and had moved on.

Henry Wikert sat on the front porch as the four riders entered through the tree line at the edge of the property. On any other day, Wikert would have shot a warning shot into the dirt in front of any rider approaching the house, but today, the man on the far-left end was William Rainsbarger, a trusted member of the Johns family. Wikert smiled at the sight, rang the bell on the front porch, and yelled, "They're here, boss! I'll bring them in, in just a moment."

"Good evening, Henry," William said as he jumped down from his horse and tied it to the front rail.

The three other men did likewise as Wikert replied his greeting to William. The men looked around and noticed several folks appearing through the timber around the property. Some of which were dressed as men but looked no older than teenage boys. Every one of them was armed. William saw them noticing the boys and warned, "They're all mine and Henry's sons, and if you thought taming a wild horse gave you a beating, I wouldn't recommend starting in with any of them boys. They're good kids, but they're just that, kids, having to grow up years in a matter of months, and it ain't fair."

"I suppose not," Waterman replied, in a voice that sounded as if he understood their pain.

Wikert spoke up, "Mr. Johns is waiting for you, men. We should head inside." They all followed him inside the quaint house and down a hallway that led to a bedroom. He knocked on the door and put his ear to it to listen for a reply. While he waited, a short man came to the door, and joined them in the hall.

"Hello, Dr. Potter," William said, "How is Henry doing today?"

"Henry is doing exceptionally better! He is still weak but healing well. The lung which took the bullet is the biggest concern right now. His arm and face may scar, but they're mostly healed now; well, they're stitched, and closed anyhow. He is ready for you."

Wikert slowly pushed open the door and guided the men inside. After doing so, he turned and left the room. Henry Johns was sitting in a large bed in a dim room. He looked tired and yet in good health. Seated on either side of the bed was his wife, Martha, and his son, Frank. Upon seeing the men enter, Henry sat upright in the bed and greeted them, "Thank you men for coming, and thank you, William, for bringing them."

William was happy to see Henry, but his heart was heavy. He sighed deeply and everyone looked at him. "Martha, you and the boy look tired. Why don't you two go on out, and get something to eat, and maybe some rest," he said. Martha didn't dare look away from Henry. She was holding his hand and rubbing it gently. William could see she was crying and couldn't bring herself to speak.

"It's alright, dear," Henry finally said, "Please do as your brother asks, at least for the boy's sake." She shook her head and rubbed his cheek where his scars would form once he was healed. Without saying anything, she took Frank by the hand and left the room. Frank hadn't cried, but all could tell he was burdened by the assault on his father, and himself.

Henry tried to sit up a bit more, but it was difficult with his arm in a sling. William gave a small laugh as Henry cursed at the pillow for moving out from under him, then laughed a bit himself. They had all been through so much hate, and prejudice that William cherished the moments that still made him feel human, or any other feeling, other than fear for his family's life. Even with the growing violence surrounding them, the Rainsbargers wouldn't leave. They weren't cowards, and even if they were, they couldn't leave Henry in this state. They couldn't leave Frank and Nate to suffer, and rot away, either.

"Henry," he said in a quiet voice, "as you are surely aware, these are the two men you hired, Detective Waterman, and Justice Harrington. This gentleman who is joining us, is Constable Clark. He will be another witness today and file your statement with the county clerk's office." All the men greeted Henry with a; *nice to meet you, glad to see you doing well*, and a handshake with the working hand.

"Thank you all again for coming! I hope the journey from Marshalltown wasn't too bad. You never know what the weather will do this time of year. How are Frank and Nate holding up?" Henry asked.

"To be honest, they're getting anxious, like a caged lion that paces back and forth, waiting to be released," Waterman said as he shook his head to show his disapproval of the situation. "I'll visit them again in a week, or so and give them an update on the case, as well as your current state. The Lord knows they're dying to know."

"It's my understanding that you know who attacked you. Are you ready to make a statement, Mr. Johns? I fear that whoever did this knows by now that you are alive and that they will retaliate. We should get a statement filed as soon as possible," Harrington said.

Henry cleared his throat, "I heard them all, but there were a few voices I recognized. James Rice shot my horse out from under us as we went. A man named John Stevenson is the one who got me in the side where the damn bullet entered my lung," he winced as he said it, "and Deputy Amos Bannigan is the bastard who shredded my arm."

Henry coughed a bit from talking so much with a damaged lung. Justice Harrington wrote down everything frantically as Henry spoke. He hoped to get it all to avoid having Henry repeat what he said.

"Was there anyone else there that you know of?" Waterman asked.

"Ash Noyes, and Charles Marx were also among the men who shot at me. Bill Hiserodt and Amos stood over me as I lay there pretending to be dead. That's all I know for sure, but I'd also like to go on record that there has to be an inner circle to the Vigilance committee that's run by the counterfeiters! Their motives are too connected!"

"How many men did you say there were?" William replied.

"I'd say about a dozen or so, maybe more."

Constable Clark removed his hat and let out a small chuckle, "Damn, Henry, you're lucky to be alive!"

Henry smiled, "I am grateful there's not a sharpshooter in their bunch! I'm even more grateful that Frank and Wikert were okay."

"So what do we do now, doc?" William asked. Everyone looked around at each other with a confused look.

"I could have sworn the doctor came in with the rest of you," Henry said, "Where is Dr. Potter—?"

As Henry finished his question, there was a crash from the other room, and a scream followed by another sound of heavy footsteps, and the clatter of the front door being shoved open. William and Constable Clark exchanged a nervous glance and ran out of the room with their guns drawn. Detective Waterman stayed in the room with Henry and Mr. Harrington. Upon reaching the main room, the two men saw a broken chair, and the front door open. With one look at Martha, who was cowering behind the kitchen counter, William was directed to the front door.

"The doctor! Something fell out of his pocket and Wikert saw! When he asked what it was, he hit Wikert over the head with a chair, and ran outside!" Frank yelled as he joined Martha in pointing towards the front door.

William ran towards the open door as he heard gunshots ring through the valley. Clark walked over to the broken chair and picked

THE RAINSBARGER BROTHERS – 163

up a small vial, tucking it away into his breast pocket. He then joined William outside who was staring into the dense woods to the right of the property. The young men stopped their gunfire and started the long run into the timber.

"The doctor, he hit me and ran! The pigeon-livered son of a gun ran into the woods!" Wikert yelled as they all ceased their firing.

"The woods drop off from there. If he made it to the woods, he would be gone by now. He would have gone down the slope and missed the barrage of bullets," William said. "What did he drop that caused all of this?"

The Constable and Frank joined them outside as William asked his question. Clark reached into his pocket and pulled the vial out, "He dropped this," he said as he handed it over to William.

"What is it?"

"I don't know, but perhaps Henry will. Let's go find out," Clark said as they all ran back to the room, following behind him.

Waterman had stowed his gun back in its holster as they entered the room, and gave them all a look that, to William said, *what the hell was that about?* No one answered Waterman's look as they rushed in.

"Henry, this was found on Dr. Potter," Clark said while holding up the small glass jar. "When it was discovered, he assaulted your hired man, and ran for it. What's in it?"

"I don't rightly know, chap, but it did have a substance in it that he would often rub on the wound in my side. I don't know the name of what was in it, but I assumed it was medicine," Henry said.

William rushed to his side, "Sit up, Henry, and let me see your side," he said while wiping his sweat with his sleeve. "Mr. Harrington, please come look at this," William added, while holding Henry's shirt up on one side.

There was a small hole on the side of Henry that was green looking and had started to puss. "Shit! That's not medicine, Henry! Whatever he's been applying has infected the wound to your lung! How long has he been applying it?" Harrington howled.

"At least a few days, *probably* since the day it happened. What do we do now?" Henry asked in a worried tone.

"We get you a new doctor!" Wikert yelled as he stormed out of the room. Wikert threw on his coat and grabbed his rifle from the sitting room in which he had just been attacked. While everyone in the room prayed for Henry Johns, the sound of Wikert's horse pounding the thick grass at full speed could be heard as he rode into the night.

II

When Henry Johns' health took a turn for the worst, Dr. Morse was called to examine him. He found unmistakable evidence that Johns was poisoned. Henry Johns then took several opiate pills that had been left by his bedside table to ease his condition. He spent his last few days alive in pure delirium.

A man named Homer Jones stated that he was lying near the road, a mere thirty feet away from the attack and knew everyone that had shot at Henry. He was not taken seriously, and his statement was never filed.

III

May 13th, 1885, at the jail in Marshalltown, Iowa...

Detective Stanton Waterman was led into a small room with a table and chairs. They barely fit into the brick room, and it made him begin to feel claustrophobic. The Marshalltown County jail was more welcoming than most jails that Waterman had visited, nonetheless, it was still as cold as any other. Prisons, and jail houses were cages for human beings, and the idea of being trapped in one made Waterman shutter.

The warden had guided him to the small meeting room and promptly closed the door. As he waited for the two men to arrive, he took two newspapers out of his briefcase, and placed them on the table. Waterman knew the brothers were expecting Henry Johns to make a full recovery, and for him to show up today. They would surely want answers about his absence. As he turned the newspapers to the articles that he wanted to show them, he heard the door on the opposite side of the room begin to unlock. Keys rattled, and the door was pushed open. Two men in oversized striped clothes entered the room. The two men looked happy to not be entering the room in handcuffs, but their smiles were lost in a look of dismay as they realized they were not meeting their brother-in-law. Frank Rainsbarger looked saddened by the fact, and Nate looked angry. Neither man said anything as they sat down.

"Hello, gentleman! How are you holding up?" Waterman asked.

"Where's Henry?" was Frank's quiet reply.

Stanton didn't reply right away, nor did he look either man in the eye. He sighed and sat back in his chair. He swallowed hard and cleared his throat. Everything about his body language made Frank and Nate even more nervous. Finally, he spoke, "We'll get to that."

"We'll get to that now! We were told he was recovering and would come," Nate said in a frustrated tone.

Waterman shifted in his seat, and looking them in the eyes, he then finally spoke the words they dreaded to hear, "Henry died last week." Neither brother said anything at all. Nate looked shocked, and Frank began to cry. Now it was their turn to not make eye contact with Waterman. "I held off the newspapers from reaching you until I could come and tell you myself," Waterman said in a tone that spoke to the defeat he felt.

"How could he die?" Frank asked, "He was supposed to recover!" he yelled as he hit the tabletop.

"There's no freeing us now," Nate remarked.

Waterman replied as the brothers consoled each other, "The wound to his lung...it got infected. He fell into a coma about a week later, and he passed away at home. We are determined to investigate the assault, and his death." He shifted in his chair again and exhaled long and hard.

Nate sat more upright and stared at the detective. "Why his death, also? You said he died from an infection from the assault," he asked.

"Well...we aren't sure how he got the gangrene, especially since he was on the mend. Dr. Potter dropped a small vial that his hired man found. The doctor had been applying whatever was in it for days prior to the coma. We assume that's how the gangrene started!"

"You mean he was poisoned? Will this prejudice against us never end?" Frank yelled.

"We don't know for sure, what we do know, is Dr. Potter has a few boys, and it looks like they're a part of the vigilante gang. He may have been threatened...," he trailed off and sighed. "Anyway," he continued, "your attorneys, Mr. Weaver and Mr. Albrook, will be meeting with you when I leave the room. I requested that they give us a moment to speak in regard to your brother-in-law first."

At their names, Frank now sat up, "Are they going to help us get separate trials like we requested?" he asked as he wiped his eyes with his sleeve.

"I should let them go over those particulars with you, but as far as I'm aware, you were granted separate trials. Unfortunately, we still don't know when," he answered.

"Thank you! We are grateful to you all for pleading our innocence," Nate remarked.

"Detective...Nettie never sent me the photo of Zella that I requested. Is there a way to get one?" Frank asked, the tears in his eyes began to swell again and this time they fell. "How is my little girl? I can't be here without seeing her face again...please!"

Nate held Frank as he mourned the loss of his brother-in-law and the idea of never seeing his daughter again. Nate began to tear up again as well and stared at Waterman. "Please, help us! We're innocent men and will maintain this resolve until we're declared as such. There's no way to link us to this murder," he said, "Enoch was my friend! Don't you have the names Enoch gave?!"

Stanton Waterman had previously felt defeated but the brothers' resolution for justice and their freedom gave him new confidence. He had become a detective of the United States government for the pursuit of justice.

"I am sorry to say that I don't have one Frank, and I'm not sure how I would get one either. Maggie and Nettie are still held up in the

Ellsworth Hotel, which is now guarded. Effie and Zella now stay with Maggie's parents away from the hotel...but...I'll see what we can do. I'll keep investigating the counterfeiters as Henry hired me to do. We are working towards finding incriminating evidence against anyone on the list Johnson gave us, but we've had no such luck as of yet. Your day in court will be up to your attorneys, who are most likely getting anxious to speak with you."

Nate chuckled, "The folks of Eldora sure are in quite an uproar over a man whose death they celebrated!"

"That they are, and unfortunately, they blamed you all. Someone has the whole town, and everyone else in a frenzy. No one mentions that even though you're both sitting here, the counterfeit money hasn't stopped circulating. Johns' attorney, Mr. Robertson, says that he was close to finishing his indictment of the gang, but who truly knows?"

"Why are you still helping us, now that Henry is gone? Who's keeping you on?" Frank asked.

Waterman laughed a little and smiled, "I thought you knew! Your oldest brother, William, he's keeping the investigation going, and unfortunately...my time with you is up, gentleman," he said as he looked at his watch. "One last thing! I brought these two newspapers with me for you to see. One of them is from this morning. I hear you're collecting articles already, Nate...these might not be ones you want to keep."

Waterman then stood up with his briefcase and left the room, assuring the men that he would send in their attorneys shortly. As the door closed, Nate took both news articles and read them to himself. The first article stated that it was a well-known fact that Henry Johns lived in constant fear of the Rainsbargers. The second article said that Finley Rainsbarger was seen on Monday morning carrying a large knife and revolver near the home of Henry Johns, insinuating that he had killed Henry.

The war against the Rainsbargers continued in a full flood of rage and hate. With their case preparing for trial, both men wondered what the true criminals of Hardin County would do next to rid the people of their family.

IV

May 15th, 1885, at the Schoolhouse in Steamboat Rock...

"I appreciate your time and you coming along with me, doctor," Rittenour said as he pulled his buggy to a halt just outside the schoolhouse.

Dr. Underwood had heard of the Vigilance Society, but he was never a part of their inner circle. He wondered why Rittenour had invited him along this evening. At first, he was concerned at the cause, but now found himself delighted in the idea of aiding in the exodus of the Rainsbargers from the county. In his private time, he often referred to the group as the 'Vengeance Society'. Even so, Underwood viewed the Rainsbargers with as much disdain as nearly everyone else in the county. He especially had a distaste for Frank after their meeting over the insurance policy. Still...he wondered why they invited him in *now*.

"Doctor, who runs these meetings, and why was I asked to accompany you here tonight?" he asked in a matter-of-fact way.

"Well, Sheriff Wilcox originally gathered the men to aid him in the preservation of our small towns. Nearly everyone in Steamboat Rock, and Eldora had something stolen from them, whether it was small objects, or livestock. The horse association wasn't able to handle the crime spree on their own."

"So, what does that have to do with me?" Underwood asked.

"Wilcox and Hiserodt need your help with something, I don't know what, they don't tell me nearly anything. After the meeting, they'd like to have a word. But seeing as we're here and the meeting is starting, we should head inside," Rittenour said, jumping down from the buggy, and waving his arm, indicating for Underwood to follow him.

Upon entering the schoolhouse, Underwood could see a wave of men with torches and weapons. They seemed calmer than usual to Rittenour, but the meeting was only starting. Wilcox interrupted the room full of men as usual, with his arms raised and a loud shout. The mob was beginning to start their uproar, but since Wilcox had to fire a shot to calm the crowds previously, they laid an ear to his shout so as to not have to repeat the method.

"Evening, men! We again meet to work towards the continued progress of our preservation of family and community! There's been a rumor about a plot to kill the free Rainsbarger brothers! I can tell you that no such rumors are true, and the county militia has been told to stand down!"

Angry shouts about making the rumors true rang like pure beauty to Wilcox's ears, and Hiserodt tried to hide his smile, but was unable. Both men had become so intoxicated by these men's fear and hate, that they lavished every shout of murder.

Wilcox continued, "No one is seeking revenge for the death of Henry Johns, which we know the brothers are responsible for! Rest assured men, they will be brought to justice! Right now, we don't have enough men to infiltrate their fortress near the Johns' homestead!"

Hiserodt interjected, "They have surrounded his home after their assault on his life in an attempt to keep Mr. Johns quiet, much like how Frank and Nate took in Enoch Johnson after his release. Both men have died at the hands of these scum!"

"They forced Henry Johns to falsify his statement," Wilcox said. "The statement in question incriminates several respected men of our community and society! Furthermore, it claims that we have an inner circle of men, run by elites, who are actual members of the counterfeiting ring!" There was noise of more angry shouts, a broken bottle, and men shoving one another. Most men laughed at the idea, but others were desperately infuriated.

Deputy Swain stepped forward, holding up the statement that was filed by Constable Clark. "This here statement names the respectable Mr. Hiserodt, loyal Deputy Bannigan, James Rice, Charles Marx, John Stevenson, and several others as the would-be assassins!" Swain shouted. Now nearly all men laughed in unison instead of listening to their anxiety. There were shouts claiming the statement to be ridiculous, and that the Rainsbargers would do anything to call good men evil and evil men good! Swain then leaned over to the nearest torch to himself and lit the corner of the statement on fire. "Let all such lying filth die right now!" All the men cheered in agreement with the idea.

Underwood watched all of this unfold and was shocked to see such *evidence* against the men. The extent of the Rainsbarger's involvement in stopping the indictment to the counterfeiting ring only aided his suspicions that the brothers were all involved. Underwood's heart pounded hard as he became enamored by the speech, and order of men who had shown up. A mob was formed but was yet to march upon their enemy. As he watched, in pure fascination, he wondered what part he would play.

Wilcox gave the closing call to the meeting, and nearly all men shouted back, "Hang them high; hang them all," and dispersed.

Rittenour leaned into Underwood and told him to wait. As the men left in hoards, Wilcox and Hiserodt came forward and greeted him. He shook each man's hand and still stood there in disbelief at what he had just witnessed.

"If I would have known the extent to which the society's arm would reach, I would have tried to join long ago," he said at last. Hiserodt laughed and removed his hat. Wilcox handed each man a small glass and then drank his quickly. "The doctor here said you requested to see me this evening! How can I be of service?" Underwood asked as he took a drink.

"Service! I like the sound of that! That's exactly what we need," Wilcox said. "Them boys are laying in a closed coffin, but we need someone to help lower the bastards into the ground, so-to-speak."

"What did you have in mind?"

"Well," Hiserodt chimed in, "We try to do things as honestly as possible, but nothing ever seems to stick to those boys! They always walk away, but this time, two men have been murdered, and we can't let this pass! We aren't asking you to help us harm anyone, but rather to incriminate them further, and as the Sheriff puts it, help slide their coffins into the ground. Seeing that you are a key member of the trial and possess the most incriminating evidence to testify with, we're coming to you for help."

Underwood smiled a creepy smile through his thick beard, and mustache, finished his drink, and replied, "Let's bury them, then!"

V

The Western House Hotel and Saloon, May, 1885...

The hotel was wild with enough drunk Vigilance Society members to rival the onslaught of lawlessness at the Ellsworth. Maggie Johnson, and William Hiserodt stood on the upstairs balcony near his office door, watching the frenzy below.

They saw several angry patrons stand on top of the saloons' wooden tables making blood-thirsty declarations about how to disband the Rainsbarger brothers. Many declared they would steal their own cattle, and hide them in Henry Finster's cave. Others vowed to shoot, or maim their own cattle, or even burn their haystacks. All men agreed to report that the Rainsbargers and their sons were responsible.

Maggie and Black Bill cheersed each other and Maggie declared, "To Enoch!"

Bill laughed and replied, "Peace to his ashes!"

VI

Just outside Irvine Liesure's store in Abbott...

"What do you want me to do with the rest of these boxes, old man?" Dan Turner shouted from the back of the store.

"Put them in the back of the wagon with the rest of it," Irvine yelled in reply.

After he had finished loading the wagon, Dan Turner joined Irvine inside his empty general store. Both men were hot and reeked of sweat and humidity. "That should be the last of it. What are you doing with everything, anyways, moving stores?" Dan asked.

Irvine laughed quietly to himself and looked around at the empty shelves, "Something like that. Thanks again for the help, Dan! You're a good Mayor! A real man of the people!"

Dan smiled and said, "I do what I can, but sometimes it's not much."

"Well...perhaps today you can do some good and not let your alms be done in public," Irvine said as he winked at Dan.

Dan gave him a confused look as Irvine reached under the counter, took out two small jugs, and handed one to Dan. "Those Rainsbargers need to be put down," he said as he began to take the lid off of the container. "They're fixing' to run us all out of the county! William's oldest boy acts like a damn hellion and like he runs the gang himself! None of them can be trusted!"

Dan laughed hard and after nearly dropping the canister, he replied, "I couldn't agree more! They've been causing trouble around here for too damn long! They're in with that Jack Reed fellow, and half a dozen other criminals running from the law! One of them is wanted for bank robbery, *in my own damn town!*" Dan then lifted the canister to his nose, took a whiff, and leaned back far away from it. "What's with the kerosene, old man?"

Irvine didn't answer at first but laughed like a maniac as he poured the fluid all over the floor and countertop, covering the worn-out register. Looking deeply into Dan's eyes he said, "Wilcox is waiting for us at the Western House to make a statement! You and I saw a few of them bastard Rainsbargers leaving this area, and when we saw smoke, we rushed over! Ain't that right, boy?"

Both men ran the story back one to another as they doused the inside and outside of the small store with the flammable liquid. Once they had finished their work, Irvine lit a small fire with his buggy lantern and a small rotten branch from a tree behind the store. With the building set ablaze, they shook hands and hollered and howled like animals.

"Let's go see Wilcox and make the report," Irvine snorted as he tried to stifle his excitement while he climbed into the buggy.

The two men shook hands again, and Dan Turner replied, "Let's go quick! First round of whiskey is on me!"

VII

On May 20th, 1885, the Eldora Herald joked:

'The Eldora Militia have been commanded to hold themselves in readiness in case an assault should be made upon the jail. The vigilantes will please take notice and not come during a rainstorm. Our militia is for dry weather.'

There were no Rainsbargers in the jail at the time, as Frank and Nate had already been removed and taken back to Marshalltown. That same day the Eldora Herald also printed:

'The Rainsbargers are old offenders and they have been a terrible curse to this county. They have lived almost exclusively by dishonesty, and when any attempt had been made to bring them to punishment, they would send out their incendiaries and thieves and intimidate persons into silence.'

'It is the opinion of those who know them that they will never leave that section at command. Their blood is up and they are not cowards.'

The newspaper concluded with a poem that was sung by a few local girls who had noticed a hanging rope late one night:

> *'O, the Rainsbargers they'll suspend*
> *Until they're dead;*
> *Oh, boys! Us you'll defend,*
> *And a girl you will wed!'*

On June 1st, 1885, three men cut down a twenty-foot maple tree and laid it near the road leading into Eldora near the Armstrong house. The next day, there was a meeting with over two hundred society members at Hiserodt's hotel.

CHAPTER 16

DR. MYRON UNDERWOOD

I

June 4th, 1885, in Eldora's town square...

The warm morning light crept up into view and laid its decadent rays upon the waking town. The early morning heat was like fuel to the damp grass, which only aided the humidity in the air. It was early, but the sun was now up, and in turn, so were the folks of Eldora. Many were on their way to their shops to open for the day or headed to the surrounding areas in which they farmed. As the town's people were preparing for another summer day, a gunshot rang through the streets. Several women screamed, and some men took cover, and drew their own weapons if they had one.

"Ambush! Ambush! People of Eldora! Set your sights on the newest assault from the Rainsbarger Renegades!" cried a voice from up the road.

Deputy Barnes was sitting in the upstairs room to the small jailhouse when he heard the shot go off. He jumped up, slid open the window, and shoved his head through. He could see gunpowder dissipating in the air and knew someone had only shot into the air and not at another citizen. "Dang nabbit! I don't know who is shouting but *knock it off*!" he barked.

A man on the roadway below him pointed at a buggy that was sprayed with bullet holes and had entered the town square. It was circling like a shark to its prey before it came to a stop. Upon seeing the buggy, and the four men get out of it, Barnes knew his presence would soon be needed below. He shoved his head back through the window, cussed, and rushed downstairs towards the jailhouse front door.

"What's happening, boss?" came the voice of George Barber, the jailhouse's only resident at the moment. He had recently been arrested for possessing and selling liquor and was a mangy-looking man.

"Be quiet, George, you damn mudsill," the deputy replied as he smacked George's room door and exited the building.

The town square was being flooded by several locals as the deputy arrived. A man was seated on the horse that had carried the buggy and was yelling *'Ambush'* like a train horn that wouldn't stop. "I swear to all that's good, and holy, if you don't stop screaming, Caldwell, you're gonna spend the night next to Mr. Barber in the iron hotel!" Barnes yelled.

Mr. Caldwell immediately stopped and gave the deputy a nod as if to say, *I'm stopping; I'm stopping!* He then jumped down from the horse and settled in with the other three men. Deputy Barnes shifted his view to Bill Hiserodt, Dr. Underwood, and Dr. Rittenour, and said, "Now what's this all about, gentlemen? Deputy Bannigan took your statement in Steamboat last night, did he not?"

"We came to show these here folks how heinous those bastards are!" Rittenour sneered.

Eldora's City Marshal, Joseph McMillan, spoke up, "What happened to the buggy? Who in Sam Hill did this?" His voice echoed through the town square, gaining the attention of more onlookers. Dozens of men, women, and children crowded the torn-up buggy. Murmurs could be heard passing from one end to another.

Underwood spoke in a loud deep voice, which everyone could hear, "It was those Rainsbarger brothers, Finley, Manse, and even Old Bill! They had with them their nephew, Ed Johns!"

"We were coming back from having a few drinks," Hiserodt said, "When they ambushed us last night! We believe they were trying to lay-way to Mr. Underwood, seeing as he's set to testify in the other brother's trial, and holds key evidence against them!"

Someone further back in the crowd yelled, "It's just like the papers said! They're trying to intimidate us all!"

"That's right, Mr. Buckner," Caldwell replied, "I thought they would surely get us, until Rittenour jumped from the buggy, and shot one of them!"

At the news of the assault and Rittenour's brave retaliation, there were mixed cries coming from the crowd. Some were in favor of storming the gates to the Rainsbarger's holdout, and some were more than suspicious of Rittenour being any type of hero. While the people in the crowd made up their minds, Sheriff Wilcox rode into the scene and dismounted his horse. "It's true! We heard word this morning that one of them dogs is licking his wound in a hole somewhere," Wilcox remarked in a way that sounded less-than convincing, even to his own men.

Deputy Barnes noticed the hesitance in Wilcox's voice and decided to step in, "Alright, everyone clear away from the buggy! It needs to be examined by the Sheriff!"

As he was trying to clear the crowd, Underwood yelled, "You, fella, get the hell out of my buggy," he finished by poking the older gentleman in the chest. A rather large man had climbed inside and was examining the wounds to the carriage. At Underwood's request, he stepped out of the carriage, and in front of the doctor. Underwood thought he was a menace of a man and wished he hadn't poked him like a sleeping bear.

"You know," William Wickham replied in almost a shout, "I find it odd that they shot your buggy, and no one is hurt, not even your horse! More than that, your buggy has burn marks on the inside, not the outside, and splinters outwards!" Everyone in the square heard his declaration and many gasped in response. Many folks had now stopped their daily tasks to listen. Mr. Wickham was a well-known older gentleman in the community, and many called him 'Daddy' Wickham. He was viewed as a man to be heard.

"Uh, well," Underwood stammered, "We...uh...did fire back you know!"

"You know what I think?" Wickham said as he leaned in toward Underwood. "I think you're all a bunch of lying bastards!"

Wickham started laughing as there came shouts from the crowd of him being a Rainsbarger-sympathizer. Others contended that he was right, and the whole matter needed to be investigated. Wickham wasn't afraid of the crowd, even though there were dozens of people. He stood over them as a grasshopper does to an ant.

"Whoa! Whoa! Let's all settle down, men," Wilcox interjected, "Easy, now! I'm sure Wickham ain't a friend to the boys, now, are you?"

Wickham let out a small laugh again, "What I mean is, those boys are sharpshooters," he said as he stepped forward towards the doctor. He then poked Underwood in the gut and said, "If they truly shot at you...they wouldn't have missed!"

At his words, the whole crowd turned into an uproar of fear, and anger. Several infuriated men grabbed Wickham's shoulders and pulled him backwards into the crowd. He was lost to them as the shouting continued. A few men at the back of the forming mob tried to start a chant of, *'Lynch them all'*, but no one joined in.

Wilcox climbed onto the buggy to address the people of Eldora as Deputy Barnes tried to keep them at bay. Wilcox shouted, "Citizens of Eldora! This will all be investigated by the Sheriff's office! There is no need to panic! The men who did this *will* be apprehended, now...everyone please step away and resume your business!"

After some more convincing from Barnes, the crowd further dissipated and continued on their business as usual. Wilcox climbed down and reached into the bag tied to the side of his horse. He withdrew a newspaper and shoved it into Hiserodt's chest.

"The Herald is already saying a lynching is to be expected! Great job, men! You come into town before I'm even here to address the men or keep them away from your *assaulted* wagon! You stupid bastards! Now the whole town will be talking about the assault possibly being a fake! *How stupid are you to shoot from the inside of the cart?*" Wilcox said all in one hurried, angry tone. He shook his head, "Who told Ross to print the story before the people even heard about it? It makes him look like he's on the inside! Damn it!"

Wilcox was angry at how stupid the men had been, and even more so at Hiserodt, who was one of the leaders in this whole cult. Wilcox spit, and cussed, then kicked the buggy wheel, and whispered through gritted teeth to Underwood, "Get this piece of crap out of here, now!"

"What do you want me to do with it?" he asked as Wilcox mounted his horse.

"Burn it!" he shouted as he rode away, leaving the men there to clean up their mess.

II

Afternoon of June 4th...

The day's dirt and sweat clung to William Rainsbarger's sunburnt neck as the heat of the day came to an end. He stood on his front porch, watching as the wagon came down the dirt road to his home and wondered why the Sheriff was coming to pay him a visit. In his heart, he thought he knew. It wasn't every day the Sheriff approached your home in the jailer's wagon with a deputy in the seat next to him carrying a rifle.

William slowly removed his gun belt and handed it to his wife, Elizabeth, who had joined him on the porch. "Go inside," is all he said in a quiet tone.

"Bill, what are they here for—?" she began.

"I said go inside. Don't come out...I'll see what he wants. I have a feeling I won't be home tonight," William replied. He stepped down from the wooden walkway, and greeted Wilcox, and Deputy Gardener as they came to a stop.

Wilcox got out of the wagon's seat and simply said, "Sorry it's come to this, Bill," he sighed as he unhinged his handcuffs. "William

Rainsbarger, I hereby place you under arrest for the assault on Dr. Myron Underwood."

William held out his hands with his wrists aimed upwards. As Wilcox tightened the restraints, William replied, "You're not sorry about a thing, Sheriff. The whole county has been after us and you've done nothing to stop it."

Wilcox just sighed again as he walked him to the back of the wagon. The carriage was a normal-sized buggy, except it had been modified to have the back enclosed. It was walled with old wood that had been painted black. The very rear had a small door with an even smaller window that looked out the far end of the buggy.

As Wilcox opened the door and loaded William inside, Gardener called, "You want me to sit in the carryall with these lowly criminals, boss? Keep an eye on them? An eye, or a six shooter?" he laughed.

"Shut your damn mouth, you stupid gull!" Wilcox barked.

"Are you going soft on these boys, Sheriff?" he teased.

Manse Rainsbarger yelled from the back of the patrol wagon to Deputy Gardener, "Well, Jimmy, what's even the charge this time?"

Gardener yelled back, "Assault with intent to murder, you stupid mule."

Manse laughed, "Oh, is that all?" he winked at William as he said it.

Wilcox became annoyed by their banter and interrupted. "Don't worry, Bill, I'm sure this is a big mistake and will soon blow over," Wilcox lied.

As the door was closed, William looked at the other two men in the patrol wagon, "Welp...evening, little brothers," he said to Finley and Manse. They had also been arrested in relation to the alleged assault on Underwood. Both men seemed in good spirits, finding the whole thing a little humorous.

Finley chuckled, "Evening, Bill, what brings you here?"

Manse laughed and added, "Is Elizabeth gonna let you come out and play tonight? It's been a minute since we've all shared some fire water!"

William smiled at the thought, "This whole thing is ridiculous! It's absurd to think that we would shoot at anyone who didn't shoot first! Well...it's absurd to think that *I* would at least!"

They all laughed again, "It's all a lie, anyways," Manse said. "I think they're scared Frank and Nate are closer to freedom, and that the real criminals will be caught. They've been trying to run us out for some time now!"

"You think they give us a fair trial? It ain't fair to my girls to have to visit their Pa' in jail, locked up for no reason," Finley stated, shaking his head as he spoke.

Williams' smile was completely gone now as they rode along, "Ain't nothing fair about what we've been through, and now I dare say, we may get a glimpse of what our little brother's soul has gone through. I know Frank is dying to see Zella again."

At his remark they all remained silent for quite some time, until Manse spoke again in a choked voice, "I don't think we'll be gone long. At least I hope not. Ruby's my world, and baby boy is obviously attached to his Ma' but...he's my little guy. It ain't fair to anyone in our family." The other two brothers shook their heads in agreement with everything Manse had just said.

"I hope they let us go by early morning," Fin said as Manse stared out the small back window, "They asked me about our nephew, Ed. I think they intended to arrest him also, but I don't reckon they could find the sneak," he laughed, breaking the tension for just a moment.

Deputy Gardener smacked the back of the buggy, "Keep it down back there!"

They could hear his muffled voice from the front and Wilcox's reply, "Leave the men alone! They ain't disturbing anybody! Besides, they'll be quiet soon enough. Look up ahead!"

The three brothers couldn't see what lay ahead as they only had the rear window that was large enough for one onlooker. What they could hear, was the sound of a crowd with applause and music. As they passed through the town of Eldora, they could finally see what the growing noise was. The town square was overcome by people from Eldora and the surrounding communities. There were several men playing music, and young boys, and girls dancing around the square. Over the roar of folks clapping to the beat of the music, the brothers could finally hear the words being sung by the crowd. It was the lynching poem that had been printed in the Eldora Herald. Manse's gut sank and William held his head low. The words of the murder song got lost in that moment as Finley looked out the rear wagon window and saw a man in the crowd who wasn't participating in the celebration of their arrest. He was holding a small party mask to his face. As Finley watched, the man made an imaginary gun with his thumb, and index finger, and pretended to shoot at him.

Finley instantly knew who it was and cursed, "That son of a b—!"

He was cut off by the abrupt stop of the buggy and the cry of Deputy Gardener, "We're here, maggots!"

Wilcox quickly opened the wagon's back door, and with his hand on the butt of his gun, rushed the brothers to the small jailhouse. As they entered the facility, they were greeted by Deputy Barnes, who was ready to accept them. Justice Hardin was also present. He looked as if this whole arrest disturbed him. George Barber, the jailhouse lonely resident, was singing along to the crowd as the brothers entered.

Justice Hardin hit the door to George's cell and barked, "Quiver your lip, Barber, or I'll add a week to your stay!" He then looked around at each brother, who seemed disheartened, gave an even harder look at Sheriff Wilcox, and then said, "You folks sure stir up a lot of trouble around these parts. The town folks seem to be having their fun today, and I'm sure more than a few would like to see you all colder than a wagon tire. But...you'll be safe enough here." Turning to William, who was looking at his feet, Justice Hardin continued, "Mr. Rainsbarger, you do have the right to post bail tonight, seeing as we aren't holding court, and there's no legal action pending against you. You will, however, still have to be tried by a jury of your peers. Is that understood?"

Before he could answer, Wilcox threw down his hat and cursing said, "Wait a second now! Old Bill wasn't taken in for some petty horse stealing, but for the attempted murder of a key witness in his brother's case!" he yelled as he pointed a pudgy finger at the judge. "You'd do well to remember that!"

Deputy Gardener took Wilcox's arm and began to lower it as it shook. Justice Hardin cleared his throat and stepped forward, closer to the sheriff. The noise of the celebration outside was still ringing through the town square. "And you'd do well to remember your role! Sheriff! Not judge, or jury. In fact," he nearly yelled as he turned back to the oldest brother, "William Rainsbarger, you are hereby released upon your word to return for your trial! You will need to be here first thing in the morning!"

"Thank you, your Honor! What about my kin?" he asked.

Justice Hardin looked at Manse and trying not to make eye contact with Finley, answered, "Unfortunately men, you two will have to stay to stand before a judge tomorrow." Their heads hung low, and before either one could ask why, Hardin was speaking with Deputy Barnes. "Manse Rainsbarger has a pending case against him about a robbery in Steamboat Rock, and the other one...well I mostly don't like him, but he's also being investigated for the harboring of notorious criminals! Now, remove their cuffs and get them booked!"

He chose to look Finley straight in the face when he said *notorious criminals*. Finley gave a small smile and pretended to bow. Gardener was in no mood for his foolishness and immediately pulled him upright. Justice Hardin scoffed in disappointment for both men, then sneered, "Evening, gentlemen," and promptly exited the jailhouse.

Wilcox ran after him and caught him as he was climbing into his covered wagon. "You're not sure about the arrest, are you, your Honor?" he said as he approached.

"It's not the arrest I'm unsure about, it's you, Sheriff. Why do you think I came tonight? I will be sending a telegram for George Cook to investigate the area of the shooting with his hounds, and you better pray he finds evidence to support your arrest!"

"When? Perhaps I can come and be of some assurance," Wilcox tried to reply.

Hardin shook his hand in a manner to convey his irritation towards Wilcox speaking at all, "Tonight, Sheriff, and your presence won't be needed. You've already let the bastardization of the scene of Enoch Johnson take place...I won't let such a thing happen now!"

Justice Hardin rode away through the town square, leaving Wilcox to reflect on the situation which he was now faced with. He was angry about William's release, knowing this would only escalate, *if* they were to ever eradicate the county of the brothers.

When the judge was out of sight, he turned to go back into the small jailhouse. Standing just outside the building was his deputy, Mr. Gardener. "We have another problem, boss," he said.

"Damn it! What now? Did a gang of ruffians assemble to burn down the town?!"

"Not quite," Gardener replied, "Since folks saw the doctor's buggy, there's been rumors of a possible lynching. The county militia has been told to be on standby for assembly. The jail may be guarded."

Wilcox shuttered at the thought, "I need to speak with Hiserodt!" he nearly cried as he climbed aboard the patrol wagon.

"Why do we need him, sir?"

"Because!" Wilcox yelled. "We need a judge to hold court...tonight!"

III

That night, a telegraph was sent to George W. Cook to bring his bloodhounds to the ambush scene for investigation. On three occasions, the hounds went over the area and didn't find anything. Vigilance Society members tried to get Cook to take his hounds up to the Johns farm in order to get a scent in that direction. D. E. Waters said that Cook refused to let his dogs lie about their findings and wouldn't make them go. After their plan to fake the ambush and have the citizens run the Rainsbargers out if the county didn't work, Dr. Underwood left the country entirely.

CHAPTER 17

ACROSS THE DIVIDE

I

Evening of June 4th...

Nearly twenty other men ran in formation next to William Scott Nutting as they assembled in the local skating rink. The Methodist church bell was still ringing through the valley as they went. At the call to assemble, Nutting, and several other local men who had joined the county militia met at the armory in Eldora and prepared for their call to arms. Many of them were still dressed in their dirty clothes from their day of work. It was early evening as they gathered to find out their assignment, and the reason for the call. The heat of the summer day was settling as the sun waited to fully set, and the crickets waited to play their musical routine that they played night after night. Only a few started their music early.

As the armed men gathered and stood in formation, Captain Pillsbury rode through the entry to the skating rink and dismounted his horse. "Thank you, gentlemen, for your quick response to the call," his voice echoed through the rink. "There's been word of possible mob violence towards the Rainsbargers. The talk has been ongoing since this afternoon about the brothers, who are now taking residence in our small-town jail. A few folks had gathered near the jailhouse, but they've been made to disperse! We will, as of right now, wait to settle any new crowds that may assemble. Is that clear, men?" They all gave a singular response and broke formation, but still remained alert to the captains' shouts. "We hope to dissuade any assault upon the jail or the brothers. Deputy Barnes is posted and is keeping watch. We are to protect the prisoners, should any violence ensue! Stick around, men, and stay alert."

After the sun began the last of its descent into the night, the men lit torches, and waited on high alert for some time. They spoke of the brothers in Marshalltown and the two who were now just a few yards away. Many men were unaware of the hurt that the brothers had supposedly caused and were even more misguided on the pain that they had suffered. Frank Rainsbarger's love for Nettie had started the family on a course destined to collide with evil men; only few knew the truth. As the torches burned, they spoke of Enoch Johnson, the counterfeiters, Henry Johns, and the accused, who now awaited trial. It seemed the militia was divided on their stance of the Rainsbarger brothers. Either way, the men who had gathered, were of one heart to protect them.

Several of them took turns in pairs riding through the small town on patrol. One after another, men on horses would leave the rink, only to return and report there was no one out waiting in the byways for vengeance. As Nutting took his patrol, he considered how the night continued ever forward, bringing about the decadent smell of fresh grass, the light of the night's stars, and the melodious noise of the night's musicians. Upon reaching the small jailhouse, he could see a small light had been on in the upstairs room. As he watched, it was extinguished as Deputy Barnes settled into bed for the night. Nutting's heart raced as he thought about the possible attack on two men that he didn't even know.

Why did human cruelty know no limits?

His horse began to turn from the jail house as he contemplated his decision to join the militia. Upon arriving back at the skating rink, he noticed Sheriff Wilcox had arrived and was speaking with Captain Pillsbury, who had a scowl, and looked in deep distress. He was pointing a shaking finger at the Sheriff as they spoke. Moving away from the Captain, Wilcox sat upon his patrol wagon seat next to Deputy

Gardener. He lit a cigar and spit out the side. He turned and muttered something to the deputy that Nutting could only consider a crude joke, as the deputy laughed. With a crack of his whip, he left the captain to ease his own frustrations and rode on into the night.

"Alright," Pillsbury's voice boomed, "listen up, men! There seems to be no threat of any mob or any violence this evening! We have been ordered by the Sheriff to disband! You are dismissed!"

Wilcox laughed at them from down the road as they all muttered and got up, only to return to the armory, unload their gear, and head home. Nutting watched as the men mumbled their disapproval at the order and called out, "What if we are needed and we aren't here? What then, Captain?"

"Then the church bells will ring, you idiot! Now return your gear to the armory! I'm not happy about it either, but the Sheriff has left a deputy at the jail and he himself is headed out on the Iowa Central railway to Franklin County. It seems he has a lead on Ed Johns, the last would-be convict. He's yet to be apprehended." Pillsbury then turned and looked in the direction the Sheriff had left. Leaning in closer to Nutting, he said, "I am not in a good way about the order either, son, but the decision has been made. Stay alert!" he replied as he clapped Nutting on the shoulder and walked away.

Upon returning his gear to the armory, and himself to his home, Nutting lay awake in bed staring at the ceiling. A time or two he convinced himself he heard the church bell in the distance, and jumped up, prepared for an assault. He feared the worst was yet to come.

Sheriff Wilcox and Deputy Gardener rode along in silence for some time until they nearly reached the train station. "Did you leave the cell door unlocked as they requested?" Gardener asked.

Wilcox threw his cigar to the side and shook his head, "Absolutely not! Such foolishness will only incriminate us all and draw suspicion from Deputy Barnes. I already advised the Marshall to leave town as well. If they want the filthy rats, they'll have to hunt them," he groaned in a disgusted way.

Gardener chuckled, "I've never seen anyone hunt an animal with a twenty-foot tree and some rope!"

Wilcox smiled at the comment, "And tonight you won't either, but it's been decided, and they'll get it done."

The two men rode along the tracks to Franklin County, drinking and laughing into the hot night. The noise of the crickets filled the air by the Eldora jailhouse with Finley and Manse Rainsbarger asleep inside.

All else was silent.

II

Just after 1am, June 5th, 1885, in Eldora...

Eldora's streets had been quiet for a few hours as its residents were now deep in sleep. Nearly two hundred masked men entered the town from two directions on foot. They had assembled near the Steamboat Rock bridge and divided upon their arrival. From the north, came the majority of the men. All of them carried a rifle on their back, or a six shooter on their hip. Eldora's one road was flooded with blood-thirsty vigilantes as they approached every business and home, and held it hostage, waiting for anyone to try and escape. As the men took their places, the world stood still until the assault was ready to be executed. Nutting and half of the sleeping residents were startled awake as the loud whistle cracked through the sky in a deafening tone.

He sat upright, struggling to remove the sheets from his body as he rushed to get ready. *Had he slept through the church bell? Perhaps!* He wasn't sure but any noise at this time of night wasn't welcome. He pried on his last boot as he reached his front door to head to the town square.

As he pushed the door open, he came face to face with a masked man holding a revolver to his head. "Go back! Judge Lynch is holding court tonight!" is all the man said as he cocked back the hammer.

Mr. Aldrich, the night watchman, had fallen asleep and was also startled awake by the sound of the whistle. He jumped and spilled his still hot coffee into his lap, cursed, and slammed his shin into the desk leg as he stood up.

"What in the devil is that racket?" he yelled. Peering out of the church's front window, he saw droves of men assailing through the town in every direction. Aldrich cursed again under his breath and ran out of the small office, and into the main room of worship. As he reached the bottom of the stairs that led to the bell, two men barged into the church armed from head to toe.

"Don't even think about it, old man!" one masked man yelled. "Judge Lynch is having court!"

Deputy Barnes awoke to the sound of the mob's chants. As they approached the jailhouse, they began shouting their own rendition of the lynching poetry. "Oh, the Rainsbargers we'll suspend, until they're dead!! Oh, girls, you we'll defend, and it's us you will wed!" they shouted in rehearsed unison.

Barnes was overwhelmed by the mob as it drove upon the land with the majority surrounding the jailhouse. In the distance he could see a dozen or-so men carrying a near twenty-foot tree that had been trimmed down. The branches were being used as handles as they approached the jail. The deputy was frozen in his place as he watched the lynch mob grow in fury. Nearly everyone in Eldora was now awake and had been threatened by a masked desperado, and were unable to leave their homes. Several of the residents were now on their rooftops, watching the madness ensue.

He could hear shouts of the mob's cry from every direction and orders for folks to turn back. He knew if he didn't act fast, he wouldn't be able to turn them away. Running towards the door that led to the stairs at the back of the jail, he yelled at Sheriff Boylan to wake up. The man didn't stir in the slightest and continued his snoring in harmony with the mob's chant. Before the Deputy could reach the front of the small jail, he was held at gunpoint while the mob descended upon them.

Finley and Manse Rainsbarger were asleep like everyone else when the whistle blew. Finley stirred for a moment but wasn't brought to consciousness by it. Manse opened his eyes at the noise, wondering what he had heard. There was no noise but the remnant of a faint echo as he sat upright.

"Fin, psst, Fin! You awake?" he asked.

"No," Finley replied without opening his eyes, "And neither are you! Go back to sleep!"

"I think something is wrong! Listen!"

Finley's head popped up from his pillow with his eyes still closed as he listened carefully. He could hear what sounded like marching footsteps and a small chant. "I think you're right! Manny, lift me up to the window," he said as he got out of his small cot, while rubbing his eyes.

The more stout, younger brother hoisted his thinner brother up onto his shoulders to peer out of the small window that was high upon the wall. Finley listened for a moment. Manse could hear the growing noise of a mob. "What the hell is going on?" he asked in a mildly scared tone.

"Drop me!" Finley yelled.

As he came down to eye level, Manse could see his older brother was terrified. Without saying anything, in a panic, Finley threw the metal bed frame to one side, and braced himself between the door and the bed frame.

"Don't just stand there! Help me!" he yelled.

Manse was going to ask what was happening, but in the span of a few seconds, he understood. The full rage of the lynch mob was upon them, and they could feel the boom of the tree as it was used as a battering ram on the jail's front door.

III

The two brothers crowded the cell door like two caged tigers that knew they would be attacked as soon as they were released. They could either fight or be killed. Panic and fear struck their souls as the ram continued upon the jail's front door.

The mob outside shouted, "The Rainsbargers we'll suspend..."

THUD. THUD.

"Until they're dead…"

THUD. THUD.

Manse tried to hold back his tears as he thought of his impending demise. It was only mere feet away. Finley was sweating through his worn out clothes and pushing with all of his might to wedge himself between the door and the bed, even though the outlaws had not yet entered the jail. His voice shook as he looked at the high open window and screamed, "HELP! HELP! MURDER! PEOPLE OF ELDORA, FOR GOD'S SAKE, HELP!" There came no aid. There was no reply, but the barrage of the battering ram. Manse began to cry as he thought of his newborn son.

"Fin, we've got to hold out until someone comes! Where's the deputy in charge?" he asked as he shook. Manse felt weak as he braced the door.

"Wilcox! Barnes! For god's sake, help!" Finley's voice cracked, his mouth dry from anticipation.

The mob continued, "You girls we'll defend…"

THUD. THUD.

"I don't think the front door is going to hold out, Manny! Be ready!" The brothers breathed in deep, full of fear and covered in sweat.

"Us, you will wed!" the crowd shouted as they rammed the door one last time. It split in the middle and made a hard splintering noise that echoed through the jail.

"Oh, they're gonna get you, boys!" George Barber hollered from his cell. The two brothers could hear him jumping up, and down on his creaky cot, and begin to sing the mob's death chant.

At George's mockery of their death, they both began to tear up, and prepare for the onslaught of the mob's hate to reach their door. Manse cried, "I don't want to die!"

"Shut up, Manny! You'll be fine, just brace! I hear them coming!"

Manse shook his head frantically from side to side, "Lord, I don't want to die and leave my kids with no Pa! Please!"

"We all die sometime, Manny, we can only determine the manner in which we will go! Man up! Now is not the time to get weak knees and go on dying on me! You hear me? We're Rainsbargers, not cowards!"

Outside, several men threw down the tree and several others came forward with sledgehammers. They entered the jailhouse after opening up the splintered front door in a barrage of anger. "Get them rat bastards out here and ready for the gallows, men," came the voice of Black Bill. "Popejoy! Get the ropes strung up!" he yelled only loud enough for Popejoy to hear.

Men ran in every direction as orders were called out in a militant fashion. George Bunger had entered the jail with Albert Leverton, and they began to beat upon the cell door. The sledgehammers hit hard and the first contact made Finley's head lift off the door and settle back against it.

"Damn! That about rattled my teeth loose," he chuckled at his brother, who was still frantic. Everything Finley did to calm Manse down only seemed to exacerbate his brother's mental decline. Finley wanted Manse to see hope, but his jokes only made him feel as if Finley was a million rods away from the ensuing chaos, and that he would die alone.

"Come on, boys! Don't make this harder than it needs to be! This was a long time coming and you're fixin' to hang!" Bunger laughed.

George Barber repeated Bunger's words as he grew wild within his cell. "Let me out to watch them hang," he laughed maniacally.

Leverton beat upon the door in tandem with Bunger and several other men, most of which the two brothers recognized. "You're all rotten carcasses and you don't even know it!" Finley yelled. "Even if you get us tonight, you'll pay for it for eternity. Murder ain't cheap on a man's soul! Trust me, boys!"

"Shut your pigeon-livered mouth, Finley!" Leverton yelled as the sledgehammers pounded the wooden door. It was beginning to sound as if it was splintering, and Finley hoped Manse didn't notice. The two brothers pressed even harder upon the door and took the brunt of the hammering to their backs.

"Hello there," came the voice of Amos Bannigan. He was waving his hand in view of the high window. "Damn it! Stand still, Turner!" he yelled.

"Don't say my name, you fool!" Dan Turner barked.

All the two brothers could see was Amos' hand in the window. Even standing on top of the Mayor's shoulders, he could barely reach. "They're gonna be dead soon, Dan! Stop your worrying!" Amos barked back.

A moment later Finley, and Manse saw the barrel of a revolver enter the window and Amos began to fire. The shot echoed loud through the cell and found its way into the wall next to Manse. He screamed, and Amos laughed hard, "We're gonna get you boys, and hang you up good, and tight until your damn necks pop!"

"F**k you, Bannigan!" Finley yelled and pressed harder upon the door.

"Don't talk to them, Fin! What are we going to do? Help! Help!" Manse shouted.

Amos laughed again and cried, "There ain't no one coming to help you!"

Amos fired several more shots into the room and a few found their mark in Manse's weakened body. He didn't even yell. His body simply swallowed the bullets and regurgitated blood out of the wounds. He clenched the hole in his chest and a gush of red spilled through his fingers and down his arm.

"Damn it!" Finley yelled with tears beginning to stream down his face, "Hold on, Manse!"

Amos laughed, "I think I got one! It's like shooting fish in a barrel!"

"Shoot 'em again!" Turner shouted with joy.

The sledgehammer workers continued, but slowed their pace as time drew on. Hiserodt could be heard calling from the outside, "Swap out and break it down, men! Don't let them dissuade you from the justice they deserve!" There were footsteps of several men in the hall as fresh workers came to the door. Barber continued his incessant wild calls and pleas to watch. Manse tried to keep his strength as his warm blood ran down his body and onto his brother.

"We're getting close now! Any last words?" Bunger cackled.

Manse was yelling for Amos to stop shooting as Finley watched the life begin to fade from his younger brother. He knew what was to come, and in a soft voice, speaking to himself, he clenched his brother's shoulder, and said, "Don't worry, Manny, you may be seeing Ma' and Pa' soon. Tell Lovina I said 'hello', too." He breathed in deep, forced back his tears, and shouted, "Barber...tell our families we died like dogs, with no one to help us!"

Manse's blood ran even more through several other gunshot wounds, and out onto the cell floor. The most deafening shot of all rang through the cell as Amos fired one final time. The slug screamed through the air and settled into the side of Manse' skull. Instantly, his body went limp, and Finley shouted in pure agony at losing his brother. Desperate, cold, unending hate entered Finley's heart as he let go of his brother and stood up to release the door to the men outside. The door slammed open and pushed Manse' body under the bed. Finley could see several men covered in sweat and breathing heavily. They looked as if they caught Finley with his pants down, until he lunged at them with all of his rage.

He had grabbed his dirty work boot off the floor, and swung it hard at them, hitting several of them across the face, and head. His other hand was a clenched fist which he drove into their jaws, chests, and throats. As Finley set his beating into action, he dropped the boot, and removed a revolver from Leverton's side, and used it as a club to fight his way to the front door, unaware of how many men he would then face. He took several punches on his way, but in his current state, he felt none of them.

Outside, Hiserodt, and the remaining men of the mob cheered as they heard Finley scream over the death of his brother, and the commotion inside. They were also unaware of the wild animal they had just created who was working his way to them with a loaded gun.

"Be ready, men! We'll hang them high and hang them all!" Black Bill cackled as they waited in anticipation for the brothers to be dragged out of the jailhouse.

The commotion inside ended, and in an instant, Finley Rainsbarger jumped through the splintered opening where the door had been and landed on the front lawn. He was covered in sweat, and blood, and torn clothes that hung from him. In his right hand he had a long barrel revolver aimed up to the sky. Hiserodt's smile dropped as he saw Finley exit the jail alone.

Grinning from ear to ear, Finley screamed, "TELL THE BOYS I DIED LIKE A MAN!" He then lifted and aimed the revolver at Hiserodt, unaware who the masked man actually was. Before he could fire a single round, nearly all seventy-five men on that side of the jailhouse took aim, and unloaded their rifles, and six shooters in his direction. A litany of slugs shattered the windows behind Finley, splintered the face of the jail, and shredded his body to an unrecognizable state.

As bullets hammered his body, Finley squeezed the trigger to his own gun, and the bullet missed its true mark. The bullet simply entered the tree to Hiserodt's right. As the storm of bullets destroyed Finley's body, Hiserodt threw back his head, and laughed, while again, mimicking shooting Finley with his finger, and thumb.

When the fusillade stopped, several men dragged his body over to where Hiserodt stood, creating a dense trail of blood. Black Bill then spit on Finley's mangled body and kicked it hard. By the time he had finished howling with laughter at Finley's death, the men who had been beaten inside the jailhouse came out, carrying Manse's limp body. Placing it next to his brother's body, the men stepped away. Hiserodt kicked Finley's body again as hard as he could and yelled, "You finally got what you deserve, you brainless, yellow belly, son of a b**ch!"

Amos Bannigan and Dan Turned ran to the front of the jail to see the murderous scene clouded with gunpowder smoke. Both Rainsbarger brothers lay dead on the bloodstained front lawn of the Eldora jail. Black Bill looked around at the masked mob and then kneeled down next to Manse's body. He lifted the mangled head up for all to see, getting blood from the wound in Manse's head on his hands. Hiserodt then wiped the blood on Manse's shirt and stood up. Removing his sidearm from its holster, he shot Manse in the back of his head two more times. Blood splattered Hiserodt's boots as he laughed again and danced up and down in pure joy like a child. Everything was silent now, except the sound of crickets and a few distant women wailing from the scene they had just witnessed. They could barely be heard from where the mob stood.

Hiserodt saw all of the men watching him as he stood there unscathed by the hellish nightmare, he had just taken part in. He turned and addressed them in a shout. "Boys, Judge Lynch held court tonight, and these rotten carcasses have stood the bar," his voice echoed. "The next raid they make, I reckon, will be against the one they served, for I guess the devil will have a lively time when they meet across the divide! Our laws and courts are a mockery, and trials are a farce! Bribery, influence, and intimidation corrupt the bench, as well as juries and Governors! Technical errors by lawyers should, for their crimes, hang upon the gallows! We have no justice, no law, no courts, no recourse, but that which Judge Lynch has given us tonight!" He paused and let them all reflect upon his words, then continued, "Let it be a warning to those who defy the people's law! Now, boys...let us go to our horses! Give the signal, mount and away!"

He watched as each man of the murderous mob fell silent, eager with anticipation for their call to disperse. The street lamp was the only light in which Hiserodt could view the mangled bodies. He looked on with disgust, and then gave the signal.

IV

Three shots were then fired into the air and the mob dissipated, leaving the two bodies in the street. They returned to their nine wagons that they rode in on and left near Shaver's Wagon Factory and Lumber Yard on Jefferson Street. The lynchers kicked the mutilated bodies as they went and shot a dozen or more rounds into Manse's corpse.

Once the mob left Eldora, Manse and Finley were found by the night watchman, Mr. Aldrich, and the local newspaper editor. Deputy Barnes, and Doctor Underwood took the body to the mayor's office, where Underwood examined them the following day. They were deemed unrecognizable. The Rainsbargers were then handed over to their families and taken to Finley's home.

Finley left behind his wife, Emily Emma Cooper, and two daughters: Jennie and Minnie. Manse left behind his wife, Ethelin Marie Seabury, and two children; a daughter named Ruby, and an unnamed six-month-old son.

Several local newspapers, and several in nearby counties, printed the same literature the following day...

'Great excitement prevails. Public sentiment, however, generally approves of the lynching. It is doubtful any prosecution will follow.'

V

On June 6th, 1885, Finley's wife went to Eldora to collect his body. She caused an uproar while entering the town as she threatened the mob, and claimed publicly that she would shoot Underwood the first chance she got.

When Manse's wife arrived in Eldora and heard that her husband had been murdered, she tore out her hair, and screamed to be lynched like he had been. She and her youngest child who was with her were then taken in by a good samaritan to be fed and sheltered. Many in Eldora said the man was a Rainsbarger-sympathizer and should be lynched as well.

Fin and Manse were buried on June 8th. At the funeral, Ed Johns made a public speech that he knew who his father's murderer was, and that he was at the funeral. He swore he would get revenge. That same day, William, and Ed Johns appeared before the court, and paid $2,000 bonds each for their part in the alleged assault on Dr. Underwood.

The U. S. National Guard was then called in to prevent any more violence or retaliation.

The Eldora Herald wrote;

'The wild shrieks of the doomed prisoners were heart-rending in the extreme. They knew too well the meaning of that gathering of earnest and determined men without, and the first blow upon the door sounded their death-knell. As the prospect of immediate death loomed up before them and their miserable lives were to pay the penalty for years of lawlessness, they gave expression to their terror in wild, despairing cries for help. When the hammering was going on the prisoners realized what it was to die, and in their frenzy called upon the sheriff, the marshall, and the people of Eldora for protection.'

James Ross would go on to print an entire pamphlet about the family's supposed criminal history that had started in the 1850's. He had fabricated the entire story and got many common facts about the family wrong. It was titled, *A Full History of the Rainsbarger Gang, and their Associations.*

On June 9th, one of the Rainsbarger sisters, Deliah, now an Estabrook, wrote in reply to the pamphlet;

'As I saw the piece in the Grundy County Republican taken from your wire June 5th, I was struck with horror and it seemed as though it would wrench my very heart from its resting place. I will inform you that we did not come from the south and was not called poor white trash. We came from the state of Ohio and was among the first settlers of Hardin County. But little did we think when we was battling through frontier life and years of sickness that some of us would have to be murdered to conceal other peoples crimes and our mother who was a Christian hearted woman but must now be called a tartar. When them men was on their road that night to stain their hands with innocent blood,...if they would have been told that the first righteous man should fire the first shot who would have been there to fire it? They would have turned and sneaked home.'

CHAPTER 18

THE EVENTS THAT FOLLOWED

I

On June 19th, 1885, the Daily Nonpareil printed a recorded statement from a Steamboat Rock citizen;

'No, that Rainsbarger trouble at Eldora is not over! I am afraid that some more good citizens will lose their lives up there, and if they do, the whole gang will be killed. The people are thoroughly aroused and mean business. They feel that they cannot get full justice in the courts. One of the Rainsbarger brothers' sisters has a quarter of a million dollars left by her husband, who was shot, and she is willing to back the gang with money for their defense in court. The gang is a crowd of desperadoes, thieves, burglars, and horse thieves, which extend all the way to Missouri, and it will take blood to wipe it out.'

On June 23rd, they also printed;

'The Hardin County gang, friends of the Rainsbargers, are cautioned to be careful in their conduct, as 1,000 men are ready to take the saddle in pursuit of any man who attempts anything in retaliation for the recent lynching in that county.'

In August, the Eldora Herald printed Delia's letter and titled it; *A Letter From One of the Gang.* They added;

'While the gang think it is so terrible to make widows and orphans, they must remember that other people are just as averse to having their families made widows and orphans as they are. The families of the three

doctors the Rainsbargers fired on from ambush are also averse to being deprived of husbands and fathers.'

In retaliation to Delia's story, the Eldora Herald ran the Rainsbarger's detectives out of town, and asked the citizens to tar, and feather them if they ever returned. A newspaper in Minneapolis would write in return, an article entitled, *'What's the Matter with Hardin County?'* They claimed that the county should be flourishing, but instead was pushing people out.

At that time, John Bunger (Bunjer/Bunyer) shot his horse and himself and claimed he was attacked by William's boys; Joseph, John, and George. They were arrested by Sheriff Allan Meader who was instructed by Judge Weaver to take them to Marshalltown. Another lynch mob arrived at the depot in Eldora to kill them, while on the way to Abbott. The mob was stopped by knowing that the Rainsbarger boys were armed. They were allowed to keep their guns when they were arrested for fear that a mob would try to lynch them. The Sheriff told the conductor to run through the station and not stop.

Deputy Amos Bannigan came to William Rainsbarger's house a few days later to try to get his three boys to go with him to set Ash Noyes' haystack on fire. They refused to go with him, even after he offered to pay them. William later found out that Sheriff Wilcox and a group of about fifteen men were waiting for the boys to go with Bannigan so they could shoot them. When William found out, he confronted Wilcox about it. Wilcox simply said that even if it was true, there was nothing he could do about it.

On January 28th, of 1886, Nathan Rainsbarger's trial began. Some sources claim his trial started on December 28th of '85. He was represented by Charles Albrook, S. M. Weaver, and P. M. Sutton. Eight members of the jury voted for life in prison and four voted for hanging. His conviction was celebrated. Henry Johns' nephews testified against him and Frank. Horse thieving in general almost came to a stop after they were arrested to add to the ploy that *they* were responsible. The jury had reached a verdict around 6am on Wednesday morning. All had found Nate guilty of murdering Enoch Johnson. He had remained confident of his release until the verdict was read, when he was sentenced to life in Anamosa Penitentiary. Upon entering the court for his sentencing, he seemed every bit confident that he was an innocent man. He bowed to the officers in the court and shook hands with Mr. Albrook. He folded his hands and waited in a respectful manner. The verdict was read;

'It is the judgment of this court that you, Nathan Rainsbarger, be taken in charge by the Sheriff of Marshall County, and by him or some proper person appointed by him conveyed will all convenient speed to the penitentiary at Anamosa, and by him delivered to the Warden of said penitentiary, to be by him confined to hard labor during the period of your natural life; and that you pay the costs of the prosecution.'

The cost was $1,816.25.

Before his trial, Frank Rainsbarger was taken by Sheriff McCord of Marshalltown, to a meeting with Judge Griffon to ask for bail. It was denied. A local newspaper wrote that many adored Frank and he should expect to be greeted by several women blowing him kisses and with flowers. Frank's trial began on July 3rd and lasted until the 17th. Up until his conviction, Frank spent the first two years in Marshalltown Jail in solitary confinement. Several women were in fact smitten by Frank, and his good looks, and would flood the courthouse to see him. A local nun wrote a newspaper article to remind the women they were all married.

The newspapers then began printing stories about William Rainsbarger and his three sons. These stories have only ever been printed and can neither be confirmed nor denied. On November 7th, a newspaper article came out entitled, *'Bill Rainsbarger and his Gang: armed men in Hardin County seek to lynch the notorious desperados'.*

The story claims that William and his three sons followed William Scott, John Bunger, and a man named Hathaway, to Steamboat Rock where they then went to Scott's home. The story was that they followed Bunger after he left and tried to kill him because he had previously testified against Joe Rainsbarger in court. The story claims that the men shot Bunger on the Steamboat Rock bridge, and that he rolled off the bridge, and played dead. Bunger claimed that William went down to where his body was and said, "We have done it, boys, now let us go quick." The story mimics that of John Bunger's other story in that they were arrested by Allan Meader and taken to Marshalltown to avoid a lynch mob as ordered by Judge Weaver.

The four men were then indicted and convicted. They posted a $500 bail, and were acquitted two months later, as the examination was done privately. Months later, they were still under threat of angry mobs until it was discovered that at some point, John Bunger shot himself, and his horse. It seems that Bunger made up the same type of story in February and in November. Dr. Nathan Morse, Dr. Livingston, and Dr. McDermott all examined Bunger's wounds, and determined that they were indeed self-inflicted.

Rumors then spread that the Rainsbargers were also responsible for the disappearance of the station depot agent, Bob Fisk, back in 1870. Another alleged story arose from John Bunger, as he stated that back in 1884, Joe Rainsbarger, and a man named Krull, entered Bunger's home, threw him down the stairs, threatened to kill his family, assaulted one of his daughters, and threatened to burn down his house. Joe was indicted and acquitted again. It seemed that Bunger was just plain scared of the Rainsbargers, and did anything he could to get them arrested. When all his plots failed, he left the country entirely.

William Rainsbarger then hired a private detective named Burke, to bring back two men from California who had shot Henry Johns. It went to trial, but no one was convicted, as Henry Johns' sworn statement was missing. The two men were Charles Marx and James Rice. On August 31st, 1886, Thomas Nott confessed to harboring the actual horse thieves for nearly fifteen years, including Jack Reed.

On March 15th, of 1887, Frank was retried and convicted to life in prison. On December 10th, Nate was retried on a technicality, and was convicted a second time. The Supreme Court had reversed the first conviction due to the fact that Nettie testified against him in matters that he hadn't been arrested for, and the jury was seen as biased. Frank's trial cost $7,000. The citizens of Eldora and Steamboat Rock held a public meeting to celebrate their convictions. Nate then wrote a letter to the Marshalltown Times-Republic, which was deemed disrespectful and they criticized his spelling.

II

On the night in question, November 18th, 1884, Frank and Nate Rainsbarger had gone to Cleves. Their travels were slow going as one of Frank's horses was sick, and the other had dropsy. They went to their brother Manse' house, and to Mr. Geottles' store, where they met their brother William, and his sons. While there, they purchased a King's Bitters bottle that was later used against them, as there was a bitters bottle at the scene of the murder. After shopping, they met their nephew, Ed Johns, on the road near Abbott and had a drink with him at his home. Traveling back near that area, they visited their brother, Finley, as well, to see if he would help work their thresher. For the most part, they had an uneventful night, contrary to the state's suggested crimes.

William Johns, Henry Johns' oldest son, threatened Ed, and Lincoln Johns, that he would lynch them if they spoke in favor of their uncles. During the trials, he put them both on separate trains headed to separate states, in order to avoid them testifying on behalf of Frank, and Nate.

On three different occasions, Dr. Underwood, not being able to keep his story straight, would state that the bitter bottle was found in different locations.

In Nettie's preliminary statement about her father's death, she told authorities that Frank, and Nate came home late from being in Cleves all night with groceries for their hired worker, Henry Williams. However, in her statement at the trial in 1887, she then said she suspected the brothers right away of murdering her father. She claimed she told Nate that she knew they wanted the $7,500 life insurance money. She stated that they acted strange when they arrived home, and when she asked what they had been doing. She also stated that there was blood on Nate's jacket, and on Frank's mittens. No such evidence was ever recovered or witnessed.

Nettie went on in the trial to say that she left the baby with Vina Fisher and went to the barn to see the buggy they took. Then she spoke with Nate and accused him of having blood on him. Vina Fisher testified that Nettie's original story was true, and that while Vina washed the baby, she watched Nettie go into the field to help Frank reset a fence, and then came directly back. Nettie never accused the brothers or spoke with Nate. Vina attested to the fact that they *did* go shopping in Cleves, and remembered what they bought; sugar, flower, soap, and a broom.

During the trial, Nate stated that he never went to Gifford until the day of Enoch's funeral. Nettie claimed what he said was true by alluding to him killing Enoch just *before* reaching Gifford. In Nettie's original affidavit at the coroner's inquest, she stated that Frank was innocent, she never noticed anything suspicious. She also stated that she never examined the buggy.

Maggie Johnson would later say she took the train from Gifford to Eldora and received a telegraph from Joshua West stating that her husband had died, while she was at the hotel in Eldora. Many began to question, that if that was true, then why did she simply go to the Rainsbarger's home and say nothing for nearly two hours, and wait for a telegram to reach them from Manse Rainsbarger? Had she truly received the telegram in Eldora, she would have stated that that was the reason she went to the Rainsbarger's house so early, not simply because she got off the train.

On September 22nd, Jack Reed was finally arrested at the home of Finley Rainsbarger. He was being harbored by Finley's wife under the name J. L. Roberts. It seemed that Finley's reputation for associating with criminals was in fact true, but the same couldn't be said about the two brothers who were now in prison, as no known associations had been witnessed.

A local newspaper then printed another fake story about the Rainsbarger family. It claimed that on November 7th, a man named Bunyon, (possibly Bunger), was shot several times in the head near Abbott.

His horse was riddled with bullets. Before becoming unconscious, he claimed that William Rainsbarger shot him. It was stated that the Sheriff had gone after William but had not arrested him. The Sheriff feared William would be lynched also.

On November 11th, the Evening Gazette wrote;

'We can smell a lynching in Hardin County, and the Rainsbargers will be in it, for there will be no peace or safety in that section until they are in prison for life or hung.'

On January 4th, 1888, it was claimed that Ed Johns began looking for John Bunger. Supposed gang member, Julius Allen, reportedly choked John Leverton, and threatened him not to give out any evidence against Frank, and Nate, even though their trials were over. William Robertson claimed he saw the Rainbargers set fire to his barn and then left the county to 'save his life'. At that time, Underwood claimed he was then warned to stop looking for evidence against them, even though he moved away three years prior, and the sentencing had already occurred.

John Crosser, Granville Arnold, Peter Bannigan, and William Haines, reported that they saw the Rainsbargers stealing cattle, and were later threatened. Ash Noyes, Wilcox, Rittenour, Nettie, Hiserodt, and Leverton were all supposedly threatened by letter, and in person by Rainsbarger '*gang*' members. With two brothers in prison, and two more deceased, it's undetermined who actually initiated any threats. Specific names of the Rainsbarger '*gang*' members were never given.

Henry Finster, Sam Stewart, and E. Noyes claimed that their property was set on fire. James Haley, Nettie's new husband, and William Scott, reported being shot at. All of the accusations against the family began to divide the community even further. Many began to question if the Rainsbarger's criminal activity was even true.

On March 15th, the Oskaloosa Herald printed a story claiming that Cedar Rapids police arrested M. Sweeney, John McCarty, Mike Moony, and P. Murphy. The men were all ex-convicts from Anamosa. They were arrested for having burglar tools on them, and hiding them in the quarries for Frank, and Nate to find so they could escape. Whether the story is true or not is unknown. No actions were taken against the Rainsbargers in the incident.

In 1889, charges were dropped against William Rainsbarger, and Ed Johns for the shooting of Dr. Underwood, as there was no evidence found against them.

III

On April 17th, 1890, the Sioux City Journal printed an article stating that Marx, Rice, and Noyes were to be tried *again* for the shooting of Henry Johns, and several others were to be indicted. On September 14th, the Rainsbarger brother's hired detective, J.C. Burke, was shot at his office, and he chased the assailant down the alley outside, and shot four times at him. He was relieving the night clerk at the Wilson House when he was shot near his heart. The slug entered his chest and left out the back. His alias was J.M. Woods. He was the detective who brought Marx, and Rice back from Visalia, California. He was previously hired by William Rainsbarger.

The detective was hired this time, by Frank and Nate while they were in prison. This was the first court proceeding with a Rainsbarger as the prosecutor, and not as the defendant. The list of men to be indicted was apparently an open letter and *'every little yellow dog on the streets of Eldora'* knew who was on the list. Burke said;

'They are the most prominent and influential men in the county. Our evidence is conclusive. We know the name of every member of the party that went to kill Henry Johns. We even know what men did the actual shooting. We have the evidence of a man that was present.'

The trial began on April 20th.

In 1891, a petition for the brothers to be pardoned began circulating in Hardin County. Three years later, Dr. Underwood, and William P. Hiserodt died within weeks of each other. Hiserodt had suffered a major stroke and slowly died from his crippling paralysis on September 25th. Underwood died from a heart attack in his sleep. The Ackley World paper said it shouldn't go without notice that the two men died close together, as they were the reason for the lynching. The newspaper also named Hiserodt as the leader of the lynch mob, and outlined how odd it was that Dr. Underwood had bullet holes in his jacket when he was 'shot at' but he himself was not injured.

The Waterloo Daily Courier printed an article on September 27th and stated that Hiserodt was the leader of the law-and-order league which *'exterminated'* the Rainsbargers. They wrote;

'He was a man of indomitable courage and great executive ability and but for him the gang would never have been suppressed.'

The Muscatine News-Tribune eulogized Underwood on August 14th. He was a surgeon in the Twelfth Iowa Infantry and a member of the Senate in 1886. He was also attributed as partaking in the *extermination*.

That same year, William Rainsbarger became a member of the federal grand jury.

In June, of 1896, several papers outlined that the Supreme Court ruled an illegal verdict against the Rainsbargers, as they were sentenced under an old policy to the court, and many believed they would both have a third trial. Frank and Nate were then tried and convicted a *third* time.

In 1897, James S. Ross sold the Eldora Herald, and confessed to Dr. Nathan Morse that he knew that Nettie's letter was a sham, and that the attack on Underwood was a fraud. He also confessed that he knew Enoch Johnson was killed by John and Milton Biggs, who had been hired by the counterfeit ring. John H. Tiser was the boy who overheard the plot to kill Enoch, and how the Biggs brothers were hired for the job. He wrote this in a sworn affidavit. In his statement, Ross also admitted that he was paid for printing misinformation about the family.

On May 14th, 1899, Maggie and Effie were arrested for robbing the Ellsworth bank in Hamilton County with a man named Sam Burch. The bank had marked twenty-dollar bills, which Effie got caught using the day after the bank robbery. They were released two days later. It seems the two women's criminal lives would finally come into view of the public.

IV

On January 2nd, 1900, Governor Shaw denied the brother's pardon.

In 1902, Milton Biggs died at the veteran's home from heart disease. Most of the Vigilance Society and counterfeit members died as free men.

On January 18th, of 1904, Nettie wrote a letter to Governor Cummins stating that Frank, and Nate threatened to kill her if she convicted them, and begged for them to not be released.

The Rockford Register wrote;

'The Rainsbarger brothers, two murderers from Hardin County under a life sentence, want to get out. It took several lives and the best efforts for years of Hardin County law officials to land these rascals where they are. Let them stay where they are, or else abolish our courts and let the people administer justice by mob law.'

In 1906, Dr. Nathan Morse, who had examined Enoch's body, started to put everything together surrounding Enoch's death and the affidavits that were coming in. He wrote a letter to Governor Albert Baird Cummins, asking him to reopen the case. Frank and Nate then petitioned the Governor for a pardon. It was denied once again.

On February 23rd, someone mistook Effie for Nettie and threatened her not to appear at the parole hearing on the 25th. Sheriff Wilcox filed Nettie's affidavit, and stated that Frank, and Nate sent the man to threaten her. He claimed that if they were released, Nettie couldn't live a safe and normal life.

On June 1st, Dr. Morse wrote a letter to Governor Cummins, and stated that Nettie knew of the plan to kill Enoch, and that she was in agreement with his death because Enoch had forged Nettie's name to gain money on Frank's mortgage. Morse stated that this was simply a matter of court record. He also outlined that Enoch was murdered at his wife's empty home in Gifford, *and then* taken to the scene of the 'accident', and then it was made to look as such. The home had not been examined to verify this claim.

On June 6th, of 1907, Dr. Morse received two more affidavits from James Ross, confessing that the counterfeit ring framed the Rainsbargers, and that the Biggs brothers killed Enoch Johnson. He continued to admit that Nettie's letter was a fake and admitted to his part in inciting the town against the brothers. He also claimed that the Vigilance Society had an inner circle that they didn't know about. He claimed they joined in good faith. However, we know he was paid $12,000 for his part.

Morse then collected several other confessions, and affidavits; some willingly, and some not. That day, Walter Harned signed an affidavit that Dr. Morse's findings were true. Deputy Joe W. McMillan's affidavit said that Underwood's *assault* was meant to drive the Rainsbargers away, not have them lynched. He attended several Vigilance Society meetings, and stated that they ran off Thomas Nott, not the brothers. McMillan also knew the lynch mob was forming but stated that he didn't go. One key point to his affidavit was that he swore that Hiserodt confessed to him on his deathbed, that he wished that Frank, and Nate would be pardoned.

Deputy McMillan, Attorney Jim Stephenson, William Buckner, and Amos Bannigan were actually the alleged assailants of Dr. Underwood. They had dressed up like the Rainsbargers to shoot at his buggy.

In May, Frank and Nate wrote a letter to the Governor, stating;

'We say that we never had any ill will or quarrel with Enoch Johnson, that we never molested so much as a hair of his head, that we have suffered these long years for a crime that we did not commit, that we have waited patiently for deliverance from prison, never having lost faith in the idea that our liberty would someday be restored to us. We have therefore joined in the above statement of facts, trusting that it may help your excellency to feel the duty of enabling us to pass the remaining years of our lives in freedom, each feeling that under such a condition we can prove to the world that we have but one controlling ambition and that is to be good and upright citizens before our neighbors and before the laws or our country.'

On June 22nd, J. W. Lynk's affidavit confirmed that all other affidavits were true, and he also asked for a pardon.

The Marshalltown Times-Republican stated on October 4th, that William Rainsbarger was very sick, and in critical condition.

In 1908, Dr. Morse wrote a letter to Governor Cummins, stating that he was told by several men with affidavits, that Milton Biggs was hidden by Maggie Johnson in Gifford, and that he killed Enoch Johnson. Additionally, John Biggs was present at Enoch's death. Dr. Morse also appeared before the parole board on behalf of the Rainsbargers.

On September 28th, Joshua West stated in his affidavit, that Maggie knew Enoch was going to be murdered the night that they went to Ackley. He also asked for parole for the brothers.

On October 1st, Deputy H. E. Gardener stated that Wilcox neglected to take any measures to protect the jail in Eldora, and that he knew that a mob had assembled.

On October 12th, a parole board member visited Frank and Nate to get their story before the hearing. The brothers mentioned a few people who were once after them, only to find out from the parole board member, that they had all either died, or lost their wealth, and were beggars. Frank and Nate said that it was the wrath of God. Whenever Frank was asked about Nettie, all he would do is shake his head and say, "O, poor, silly woman; she was coerced."

V

Hundreds of citizens from Eldora appeared before the parole board and gave strong evidence for the brothers' release. In December, there was a flood of volunteer affidavits before the Iowa State Board of Parole was scheduled to reopen the case. Many claimed they were under threat from Hiserodt and Wilcox to frame the Rainsbargers. Wilcox, who sat in with the board, said that their release would be a gross act of injustice.

On December 26th, W. F. Clover signed an affidavit, stating that he bought his home in 1899 from Irvine Liesure. While renovating the house, he found the key to Liesure's store in one of the walls; the very key that Liesure claimed the Rainsbargers stole to break in and burn it down. That same day, John and Catherine Deemer signed a statement that Frank and Nate were at their house in Cleves the night of the murder as late as 8:30-9pm. L. W. Daniels' affidavit claimed the same thing.

Wilcox, Nettie, and Stevens met in Des Moines, and started spreading misinformation to create doubt within the community. It was stated that Sheriff Wilcox did not want the pardon, and that he knew the lynch mob was going for Fin, and Manse Rainsbarger. He was also aware that the assault on Dr. Underwood was fake. Wilcox later stated that he wouldn't stand in the way of the brothers getting pardoned. However, Frank's daughter, Zella, was now grown, and worked tirelessly to stop any pardon from taking place.

When Zella was three years old, she was brought into the court, and refused to acknowledge Frank as her father, as she had not seen him since she was only a few months old. Nettie had also remarried and changed Zella's last name. It caused such a scene in the courtroom that they had to stop the court proceeding. That was the last time Frank saw her in person. Frank was later shown a picture of Zella while in prison as he hadn't seen her as an adult. It is reported that he cried. He wrote to her often, begging for her to write back. She never did.

The Iowa Supreme Court Justice, Silas Weaver, then began the steps of petitioning the state parole board, asking that the brothers be released as he believed they were innocent. He wrote the parole board;

'After more than two years of investigation of the case and close observation to their conduct and demeanor, their unhesitating frankness and clearness of statements in consultation with counsel, their consistency of their story and their denials, with facts of which I had independent knowledge, impressed me very deeply with the belief which I still retain of their innocence of the alleged crime.'

In anticipation of their release, Frank and Nate made wooden souvenirs in the carpentry shop to sell to help pay their legal fees. The parole board denied their release again.

W.H. Berry, and John E. Howe voted against their release, but David C. Mott was for their release. Detective Waterman accused Berry of being paid off to deny the request. At that time, former prosecutor, John Stevens, made a newspaper writer for the Des Moines Register, write a newspaper article against Waterman.

On December 30th, B. F. Surles wrote in his affidavit that his brother, Ralph, lied during the trial, as he was threatened by Hiserodt, and Wilcox. He stated that he was with his brother at the bonfire the entire night of the murder, and that Ralph never saw Frank, or Nate that night.

Henry Rubbendall also signed an affidavit that day as he was Maggie's neighbor and was there when she died. He stated that she expressed several times to him that she needed to confess that Frank and Nate didn't kill Enoch Johnson, her former husband. She repeated on her death-bed, "They didn't do it." Effie then told Rubbendall to get the book out of a trunk. It was Maggie's diary, and it outlined that Milton Biggs killed Johnson. Effie burned the book and said that Hiserodt brought all of the troubles they had upon her family, and that Frank, and Nate were innocent. Nettie stopped Effie from speaking and wouldn't allow Reverend Stanley into the house to get a confession until after Maggie had died. She was taken care of by Dr. Whitney, who was present when she died from pneumonia.

On January 2nd, 1909, J. C. Robinson, William Rainsbarger's son-in-law, and county surveyor, wrote in his statement that he traveled the thirty-four-mile round-trip that the brothers supposedly took on the night of the murder with two sick horses. He stated that it wasn't possible in the time that the court indicated. The next day, Elizabeth Schiehtl wrote an affidavit to verify Joseph McMillan's affidavit, after Wilcox tried to discredit it.

On February 2nd, James Ross wrote a statement that the Bolder Gang, composed of Finley Rainsbarger, Nate Thompson, Enoch John-son, Ed Cheney, Thomas Nott, John and Milton Biggs, and Jack Reed, were responsible for most of the crimes in Hardin County.

Another local writer wrote, *"Suspicion, not being tangible evidence, led to the war against them."*

On March 2nd, a member of the state parole board wrote to Dr. Morse, stating that he would be happy to give them freedom, but they had an opposition that they didn't know about yet, and that he couldn't say what it was.

On July 30th, Governor B. F. Carroll was met by a man named W. P. Soash, who said that he had information regarding the Rainsbarger case. The men reviewing the case agreed for release, and so did the majority vote with the board. However, this meeting blocked the pardon from moving forward for six years. During that time, Howe and Mott died, and the state board needed to meet again. It was later found that Soash was Hiserodt's nephew, his sister's son. It is unknown what he told Governor Carroll, but it led to the papers not being filed, and the pardon not coming to pass. It's assumed a bribe was given, as he owned a large portion of land that new homes were being built on, and a possible percentage was granted to the governor.

On January 31st, 1910, Ed Johns signed an affidavit stating that he went with Frank and Nate to the Deemer's house around 8:30 or 9pm on the night of the murder. At 10pm, they arrived at his family's house, south of Abbott, and then went to Finley's house as late as 10:30pm. They were not anywhere near the scene of the crime. On February 1st, W. A. Young testified in their affidavit about Ed Johns' character. On the 2nd, Lincoln Johns wrote an affidavit confirming Ed Johns' statement. W. H. Leslie testified to Lincoln Johns' character.

On March 23rd, Deputy W. S. Nutting's affidavit stated he was ordered by Captain F. W. Pillsbury to assemble at the armory in Eldora on June 4th, of 1885, at 7pm. They were ordered to protect the Rainsbargers in the jail. The captain then ordered for them to disperse around 9:30-10ish. He stated that the captain was not happy with Wilcox's order to leave. Wilcox then left on the Iowa Central Railway. They were told by the captain that the Methodist church bells would ring if they were needed.

On March 26th, Maggie's lawyer, W. J. Moirs' affidavit stated that he kept record of all of Maggie's insurance policies, and that the insurance companies suspected her for Enoch's murder. She was only paid

$2,767.88 in total from the $16,000 life insurance policy. This left her with almost no money to pay off the two men who killed her husband. Nettie was only paid $1,200 out of the $7,000 life insurance policy. In her testimony, she lied, and stated that she didn't have the policies, as that they had been taken from her desk. Frank was never awarded any money from any insurance policy.

On July 2nd, George S. Rush wrote an affidavit saying that John Bunger confessed to shooting himself, and that the story about the Rainsbargers attacking him was a lie. He stated that he knew that the Rainsbargers were framed for stealing horses and that the missing person, George Boyer, was found in Tulware County, California. He had left under threat by Hiserodt. Rush lived near where the assault on Underwood took place, and he stated that the shots were planned. He also saw Underwood go to Albert Leverton's house to get the horses they staged after the shooting, and that Underwood was fine. He confessed that the Rainsbargers stealing, shooting, and maiming animals, was a lie.

On August 27th, the affidavit of Mayor G. L. Tyler stated that he knew Nettie, and she was a liar, and had bad character. He stated that Nettie was led to believe that she wouldn't get the $7,000 life insurance money unless Frank was convicted, so she lied in her testimony. Nate never knew he had a policy, or that Enoch had created one for him.

On October 17th, Frank and Nate were transferred to the prison in Fort Madison.

VI

Sometime in 1911, Dr. Morse collected one thousand signatures from people from Steamboat Rock, and Eldora to free the brothers. Governor Carroll denied the request. Carroll said that the case had become less favorable for the brothers, even with the affidavits. He stated, *"Neither the board nor myself, after the most careful investigation, believe them worthy of much credence."* He denied the clemency, declaring that a life sentence should be commuted, only in the most extraordinary circumstances, and that the brothers didn't qualify.

An unnamed man then visited Frank and Nate in prison to ask for forgiveness about what he did against them. He claimed that he did not know that the Vigilance Society had an inner circle committing the crimes with which they were charged.

On December 19th, the editor for the Hardin County Ledger, Mr. Kneedler, said that he knew Frank, and Nate didn't kill Enoch. His claims drove Governor Carroll to reopen the case, and travel to Fort Madison for further investigation. Kneedler stated, *"What at first was a good deal of a mystery is readily explainable now."* Dr. Morse then found Detective Waterman and they worked together, gathering evidence. At the end of the year, Morse left the case in Waterman's hands.

Over 3,000 people of Eldora signed a petition for the brother's release and sought to charge Governor Carroll for not expediting their clemency as he said he would in the previous winter term of the parole board. After several years of the petition for a pardon being transferred between the Governors, and the parole board, Carroll denied the clemency once again, and stated that this was the final say in the Rainsbarger sentencing.

In 1913, Dr. Morse, and Waterman then reconvened, and located Henry Martin. Martin sent them his notebook that he had kept while at the Ellsworth Hotel. They used it to locate the hotel maid, Eva Danforth, and several others who gave affidavits about what happened at the hotel.

On September 29th, Detective Waterman released all of his findings, reports, and affidavits to the Des Moines paper; The Register, and Leader. His reports stated that he was a Secret Service detective during the time of the counterfeiting rise to power and was already investigating them before he was hired by Henry Johns. He also claimed that the Rainsbargers' hired man, George Winnans, was a secret informant for the counterfeiters before Enoch was even to be murdered. The Rainsbargers were always to become the scapegoats if they ever got caught. Further, he claimed he also had a counter informant inside the Vigilance Society.

In October, the Mayor of Eldora wrote the Des Moines Register about their release. He said that nine out of ten people believe they are innocent, and money surely passed hands to convict them. It had no effect. Waterman then discovered that John, and Milton Biggs were actually the leaders of the counterfeit ring, and Hiserodt was their trusted associate. George W. Clarke became Governor and was then asked to pardon Frank and Nate. Frank at the time was extremely sick, and this led his supporters to call for release on humanitarian grounds. That too, was denied.

On December 3rd, the brothers were allowed to attend their brother, Williams' funeral, but with a pardon on the horizon, they refused to go, expecting that while they were out, their enemies would trump up something new about them, so they would never be released. They said that the next time they would leave the jail, they would need to be free men. Frank was still very sick, and Nate said he wouldn't go alone. William had requested to see them before he died, but he was never able to. The newspaper stated that William died from his brothers' sins and became sick with stomach issues. They said worry created his sickness.

He died at 73 years old in November. His service was at the Congregational church in Steamboat Rock. Reverend Rosenberger was in charge of the service. So many people came, that they couldn't all fit into the church. It's reported that there has not been a larger service for a private citizen in that area since. Many citizens then petitioned Governor Clarke to release the brothers and to 'let them die decently'. Instead, they were sent back to Anamosa Penitentiary as Frank had started to become ill. Frank needed to be in the reformatory, but refused to go without Nate, so they were both transferred. Many requested for the Governor to free them and 'let them die in the sun'.

On January 3rd, 1914, Frank developed liver problems and the local newspaper stated that officials thought he would die. In April, detective Waterman met with Governor Clarke to request a pardon. He presented Clarke with 2,000 signatures, and a telegram from an anonymous counterfeiter, stating that Enoch Johnson was dead. He received the letter on November 17th, a whole day before Enoch died.

On March 11th, Nettie, Zella, Dan Turner, Henry Finster, W. P. Soash, William Johns, Judge Stevens, and Wilcox all went to the board of parole and requested they deny the pardon. They claimed Waterman led attacks on the parole board members, so he shouldn't be heard.

On April 30th, Clarke wrote a letter stating that Waterman's case, and affidavits had no bearing, and that he didn't understand what he was researching. This was after the parole board again denied their parole on the first of April.

On October 5th, Columbus Lundy signed an affidavit stating he was friends with the counterfeit gang and knew who was in it. He knew where they hid stolen goods, and that they were responsible for the Shintiver family's disappearance. The counterfeit gang killed them; they were not run off by the Rainsbargers. He knew that Enoch married Maggie when she was eighteen, and he was forty-one. She was only thirty-five when he died and remarried twice since then. He said Maggie was a hussy with boys in school and was a whore when she was married. He claimed that Hiserodt was the leader, Leyman F. Wisner was the banker, known as the Land Pirate, the Biggs brothers were cattle runners, and that Henry Finster, owned the cave where they hid their stolen goods. D. W. Ballard was the chief of the gang in Des Moines.

After that, Governor Clarke took an interest in the case and re-read the affidavits. He then drove the supposed route Frank, and Nate took to kill Enoch in a horse, and buggy, where he found that it was impossible, given the times in the trial by the prosecutors. He did all of this *after* he denied clemency for the brothers and the citizens of Eldora brought charges against him for denying it. It would still take nearly a year to pardon the brothers.

On November 30th, Detective Waterman then filed a claim against William Rainsbarger's property for $1,600, claiming that they had a verbal agreement about aiding Frank and Nate starting on March 12th, 1913. William had already spent thousands before his death to hire Waterman and other detectives to appeal to the parole board for a pardon. Even after being denied the claim, Waterman continued to face the Governor and parole board to petition their release.

CHAPTER 19

GODSPEED AND GOODBYE

In April, of 1915, Frank and Nate were allowed to leave prison to see their sick sister, Martha Johns. She died while they were there, and they were allowed to remain for the funeral. While at the train station, they were met by many people who were excited to see them. Most of the people the Rainsbargers' didn't know. One man was Mose Arquette, who ran up to them with great excitement. He was the engineer for the fastest train in Iowa, the Cannonball. Frank and Nate used to ride along with Mose on the train.

In June, Nettie begged Clarke to not release Frank, but he ignored her. She then went before the parole board with letters she claimed were from Frank, threatening her, however, the brothers had become model prisoners, and were trusted at the prison. Frank was in charge of the carpenter shop, and was the only inmate allowed to keep a dog named Trilby. He nicknamed him Toots. Nate was a pattern-maker in the machine shop. The guards at the prison called them their *friends*. Frank once wrote to the Police Chief, Mr. Leighton, and asked him to assist a young prisoner who was about to be released to find a job. He had no family, and would either have to beg, or steal, and Frank didn't want that for the young man.

Nearly 30 years after their imprisonment, on August 23rd, Governor Clarke granted Frank and Nate parole that would become a full pardon after three years. They had no supervision on parole, but had to remain as upright citizens, and not seek revenge on anyone who had a part in their convictions. Nate said that he wouldn't leave unless he had a pardon. He said he entered a free man, and would leave as such, or not at all. Warden C. McLaughry stayed up all night to persuade him to take it.

Clarke wrote and had printed in several local papers;

'I can not see why I should not be perfectly frank in stating my conclusions with reference to these cases. I can not understand how, upon the record as I have it, it was possible to find these defendants guilty beyond a reasonable doubt. I can not see how it can be said that their guilt is inconsistent with any other reasonable hypothesis or any other rational conclusion. These men were tried at a time of great public excitement and indignation. To write the whole story of these cases would require a volume of several hundred pages. I have only touched very briefly the outline. I can not, on the whole, possibly divest myself of the feelings that there was an organized effort and a very direct motive to get rid of these men and others as well as Johnson. I may be mistaken in my conclusion, but I am irresistibly driven to it. Others may have been right and I may be wrong. But if there is doubt in the minds of any, these men are entitled to the benefit of it. For more than thirty years they have stoutly maintained that they were innocent. They have challenged investigation. They have been fearless in inviting the closest of scrutiny of every fact and circumstance that could be suggested. Their conduct at the prison has been faultless. They have always been referred to as model prisoners. They have been deprived of their liberty since Jan. 16, 1885. I can not but think in any event this would be punishment enough, but in the face of great doubt of their guilt which fills my mind, amounting practically to a conviction that they were not guilty, it is far beyond anything they deserve. No good purpose can be served by imprisoning them longer. I can not agree, therefore, with the conclusion of the majority of the board of parole recommending to me that no clemency be extended...'

Their release was further delayed by several hours, as the prison tailor hadn't finished making their civilian clothes. Upon leaving, they were given their belongings with which they had been arrested, a five-dollar check, and their pardon letters from the Governor. The warden said to them as they left, *"You are again master of your own destiny. The front door of the prison is open to you. Godspeed and goodbye."*

They were released to their nephews on August 30th and were not required to follow the normal terms of parole. As they left, they took a photo in front of the prison. Frank was nervous about having his photo taken, and made the photographer promise to send him a copy, and to get his suitcase in the photo to show that he was leaving. They planned a dinner with Mr. Gould at his house across the street from the prison. They also visited Mr. Gorrisk who was once imprisoned with them and was now 90 years old. They visited A. A. Fife, who was once head of the prison carpentry shop. Enjoying their freedom, they took their first automobile ride to the train station to take the 7:15 train to Cedar Rapids.

The Gazette wrote;

'Rainsbargers, deprived of their liberty nearly thirty years ago for a crime which probably a majority of the people of Iowa never believed they committed, today for the first time in a generation, breathed the air of freedom.'

By December of 1916, Nathan was living in Marshalltown and working the elevator for the Western Grocery Co. Mills, while Frank did contract work near Ackley. At the end of 1916 they returned to Iowa's capital as Clarke made an announcement to end his term as Governor. To thank him personally, they showed him they were making good on their parole.

On January 5th, 1917, one of Clarke's last acts as Governor, was to visit Hardin County, to see Frank, and Nate. He then granted the two brothers an early full pardon as a New Year's present.

CHAPTER 20

ENOCH JOHNSON

Near Gifford, Iowa, the night of November 18th, 1884...

The horse tried to maintain a steady pace as it pounded the hard road under Enoch's heavy hand. A second cannon was fired, sending panic into the old man. He had no doubt that the whistleblowers and the cannons were linked together, but he had no idea what exactly they meant. As he drove the horse onward, he never noticed his busted front wheel.

The road was hard, but the grass and sides of the road were slippery and muddy from the rain the night before. The horse made easy work out of the crusted road but slid every now and then when it came too close to the path's edge and clipped a wet spot of grass. At intervals, Enoch looked behind him to see if any of the gunmen were following him. He was still breathing heavily and sweating through his overcoat. With one hand on the reins, he took it off, took another gulp of gin, and threw the flask in the back. He tried to think of what to do next. Was going to Gifford the best for him now? He was sure he would be killed by Hiserodt or his men.

A third cannon blast rang through the air like a death knell. Enoch thought that if the gunmen were out on the main road, and lining it, hiding by the fires, it may be best if he wasn't. Coming up the last hill heading into Gifford, he decided to take the side road that was used mainly by men on foot. The road was narrower and was covered overhead by tree limbs. As he entered the path, the beginning branches were lower, and they took off his hat, scratching the side of the buggy. His judgment was clouded from the gut-warmer he had been drinking, and the horse's skittishness only grew from his frantic state. He looked back again to see if anyone was biting at his heels. As he turned back around, he was whipped on the side of his face by a low branch. It cut open his cheek near his left eye. He yelled out and grabbed his face. With only one hand on the reins, he started to lose control.

Enoch tried to regain the reins as the horse came around a sharp bend at full drive. The bend turned to the right side into the cliff wall. Off the left side was a steep ravine that led to a small creek about fifteen yards off. The reins slipped from both hands as the horse slid the buggy's left side, off the path, and into the slick grass and mud. The damaged front wheel had all it could take. The grass gave way, and the horse and buggy were led off the side of the ravine. They hit hard at the bottom and Enoch was thrown from his seat.

The landing didn't throw him far enough to escape being run over by the carriage's back left wheel. It had bounced, and then hit Enoch in the back, crushing him into the ground. The air was taken out of his lungs as his diaphragm was squeezed, and three ribs cracked under the weight. The middle rib snapped instantly and punctured his lung. He gasped for breath after rolling over. The buggy had continued going after mauling him. The skittish horse kept pulling it for another fifteen feet before coming to a stop. Its head jerked forward and back as if it was trying to stop another fit from happening.

Rolling to his side, he gasped in fresh air, and spit up a mouthful of blood at the same time. The cool winter air was dulled in his mouth by the taste of iron. Enoch cursed as he got up and limped over to the horse. He knew he had to leave before any of Hiserodt's men showed up, but hurrying wasn't an option. Enoch hurt, and he hurt bad, even with the winter air, and gin numbing his skin. He choked down more blood as he reached the horse and buggy. Enoch wanted to beat the old horse, but he knew it wouldn't help, and that the accident wasn't his fault.

After a quick glance around, he hung himself over the buggy side, and tried to regain some strength, wondering how much blood could be mixed with the gin before he got sick. Another cannon blasted in the distance, and the urge to run returned. With his head hung low from leaning over the buggy's side, he finally saw it. The front wheel was broken and splintered. He cussed again as he tried to regain his breath. His chest and left side hurt, but he continued on. Perhaps the gin and beer had dulled his senses enough to keep him moving through the pain. He knew he didn't have the time or the ability to fix the wheel. Enoch began to untie the horse from the carriage, when he heard a noise, loud and sharp, just up the hill from him. The whistle cut the winter air as well as Enoch's hope of making it to Gifford. The whistle startled the horse again, and Enoch was knocked off his feet. At full drive, the horse started sprinting up the hillside off of which they had just driven off of. With the reins still in his hands, he hit the ice-covered grass hard on his back. In an instant, he felt the rope that was the reins, tighten around his left foot. He was tangled in the harness equipment as the horse ran on.

He was flipped over onto his stomach, near his left side. His broken ribs dug deeper. Enoch tried to scream out in pain but wasn't able to make a noise. The only thing that came to his mouth was more blood. He could hardly breath, let alone make any noise to stop the horse. The ice on the grass blades cut his left cheek, eye, and arm. His scarf bundled up over his mouth and choked him, as more blood joined it. His shirt and overcoat followed the scarf's lead.

As the horse hit the hardpan path that led back to the main road up the hill, Enoch's skull bounced off a jagged rock. Warm blood poured out of the side of his left temple and coated the dirt. His body was pounded by the jagged road as the horse continued on. His old body couldn't take any more. Enoch fainted and knew nothing more about the whistleblower.

With a loud bang, he awoke. Enoch guessed another cannon shot was fired. Judging by that fact, he assumed he had been unconscious for several minutes. Looking over, his horse was no longer attached to his left leg.

It was hard to breathe, and he expected to be in pain. Having laid on the near-frozen ground for some time, had stiffened his body. He could barely move. Lifting his face up out of the small pool of blood, he saw someone in the distance. He was carrying a bottle and was wearing a celebratory mask.

"Well hello there, you old coot. I'm glad I found ya. I was worried I wouldn't. When I didn't see you on the road, I thought I lost ya," the man chuckled. He took a drink of the bottle and stepped closer to Enoch.

There was near silence now. Enoch couldn't hear the folks at the bonfire, only the chirps of the insects of the night. He spat out a little blood and drew in a gurgled breath. He could see his breath in the cool air and wondered how he was even able to breathe. He still couldn't move. He felt weak. At that moment, he thought of Nettie, his beautiful girl. She would most likely never see him again, neither would Effie. He wanted to cry but couldn't.

The man came all the way to Enoch's face, and knelt down. He finished his drink, and in the dim starlight Enoch could see it was a King's bitters bottle as it tumbled through the air. It hit the wooden rail near the horse, the neck shattered and landed in the field over, scaring the horse yet again. The man took off the party mask and threw it aside. In that moment, Enoch's heart skipped, and his chest clenched. It was John Biggs, his wife's uncle; Hiserodt's leading confederate.

"Shhh, shhh, calm down, you old cuss," he said. He rubbed Enoch's hair gently, and gave him a look of pity, and hate. John pulled Enoch's face up toward his. Enoch groaned and choked at the movement. "Little Nettie, and Maggie asked me, when the time comes for you to be put down like a good for nothin' horse, that *I* be the one to do it. I promised them I would, but I don't think I will."

Enoch's heart began to give up the ghost when he realized that Nettie knew he would be murdered. *Why? Did she hate me that much? Was she under a death threat as well?* It pained him all the more, knowing he could do nothing to help her.

Enoch sat up a bit on his hands. He let out a small sigh of relief and blood from his lower lip spotted John's face. John closed his eyes and wiped the spots away with disgust. Trying to catch his breath, he replied, "You ain't? Thank goodness. Help me up, boy, I need you to take me to Maggie!"

John made no move to help him. He spit, and it landed in front of Enoch. He understood by John's face that he wouldn't get any help. "No, no...I don't think *I'll* kill you. But...Milton will." Enoch's head cocked to the side to demonstrate his confusion. John looked up, and behind Enoch. Before Enoch could fully turn to see what John was looking at, he felt a boot on his back.

Milton Biggs stood behind him and held him to the ground with his big boot. In an instant, Milton lifted his rifle, and cracked Enoch in the back of the head with the rifle butt. Enoch's skull cracked behind his right ear. His head fell down instantly into the pool of blood he had fainted into. He tried to scream but couldn't. Even if he managed to make a noise, another cannon was fired at that exact moment.

Enoch looked up at John, blood and spit on his lips, tears in his eyes. "Help me, please," he croaked, as his voice gave out.

"Well, see now, Milton, that wasn't near hard enough. The horse-thieving bastard ain't nearly dead yet. *HIT HIM AGAIN AND HIT HIM HARD*!" John yelled.

In full swing, Milton brought the rifle's butt down again, this time creating an even larger split in Enoch's skull near the left ear. Milton howled like a wolf into the winter air as he stood over Enoch's body. He took out a pair of iron knuckles and continued to beat Enoch to death.

"It's time to meet your maker, you lily-livered son of a gun!" he yelled.

Lying there, drowning in a pool of his own blood, Enoch died, wondering why his wife and beloved daughter hated him so much. His heart was crushed far worse than his body. The last thing to run through Enoch's mind was the face of his beautiful little granddaughter, Zella.

The bonfires raged on through the night, but the cannon fire stopped. All alone on an old forgotten road, Enoch Johnson was murdered by his own family. Milton and John Biggs laughed at his death. They staged the body to look as if he was dragged even further and trampled by his horse. They spit on him as they left him, beaten to death, and facedown in an ever-growing pool.

Silence ensued, and only the noises of the night were left to keep Enoch Johnson company.

CHAPTER 21

FRANK AND NATE RAINSBARGER

No one was ever charged for the murder of Henry Johns. Governor William Larrabee put out a $500 reward after Henry's death for any information, but no one came forward. No one was charged for the murder of Finley and Manse Rainsbarger. No charges were ever filed against Sheriff Wilcox, William Hiserodt, Nettie, or Maggie Johnson, John or Milton Biggs, James S. Ross, Dan Turner, John Bunger, Ralph Surles, Amos Bannigan, James Rice, John Foy, or Charles Marx.

No one was ever prosecuted for shooting at Finley or William Rainsbarger during the events of 1885. No charges were ever brought against Dr. Rittenour, Dr. Underwood, Dr. Caldwell, Ash Noyes, William Johns, Henry Huff, Attorney John Stevens, Judge Henderson, or Mr. Deyo.

No charges were ever filed against Leyman Wisner, Henry Martin, Irvine Liesure, Joseph McMillan, William Buckner, William Scott, or William Haines.

No charges were ever made against Mr. Hathaway, John Leverton, Albert Leverton, or George Leverton.

No indictment was made against Henry Finster, James Haley, Governor Cummins, W. H. Berry, W. P. Soash, Governor Carroll, or D. W. Ballard.

The counterfeit gang members, Mr. Popejoy, and G. W. Edgington were never charged with a crime.

Three years after their release from prison, Zella died from unknown causes. She never saw Frank before her death. Ash Noyes was ashamed at the part he played, and was afraid people would retaliate, and vandalize his daughter's grave. He posted guards to watch it day and night, for a year. Eventually, he decided to leave the state. After his death, he was cremated, and returned to Steamboat Rock to be buried. Nettie died of unknown causes in January of 1919.

Frank got married to Laura Cox in 1922 and bought five acres of land in Abbott. He and his wife then invited Nate to come live with them. Frank died of a stroke in his front yard on November 15th, 1926. The brothers had still never spoken to the press about their case.

Ed Johns died the same day as Frank's funeral. He had a stroke when he arrived home from being at the funeral.

The Des Moines Sunday Register wrote on December 12th, of 1926: *Last of the famous Rainsbarger Gang tells their story.* Nate finally spoke about the case after Frank's death and after Frank had been buried. He told the press who actually murdered Enoch Johnson.

On March 12th, 1929, Frank's second wife, Laura, took Nate to court to gain ownership of their house in Abbott.

Nate died in 1940, at 88 years old in Marshalltown at his niece's home. He was never married. At the time of his death, he said, "I'm not afraid to die. Why should I be? God knows who killed Enoch Johnson. He knows that it wasn't Frank or me."

'The only thing necessary for the triumph of evil, is for good men to do nothing.'

-Unknown

'When bad men combine, the good must associate; else they will fall, one by one, an unpitied sacrifice in a contemptible struggle.'

-Edmund Burke

•In 1879, William Hiserodt started a get-rich scheme and hired Enoch Johnson.
•August 16th, 1883, Enoch was arrested for getting caught with counterfeit money.
•April 14th, 1884, Enoch was bailed out of prison by his son-in-law, Frank Rainsbarger, at the request of Nettie Rainsbarger, as the counterfeiters left him to rot in jail.
•November 16th, 1884, Enoch's death was planned by the counterfeit gang since Enoch was working with the federal grand jury and Henry Johns to indict the counterfeiters.
•November 18th, 1884, Enoch received a bait letter from his wife, Maggie, to meet her in Gifford, Iowa. He was murdered on his way there. Maggie was then a suspect and needed someone new to blame.
•January 14th, 1885, Nettie met with Maggie Johnson and Hiserodt to agree to frame the Rainsbargers.
•January 16th, 1885, Frank and Nate Rainsbarger were arrested for murdering Enoch Johnson. The Eldora Herald and Vigilance Society instigated hatred towards the Rainsbarger family to throw scent off the real counterfeiters.
•April 1st, 1885, Finley Rainsbarger was shot at.
•April 6th, 1885, William Rainsbarger was shot at.
•April 8th, 1885, Henry Johns was shot at.
•April 16th, 1885, Henry Johns was shot and left for dead by the counterfeiters to stop the indictment; Henry Johns knew the Rainsbargers were innocent, and held a list of names of counterfeiters, given to him by Enoch Johnson.
•May 8th, 1885, Henry Johns died while in a coma.
•June 4th, 1885, Dr. Underwood claims he was shot at by ambush the night before by the Rainsbarger gang. William, Finley, and Manse Rainsbarger were arrested for the assault. William was released on bail.
•June 5th, 1885, Finley and Manse Rainsbarger are murdered at the jail in Eldora by a lynch mob.
•Nate and Frank Rainsbarger remain in jail for nearly 30 years.

-
-
-
-
-
-
-
-
-
-
-
-

COUNTERFEITERS
•Hiserodt- counterfeit leader
•Ash Noyes- banker
•Dan Turner- Steamboat Rock Mayor
•Sheriff Wilcox- Vigilance Society leader
•Popejoy- counterfeit member
•John and Milton Biggs- counterfeit members; Maggie Johnson's Uncles
JOHNSON FAMILY
•Enoch Johnson- counterfeit member
•Maggie Johnson- Enoch's wife
•Effie-Nettie's illegitimate child
RAINSBARGERS
•Nettie Johnson/Rainsbarger-Enoch's
daughter and Frank's wife
•Frank-Son-in-law to Enoch Johnson
•Zella-Frank and Nettie's daughter
•Nate- Rainbarger brother
•William- oldest Rainsbarger brother
•Manse- Rainsbarger brother
•Finley- Rainsbarger brother
•Henry Johns- brother-in-law to the
Rainsbargers
•Henry Wilkert- Henry Johns' hired hand
•Waterman- Rainsbarger's Detective
•Dr. Nathan Morse- Rainsbarger advocate
SOCIETY MEMBERS
•Albert Leverton-Vigilance Society member, counterfeiter
•John Bunger-Vigilance Society member
•Cady Swain- Deputy, Society member
•Amos Bannigan- Deputy, Society member
•James Ross-owner of the Eldora Herald, counterfeiter, Society member
•Ben Deyo-owner of the Ellsworth hotel, counterfeiter, Society member
•James Rice-counterfeiter
•Dr. Ben Rittenour- Society member
•Dr. Myron Underwood-Vigilance Society member

Fannon-Langton, Diane. "Time Machine: Did 2 Iowa brothers spend almost 30 years in prison for a murder they did't commit?" *The Gazette*, 2022.

Folerts, David. *The Rainsbargers Trials*. Amazon, 2022.

Moir, William. *The Past and Present of Hardin County Iowa*. B.F. Bowen & Company, 1911.

"NewspapersbyAncestry."www.newspapers.com/search/?query=Rainsbarg-ers&_province=us=ia&_year=1860-1940.

"Steamboat Rock Historical Society: SRHS."www.steamboat-rock-historical-society.com.

Tinnan, Raymond. "The Rainsbargers Revisited: County Crisis and Historical mystery." *The Palimpsest*, 1992, pp113-132.

Wallace, Jocelyn. "An Iowa Doone Band." *The Palimpsest*, pp267-280.

Other resources have been referenced in this text that have been simply passed down from one generation to another and can not be fully cited. These sources include William Rainsbarger's letter to the State of Iowa, Nathan Morse's letter to the parole board, and Frank and Nate's letter to Governor Cummins. This also includes Nate Rainsbarger's pardon letter from Governor Clarke, and dozens of affidavits.

Printed in the USA
CPSIA information can be obtained
at www.ICGtesting.com
LVHW021119060424
776631LV00014B/761